I0680761

Erector Set
Erected
Hammered
Nailed

Antholgies
Night of the Senses: Carnal Caresses
Christmas Goes Camo: Melting the Ice
Treble: Trouble at the Treble T
Subspace: Head Games
Bound to the Billionaire: Made for Him
Three's a Charm: Double Entry

Collections
Heatwave: Summer Spice
Feral: Black Cat Fever
Clandestine Classics: Northanger Abbey

Corporate Heat

MASQUERADE

DESIREE HOLT

Masquerade
ISBN # 978-1-78686-381-2
©Copyright Desiree Holt 2018
Cover Art by Cherith Vaughan ©Copyright October 2018
Interior text design by Claire Siemaszkiewicz
Totally Bound Publishing

MASQUERADE

Dedication

So many, many people help me bring a book to my readers, but there are always special ones that are with me through it all. So, a huge thank you to the unequaled Margie Hager, Joseph Patrick Trainor—who answers my endless questions about procedure and logistics with unfailing patience—Janet Rodman; my wonderful group—Denise Hendrickson-Chapman, Misty Dawn, Courtney Kinder. Fedora Chen, Deb Diem, May McCoy; Maria Connor, my VA, who deserves a medal for putting up with me. To all of you, from the bottom of my heat, thanks for being you. No books of mine would be born or succeed without you.

Prologue

The night was hot and muggy, typical of Florida any time of the year but especially in the summer. The force of it hit Craig Wainwright as he emerged from the air-conditioned office building into the sticky heat that surrounded him. He was glad that years ago he'd learned to dress for comfort, favoring lightweight slacks and soft-collar shirts with the Elite Marketing logo on them as opposed to more formal ties and button-down shirts.

He'd hoped that because he worked late, the oppressive heat of the day would have faded, but no such luck. Just something else to add to his itchy mood, one that had plagued him for more than a week. He had some decisions to make, very unpleasant ones that he wasn't looking forward to. He definitely didn't want to have the talk he planned with Lindsey, but it couldn't be helped.

Making Lindsey Califaro executive vice-president of Elite was one of the smartest things he'd ever done. It allowed him to pursue side projects without worrying about the agency's operation. But he hadn't been fair to her and the day of reckoning was coming far too soon. The headache he'd been fighting all evening was a sign that he couldn't put a lot of this off any longer. He had called her tonight and asked her to meet him early for coffee at the office. Maybe he'd stop and pick up some of those French breakfast rolls she loved so much. Something to put her in a good mood.

How the hell did I get myself into this fix, anyway?

He was glad his car had the ability to start remotely, letting the air conditioning kick in and cool off before he had to climb into it. Hitting the button on his key fob unlocked the door and he slid in behind the steering wheel. Modern science was wonderful, providing every possible creature comfort imaginable. And Craig was all about comfort.

As he pulled out of the parking garage and headed toward Las Olas Boulevard and home, his thoughts shifted in another direction. The pressure from the other Elite activities was getting to him. He wasn't sure how much more he could take. It forced him into a crazy schedule and the pressure of dealing with it was affecting him physically. In the past few weeks, he'd developed a tendency toward blinding headaches. A checkup with his doctor had revealed just what he thought — they were caused by tension. Now he had a small bottle of little blue pills that could attack the pain the moment he took them. He'd popped one during his last half-hour at work, just to take the edge off.

Too bad they aren't the other *little blue pills.*

He smiled at the thought. Maybe he'd get a prescription for those, too. Not that he needed them all that much. He was positive that his problems in the bedroom had the same cause as his headaches. What he should do was take two weeks off and spend them with

Natalia, his wife, straightening out their lives. He had never dreamed the situation would escalate the way it had. He wanted to go back to the way things had been *before*, even if it meant shrinking his income. He had accumulated more than enough to spare.

Yeah. Fat chance.

He sighed and turned on the radio, searching for one of his programmed stations. *Ah. There. Soft instrumental music.* That would help him relax. He was as tight as a drum and he wanted to ease up before he got home. Maybe he'd take a little detour. The major thoroughfares saw little traffic this time of night. *Yes, that's it.* He'd take a drive on I-95. Maybe he could put off the inevitable a little while longer.

Changing direction, he entered the highway, turned up the radio a little and rolled down the windows. A soft breeze blew through the car. Maybe it would soothe him even more. The pill hadn't done as much as usual. In fact, his headache seemed to be getting worse. The familiar band tightened around his skull, shooting pain into his eyes. And now a sharp stab in his chest had been added.

Can't breathe. Can't breathe.

Maybe he should pull over on the verge. There wasn't much traffic this time of night. He could sit there for just a few minutes until the worst of the pain subsided. He turned on his signal and began to ease toward the right. As he did so, a car behind him was suddenly on his bumper, bright lights flooding his car and exacerbating his pain.

What the hell?

"Hey, buddy. Back the fuck off."

As if he'd heard him, the driver did just that, but the moment Craig began to ease to the right again, there he was, just about kissing Craig's rear bumper. Thank god there were so few cars at the moment. He didn't want to crash into any of them. Then, all of a sudden, the driver behind him began flashing his lights from bright to regular to bright. On, off, on, off. It only sharpened the pain in his head and his chest, which was becoming intolerable. He'd have to pull off and figure out how to deal with the idiot behind him.

Without signaling, he cut across two lanes and headed for the shoulder. At that moment the pain spiked and he thought his body would explode. He tried to maintain control of his car, but the pain stole his breath and shut down his brain. He barely even felt the impact of the crash as he hit the barricade wall.

Then he felt nothing.

* * * *

The ringing of her cell phone woke Lindsey Califaro from a deep sleep. She looked at the clock. *Midnight. Who on earth is calling me at this hour?* The phone chimed again and she checked the readout, her eyes widening. Wainwright. *What the hell?* Why would Craig call her from the landline at his house?

"Lose your cell phone, boss?" she asked. "And by the way, did you check the time?"

"Lindsey?" The words came out in a rush. "Oh, thank god. This is Natalia."

Natalia? Why would she be calling? Where's Craig? Did he ask his wife to call because he was busy? At midnight?

"Yes. Natalia. What's going on?" She pushed her hair out of her eyes and tucked it behind her ears.

"Oh, Lindsey. I need your help. The most awful thing has happened. Craig's dead."

Shock reverberated through her body and for one second she thought her heart had stopped beating.

"Craig's dead? Did you say he was dead?" Even repeating the words did not make sense. She must be hearing things. She tried to remember her last conversation with the man tonight. Had there been a problem she'd failed to catch? He'd seemed distracted and tense, but no more than usual. "But when I left him earlier tonight, he was fine. What happened?"

Maybe those headaches he'd been complaining about were worse than she'd thought.

"An accident on I-95." Natalia's voice was shaky. "A one-car accident. What was he doing there? He was supposed to be on his way home. To me."

A good question. Something was very, very wrong here.

"The police were just here." Natalia's voice sounded less than steady, unusual for her. "Lindsey, they wanted to take me to identify the body. I-I don't think I can do that by myself, and they insisted I come down there now. Could you please go with me?"

Her voice broke a little. Lindsey wasn't used to hearing the woman in an emotional state.

"Are you sure you wouldn't rather call one of your friends?"

"No. No, you're the person I want." Her voice dropped. "Please do this for me. If it is Craig, he'd want it to be you with me."

"Of course." As she spoke, she was pulling clothes out of drawers and her closet. "I'll be on my way in just a few. Hang tough, Natalia. We'll get through this."

Hang tough? What kind of advice is that to give to a brand-new widow?

It was strange to hear Natalia Wainwright so unsettled. The woman could be the poster child for self-control. Smart, beautiful and rich. Her money had funded Elite Marketing. And her connections that had brought them to the attention of the vast international conglomerate Arroyo. Lindsey had joined the firm four years earlier and had immediately been given specific accounts to handle that kept her more than busy.

All the lights were on in the Wainwrights' huge home in Idylwyld, the very exclusive community where they lived. Natalia must have been watching for her, because the gate at the foot of the driveway swung open before she could touch the control box. She had just pulled up to the front of the house before the door opened and Natalia hurried out, purse in hand.

"Thank you for coming." She drew in a breath and let it out. "I think I'm still in a state of shock. Craig was such a careful driver. I cannot imagine how this happened."

Lindsey glanced at the woman as she settled herself in the passenger seat. Dressed in her usual impeccable style in black slacks and a black silk blouse, she wore no makeup and her hair was pulled back in a tight ponytail. Not her usual look. A good indication of her state of mind that she hadn't taken the time to primp and fuss.

"We'll find out everything," she assured her. "Okay? Just take a deep breath."

"I keep hoping this is just a big mistake." Natalia had a death grip on her purse. "That I'll take a look at…whoever this is and we'll see it's the wrong man. That's why I need you with me."

"Unfortunately," Lindsey said, "they wouldn't make the notification unless they were pretty sure. They could at least match his driver's license photo."

"Of course, of course. You're right." Hands gripped tight together in her lap, she was silent for the rest of the ride.

Lindsey had little in common with Natalia Wainwright and neither of them seemed to have much to say to each other at the morgue, either. She recognized Craig's body right away. Beside her, Natalia just stared for a long time before giving a sharp nod and turning away.

"Can you tell me what happened?" Natalia asked the cop who met them at the morgue.

"I wish I could. Someone saw the wreck and called it in. It looks like, for whatever reason, he ran full-tilt into the retaining wall."

Natalia's eyes widened. "Deliberately?"

"I can't say, ma'am. There are still a lot of details to sort out. Someone will be in touch with you."

"What about...the body?"

"As soon as they finish the autopsy, they'll release it to you."

"A-autopsy?"

The cop nodded. "To determine if the accident was alcohol or drug related."

Natalia's face paled, but she just nodded. Lindsey waited as the woman signed whatever papers they needed then walked in tight-lipped silence to the car. The drive back to the house was as long and uncomfortable as the one on the way in.

"Thank you again for this." Natalia climbed out of the car, her face expressionless.

"If you'd like some help with the funeral arrangements..." Lindsey began.

"The funeral? Yes, yes, of course. Thank you. I'll let you know when they tell me I can move forward with it." She started to close the door, then turned back. "I suppose we'll have to meet to discuss Elite, also. After I've figured out how to deal with this nightmare, of course."

"Elite. Of course. Just let me know. I'll make myself available."

"Thank you. Right now, I'm still trying to make sense out of tonight."

Lindsey wasn't sure if she should just drive off or not.

"Would you like me to call someone to be with you? I'm not sure you should be alone right now."

Natalia shook her head. "No. Thank you, but…no. I think at this moment I just need to be by myself. Try to figure out how this happened. But again, thank you."

"Of course."

Lindsey watched the woman until she walked into the house and closed the front door. She sat for a moment, rubbing her forehead, wondering if she'd imagined the entire thing.

Well, that was totally weird. I still don't know why she called me instead of a friend. And what was that about Elite? Has she forgotten it's not an independent corporation any longer?

When she was far enough away from Idylwyld, she tapped the controls on her steering wheel. She had all the Arroyo numbers programmed into her cell. It was close to two o'clock in the morning, but she knew she couldn't wait to make this call to the person who'd put her where she was and always wanted information delivered yesterday.

"Siri, call Taylor Cantrell."

She wasn't surprised when the woman herself picked up on the second ring.

Does she ever sleep?

"Hello, Lindsey. It must be pretty damn important for you to call me this late at night."

"I'd say it is." She blew out a breath. "I have some very bad news. Craig Wainwright died in a one-car accident tonight."

There was silence for one second. Two.

"Was he drunk?"

"Absolutely not. He would never drink and drive. He was a maniac about it. In fact, he was working late at the office, still wrapped up in something when I went home."

Now she heard the murmur of voices, soft in the background.

"I've had some questions about Elite lately myself," Taylor said when she came back to the conversation. "And about Craig himself. Who made the identification?"

"His wife. She called me after the police notified her and asked me to go with her. It was definitely him, unfortunately."

"How's Natalia doing?"

Lindsey thought for a moment. "Hard to say. She's always been a very controlled person, and I could tell she was doing her best to hold on to her emotions."

"All right. Give me a minute." More talking in the background. "We'll be arriving at the Fort Lauderdale airport in the morning. We'll have transportation, so no need to pick us up, but I would like you to meet us at the office. The employees have to be notified and you and Noah and I need to have a closed-door meeting."

Lindsey made a turn, heading toward the area where she lived.

"I have to ask. Am I in some kind of trouble?"

"Far from it. In fact, you're probably going to be our most important person in the days to come. Get some sleep. We'll see you there at seven."

Lindsey disconnected and checked the time. It was already two a.m. She'd have to sleep fast at this rate, but her brain was buzzing, wondering whatever it was they wanted to discuss just with her.

She had a feeling in the pit of her stomach that the coming days were going to be anything but fun.

Chapter One

Lindsey turned over in bed and checked the time on her little clock. Five a.m. *Holy hell.* She was sure she hadn't gotten more than an hour's worth of sleep combined all night. Most of the time had been spent tossing and turning, trying to get the picture of Craig Wainwright's dead body out of her mind. Seeing the man she'd worked with for the past four years lying in the morgue, battered and bruised, with all the life drained out of him, was painful and gut-wrenching. A sick feeling lodged inside her even as questions kept rattling around in her brain, bumping into one another.

She didn't know which shocked her more — Craig's death and the circumstances, or the fact that his ice-queen of a wife, Natalia, had chosen to contact her as opposed to one of her friends. Or intimate acquaintances, as she called them. After all, their relationship was distantly cordial at best. According to what the police had told them, he'd been killed in a one-car accident on a stretch of road that was not even close to the route to his house. What had he been doing there, anyway? And at that hour of the night?

She looked at the clock again. Five-fifteen. With a sigh, she gave up any attempt to get some sleep and pulled at the covers, which were now all twisted around her body. Disentangling her legs, she pushed herself to a sitting position and dragged herself out of bed.

Today it was important that she be alert and to have all the parts of her brain in maximum working order. As vice-president of Elite Marketing, she was expected to have her shit together all the time. No matter what. Taylor and Noah Cantrell were due at Elite at seven sharp, and that meant being alert and in charge.

When Taylor had brought Elite into the mega-structure of Arroyo Conglomerate four years ago, one condition of the arrangement had been to add another executive-level position to manage the fast-expanding business. Lindsey had been recommended by a business friend of Taylor's. She was well-respected in the industry and had a great understanding when it came to marketing. Plus she had a well-honed business sense. A high-priced education at the University of Pennsylvania and Wharton School of Finance had seen to that.

She recalled worrying that Craig would think his toes were being stepped on, but he'd told her again and again how glad he was to have her there. He was smart enough to see he needed someone who could shoulder the load with him.

"Some of my clients are taking up more and more time," he'd told her. "This will really help a lot, especially managing the staff."

It was important that the Cantrells knew their faith was not misplaced. Besides, she owed it to Craig.

Keeping the agency running and increasing revenue was the best tribute she could give him. She was sure the staff, when she told them, would be in upheaval, so she needed to be the steadying hand on the wheel.

She'd hated disturbing the Cantrells last night, and the late hour hadn't helped. However, it was a standing rule with all executives in every Arroyo division that Taylor Cantrell was to be notified at once of anything out of the ordinary relating to her top people. This more than met that qualification.

Although she and Taylor had only had sporadic contact in person since Lindsey had joined Elite, they had a relationship so strong that video and phone calls handled any business without a problem. But the woman had a way of letting people know if they'd disappointed her, even while she was smiling and being polite. Lindsey wanted to make sure she was ready for anything today.

They'd have some decisions to make, and fast, the most important being about who would step into Craig's position. Would Taylor look outside the agency again, and bring in someone new the way she had with Lindsey?

She wasn't looking forward to gathering the staff when they arrived at the office. Giving them the sad news would be extra tough since she had no answers for them. She could visualize organized chaos while everyone absorbed the news and Taylor dug into Elite to make sure nothing was wrong. It wasn't, after all, as if this was a normal auto accident, which in itself would have been bad enough. No, there'd be questions, the same ones she kept asking herself.

Lord, please don't let me lose my shit today.

A hot shower washed away most of the cobwebs, and by the time she had dressed and applied makeup, she felt halfway to being human. By seven o'clock, she had the single serving brewers set up in both the break room and her office, the carousels stocked with a variety of flavors and trays of her favorite pastries set out beside them. The answering service was on notice to continue taking calls for an additional hour. That was all she could do to prepare for what was coming.

She had just taken a deep breath when she heard knocking on the glass doors to the suite of offices.

Here goes.

Stepping into the reception area, she saw the Cantrells standing in the hallway. They were a striking couple, the tall man whose Native American heritage gave him dark, exotic good looks and the woman, with her wavy auburn hair, ocean blue eyes and milky skin a direct contrast to him. They were the quintessential power couple, looking for all the world as if they'd had eight hours' sleep and had nothing more to worry about than where to go for lunch.

How do they do it?

"Good morning." She swung the door wide for them. "I'm sorry, I thought for sure you had keys to the office."

Taylor smiled at her. "Only to be used in case of emergency. I don't want people to think they have no privacy."

And who else would consider that important?

"Please come into my office. I have coffee and pastries. I didn't know if you'd have had a chance for anything on the plane or not."

Taylor smiled. "Very thoughtful of you. Thanks."

Lindsey made sure everyone was served before indicating they should sit in the arranged conversation grouping. She waited for them to take the lead.

Taylor took a swallow of her beverage and set her cup on the little table in front of the couch.

"Okay, Lindsey. Tell me everything you know about last night, starting with when you left the office. I'm assuming Craig was still here?"

Lindsey nodded. "I worked until a little past seven before packing it in. He was in his office, working on a project. Maybe more than one, considering the amount of material spread over his desk. I'm sorry I have no idea what it was, but it might have been photos for a couple of magazine layouts. Or he could have been deciding which models to use, since we had three scheduled for different clients."

"Did he supervise all of them himself?" Taylor asked.

Lindsey wrinkled her forehead. "I don't think so, but we operated independently so it was hard to tell. Jerry Ortiz worked on a lot with him and we met once a week to catch up. Last night I asked Craig if he needed any help and he said no, he was good. He just wanted to wrap up some details before he went home to spend the evening with his wife. I have no idea how he ended up where he was or why. Obviously, something changed."

Why didn't I press him harder? Ask more about what he was doing?

But she'd been tired and more than ready to get out of there. She'd remember that for a long time.

Taylor took another swallow of coffee. "Noah called the police station and had them fax a copy of the report to the house before we left."

"And they did it just like that? I thought the police were cranky about doing things like that, especially for someone they don't know." Then she stopped and heat skimmed her cheeks. "Sorry. I forgot who I was talking to."

Taylor laughed. "Sometimes being who we are has its advantages."

Lindsey nibbled on her lips. "Did it show anything?"

"Not much, but it's just the preliminary report. But at that location, he wasn't even close to being on the way home when he had the accident. I haven't spoken to Natalia, but did she have any idea where he might have been headed? Or why he ended up staying so late at the office?"

Lindsey shook her head. "None at all."

"Had you noticed anything different about him lately?" Taylor asked. "Any change in habits or behavior?"

What could she really say? All she had were vague suspicions. Still…

"Anything you can share," Taylor prompted, "no matter how small, could be helpful. You know I have a lot of confidence in your opinion."

"I just want to make sure I'm not mistaking pressure nerves for something else." She got up to brew another cup of coffee. She'd have to be careful not to drink herself into caffeine overload today. "Craig was smart and savvy, and knew what he was doing. But lately I got the feeling he was dealing with a lot of pressure. Maybe because of some of the large accounts he'd taken on. People who wanted more campaigns and bigger ones."

Taylor frowned. "Do you think they were too much for him to manage?"

"No." Lindsey shook her head. The last thing she wanted was to damage Craig's reputation as a top marketing person in his field. "And you know yourself how good the money was." She paused, choosing her words with care. "But if I'm truthful, the last couple of years he seemed, oh, antsy, I guess, is the best way to put it. Like he was walking some kind of fine line. I have no idea what it could have been, though. Elite is doing extremely well. We almost have more clients than we can handle, especially as we're expanding our international market. In fact, we even discussed bringing another person on board to handle some of the smaller accounts."

Taylor smiled. "An abundance of business is always good to hear. But..."

"Yes." Lindsey nodded. "But. I kept getting the distinct feeling something was off. I was hoping to have something more concrete than just a feeling before I approached him about it."

Noah leaned forward and placed his coffee mug on the table.

"Was it financial, Lindsey? If he was keeping things from you, that could be a problem."

A tiny knot tightened in her stomach and she did her best to keep her voice even. "Truthfully, Mr. Cantrell—"

"Noah," he interrupted. "I think it's time we dispense with formalities."

"Noah." *Can I express my reservations to him without being sure?* The last thing she wanted was to create trouble where there was none.

"Lindsey." Taylor's voice was friendly but firm. This was, after all, business. "The president of a viable marketing company that is a component of Arroyo Enterprises has died both unexpectedly and in odd circumstances. It may turn out to be a sudden heart attack and he may have just been taking a drive to clear his head after a long workday. But I trust your instincts. If there is even a hint of something bothering you, then you need to share it with us. I have to know how we're going to handle things going forward."

23

The knot in her belly got a little tighter. "Going forward? Do you think you might close the agency?"

"No." The other woman shook her head. "Not at all. Not even a consideration, unless we find something really dire. But we can't have a vacuum here. You know yourself this agency is a moneymaker, and that looks good on the Arroyo balance sheet and to the board of directors. If we need to get in front of something, now is the time to do it."

"And there may be nothing at all to worry about." Lindsey cleared her throat. "Please keep in mind that this is just my impression."

Taylor nodded. "Understood."

"Okay. Like I said before, for the past two years or so, Craig has seemed edgy. Jumpy even, at times. As if he was wrestling with some kind of problem. He was traveling a lot for these photo shoots, much of it out of the country. That wasn't a bad thing. We've expanded at a rapid rate in the global marketplace, which means customers with a wide variety of tastes. Plus, a lot of our clients like the tropical settings for layouts. I offered several times to help ease his load, but he was very proprietary about his clients and insisted on managing everything himself. I had little to do with the foreign trips. Now and then, Natalia went with him on the trips—I think to help corral the models."

Noah lifted an eyebrow. "He didn't ask you to go with him? Or one of the account managers?"

"Sometimes Jerry Ortiz, who worked closely with him, but he usually made it plain he preferred doing it himself." Lindsey shook her head. "I was busy overseeing everything else when he was tied up with one of these projects, and the models were, well, a handful for one of the account managers to handle. They were strictly Craig's baby."

The Cantrells exchanged a glance.

"Would you say there was anything improper going on between Craig and any of the models?" Taylor asked.

"No, nothing like that." Again, Lindsey shook her head. "Not at all. But something was on his mind."

"All right." Taylor leaned back in her chair and again something passed unspoken between her and her husband. "Here's what I'd like to do. Noah's heading to the police station to see if they've learned anything else. They'll have gone over the car by now, to see if there were any mechanical problems."

Maybe that was what it was. But... "Craig kept that car in tiptop condition."

"Mechanical problems can still happen," Noah pointed out. "I want to make sure they've checked every single thing."

Taylor turned to Lindsey. "You and I need to decide what we're going to tell clients and share that with the staff. Additionally, because Elite has a high public profile, as soon as word gets out, the media will be like starving wolves at your door. How about if you draft something and run it by me?"

Lindsey nodded. "I can do that. Are you thinking about a press conference?"

Taylor shook her head. "No. I want to low-key this. In fact, I don't want to make a general announcement. We'll need to call his list of clients, something I think is best you handle. If they ask, we'll send them a brief statement electronically. And we should get ready for calls from others as word trickles out. Maybe even the media, although I hope not. He had a pretty high profile in the Miami–Fort Lauderdale area, right?"

Lindsey nodded. "Okay. I'll get something put together for you to take a look at. Before we do anything, however, I'd like us to meet with the staff. We have to tell them right away. When Craig's in town, he's always in his office early. His absence will raise questions. How about I get them in the conference room as soon as they arrive at work?"

Taylor nodded. "Yes. Let's do that."

Lindsey wet her lips then asked the question she'd been battling with. But it was important that she knew. "I should probably wait until we get past this immediate crisis, so I hope you'll forgive me for asking." She put on her best professional face. "Are you planning to bring someone in from the outside to take over in Craig's place?"

The Cantrells exchanged a look and Noah gestured to his wife.

Your deal, he told her in unspoken acknowledgment.

"We discussed this on the way over here from Texas," Taylor answered. "We'd like you to step in as head of the agency. Think about it. You know the operation and the clients. And we know you. It would be one less thing to worry about. Elite would be in very good hands and both the clients and the staff know you." She paused. "Unless you'd rather not do it. But, Lindsey, you're the logical person."

For a moment Lindsey wasn't sure she'd heard right. "Take charge of Elite?"

"That's not a problem, is it?" Noah asked, his face expressionless.

"Of course not." She was stunned. "But what about Natalia? Won't she inherit Craig's share of Elite? She might not like having me around."

Taylor shook her head. "We prepared for that. In all the Arroyo subsidiaries, if the partner passes away, Arroyo does a buyout with the surviving spouse. If there's no spouse, then with the estate. We can't have unqualified people suddenly in charge of our subsidiaries just because they inherited."

"Makes sense. That means you're buying the other fifty-one percent of whatever business it is, right?"

"That's correct. It then becomes a wholly owned subsidiary of Arroyo, so you don't have to worry about some idiot coming in and making a mess of things. It's your baby, at least for now."

Lindsey didn't know whether to be thrilled or terrified. "Thank you both for having such faith in me."

"Your reputation and history speak for themselves. That's why we sought you out to begin with." Noah rose from his chair and held out his hand. "We know you'll do a great job, Lindsey. And now I'm going to leave you and Taylor to dig into what's going on here and keep things running smoothly while I get on with my business. How about dinner at eight to recap the day and see where we are?"

Lindsey's head was spinning, but she managed to nod. "Whatever you need, I'm there."

"Good. I'm glad we got that settled." Taylor grinned at her husband. "I knew we'd made the right decision."

"Okay, then. I'm out of here."

It said a lot that Noah Cantrell did not leave without kissing his wife goodbye. It was a good indication of the strength of their relationship and how comfortable they felt in their own skins.

As soon as Noah was gone, Taylor refilled her cup. "Okay, Lindsey. Let's get to work."

Chapter Two

Lindsey scanned the faces of the staff gathered around the big conference room table. Their expressions ran the gamut from blank to stunned. Taylor had just laid out the facts of Craig's accident, telling them that was all the information they had at the moment, and asking if anyone had any questions. Lindsey had felt the announcement was better coming from the chairman of Arroyo, and anything she said would have more impact. She was, after all, the head honcho.

For a very long moment, no one said a word. Sarah Colt, Craig's administrative assistant, was the first one to find her voice.

"Dead? Craig's dead? I don't understand. What do you mean he's dead? How is that even possible? I was just working with him in his office yesterday."

Her eyes were wide in her face which had gone pale. Lindsey knew just how she felt. Again, the silence in the room was so thick it was almost tangible. Then everyone began speaking at the same time.

Lindsey held up her hand, calming the babble of voices. "Please. I know this has shocked everyone, but one at a time, please."

"Did he have a heart attack or something?" The question came from Jerry Ortiz.

"We're waiting for the final autopsy report to give us some answers there," Taylor replied. "We'll know more after that and I'll share with you as much as I can. Does anyone know if he had health problems he was hiding? Was he suffering from more stress than usual?"

Lindsey looked around the room. "Anyone? Any hint at all?"

No one said a word, just looked at one another and shook their heads.

"Jerry?" Lindsey prodded. "You'd have the best read on him. Did you notice something off lately?"

Jerry shook his head. "Sometimes he'd be a little more uptight than usual, but when deadlines are approaching, I think we all get that way."

"Fine." Lindsey referred to her notes. "The first thing we need to do is notify all the clients. If they hear it through the gossip grapevine, they will immediately suspect something is wrong. We don't want that to happen. I'll be drafting some guidelines," Lindsey told them. "We'll send them electronically to each of you when I have something."

"We'll want to meet with each of you separately this afternoon," Taylor added. "It would help if you could get your client lists and current projects together. I know Lindsey no doubt has a cursory idea of projects other than her own, but we'll both need a working knowledge of everything."

Annie Balboa raised her hand. "Will you be switching account managers around?"

"The only change we expect to make is handing most of Craig's accounts over to Lindsey," Taylor answered. "Otherwise there's no reason to. If something's not broken, don't try to fix it." She paused. "Another question. Do any of you happen to know why Craig would be in the area of town where he was found? Especially that late at night?"

There was some head-shaking and more bewildered looks, but no one had an answer for her.

"All right, then." Lindsey looked around the table at everyone. "We have important projects in process and clients who expect them to be uninterrupted. It's important that we keep things running here while we search for answers."

"I'll be working out of Craig's office while I'm here. If you have any questions, you should direct them to Lindsey, but I'm around for backup." Taylor turned to the admin. "Sarah? It would be a huge help if you sat in with me. I'm sure your position gave you a good handle on the office operations. Right?"

Lindsey noticed a slight hesitation before the woman nodded, and made a mental note to discuss it with Taylor.

"Thank you." Taylor surveyed the group seated around the table. "As soon as we have something to share with everyone, we will. Once the word gets out, we may get some calls from the media. I'm sure we don't need to tell you all to stay away from them and also not to discuss anything outside this office."

Everyone nodded.

"Okay." Lindsey let out a slow breath. "I'll draft something as a guideline for each of you to use when you speak to your clients. It's important we're all on the same page. If you have a question, please don't hesitate to check with me. Clients will have questions.

Whatever you can tell them will be in the memo I give you. Nothing more. We're still waiting for more information ourselves."

She rose from her seat, a clear indication the meeting was over.

Taylor also stood, picking up her tablet.

"Sarah, bring everything you have on Craig's upcoming schedule and what he's had you working on. We'll have to split up his projects, but before that we need to get a handle on what each one was and how he was working it."

"Okay." Sarah nodded. "Let me just get my things together and I'll be right there."

Taylor started across the hall to what had been Craig's office. Sarah moved toward the door as well, but Lindsey stopped her before she could leave the room.

"You looked a little hesitant when Taylor asked you to work with her this afternoon. Is there a problem?"

Sarah shook her head. "I just hope I can tell her whatever she needs to know. Craig didn't always keep me in the loop on things, especially lately."

Lindsey cocked an eyebrow. "You mean he kept things from you?"

The other woman shrugged. "It's just a feeling I had. With some accounts, he didn't always share the same details he did with others."

The funny little feeling flopped around in Lindsey's stomach again. What on earth can Craig have been hiding? And why?

"Don't worry. If something weird turns up — and I'm not saying it will — none of this falls on your shoulders. You're a real asset to Elite and I want you to keep that in mind."

"Thanks, Lindsey." Sarah gave her a weak smile. "I appreciate it."

The morning passed in a blur. Once Lindsey had something put together and distributed it, everyone was busy making calls, even as they continued to take care of the details of business.

Lindsey spent a lot of time reassuring her clients and Craig's that nothing would disrupt anything that was in process. Everyone had questions, and of course they were concerned about their ad campaigns and other promotional activities.

While Lindsey made her own calls, she fielded questions her account managers needed answers for. There were a lot of unhappy campers. All the clients they spoke with were shocked by Craig's death and expressed sympathy for his wife, but they wanted to know if it would affect their account at all.

It soon became obvious those clients were contacting other people to share the information, because the phone at Elite began ringing nonstop. Lindsey had Felice, her own admin, helping with the sheer volume of calls that came in to the main number, sifting out those that needed Lindsey's personal attention and those that could be handed off to others.

It was late morning before she managed to find five seconds to catch a breath. She had just leaned back in her chair when Taylor buzzed her.

Lindsey picked up her phone. "Do you need me?"

"Not yet," Taylor said. "I just wanted to let you know I heard from Noah. We should get the final results of the autopsy later this afternoon. It might take until tomorrow for any lab results. And Natalia was definitely not pleased with that."

"What do you mean?"

"She called this morning about getting the body released to the funeral home, and pitched a holy fit when they told her she'd have to wait until the autopsy was finished."

"I'm not surprised. She thinks the world revolves around Natalia. I'll tell you, I only tolerated her because it was obvious she loved Craig and went out of her way to make his life pleasant. Has Noah spoken to her?"

"He's heading out there now, to see if he can help with the funeral arrangements. To let her know Arroyo has resources available." Taylor gave a ladylike snort. "I can hardly wait to hear about that at dinner."

"Better you than me. I have a feeling she sees me as little more than the hired help, last night notwithstanding. Does she know yet she doesn't get Craig's share of Elite?"

"Oh, she's known all along. We discussed it at our first dinner meeting with them. But Natalia has her own money and plenty of it. I think without it, Craig would not have gotten to where he did."

"Good. I'd hate to be in the middle of a fight over it with her."

"Never happen."

At noon, Lindsey finally had the receptionist take over the phone and sent Felice off to lunch. She was about to fix yet another cup of coffee for herself when Taylor buzzed her and asked her to come to Craig's office

Taylor nodded at her when she entered the room. "Close the door, please. I assume you have the phone handled for the moment?"

Lindsey dropped into one of the client chairs in front of the desk, pushed her thick blonde hair out of the way behind her ears and took a deep breath.

"Yes, but it's only a short reprieve. Craig was a very visible figure in the community and the industry, and Natalia even more so. I'm sure you know they socialized with the absolute cream of society in this area. Think those massive houses on the water. It's a good thing Elite makes the money it does, or I think she would have pulled the plug. Still…"

Taylor cocked her head. "Still what?"

"Elite is a huge moneymaker, but not in the class with, say, Frank Podesta's international shipping corporation. I sometimes wonder why Natalia funded this to begin with and encouraged Craig in his work. He was very good at it, but did she just want him to have a toy to play with so he felt useful?"

"Strange situation," Taylor agreed. She took a sip from the bottle of water on the corner of her desk. "I've gone through all Craig's files, both print and electronic." She pointed to a pad on her desk which was filled with notes. "I thought I'd find some answers but all I have is more questions."

Lindsey frowned. "About what?"

Taylor sighed. "I wish I knew. Everything looks to be in perfect shape, but I just have a funny feeling about things. Maybe it all looks too perfect. Do you know what I mean?"

"I do. I've had the same feeling myself, and I can't tell you why, either. It's just there, slithering along beneath the surface."

"Well. If two smart women have the same feeling, I'd say it's not just chasing ghosts."

Lindsey raked her fingers through her hair. "I just keep asking myself, what could possibly be wrong? Craig had the major responsibility for the agency, but he was supposed to read me in on everything. Help make sure there were no glitches or problems, especially with the major clients. I thought that was what was happening, so why do we both suddenly have this weird feeling?"

Before Taylor could say anything, a phone rang from somewhere deep in the desk, a strange double ringtone. She frowned and started opening drawers, searching for it. By the time she located it, buried in the bottom right-hand drawer and enclosed in a small mahogany box, the ringing had stopped. But as soon as she lifted it out, the sound began again.

She pushed Accept then pressed the button for the speaker so Lindsey could listen. "Hello?"

No one said anything on the other end, so she said hello again.

"Where is Craig?" The voice was male, deep and with a slight accent. "And who is this answering the phone?"

"Who is this?" she asked.

"Let me speak to Craig."

Taylor exchanged a look with Lindsey. "I'm sorry, but he's not available. Can someone else help you?"

"It is important that I know where he is."

Taylor paused for a moment. "I'm sorry to tell you that Mr. Wainwright was killed in an automobile accident last evening."

Another long pause. Then the connection went dead.

Taylor stared at the phone. "Well, that was weird."

"He didn't even ask for any details," Lindsey pointed out.

"You're right. As a matter of fact, he didn't ask anything. I'd like to know what the hell Craig was doing with a cheap burner phone and why it was in a drawer. And why whoever who called did so on that phone instead of the regular number." She hit Redial, but all she got was the fast busy signal that indicated an out-of-service number. When she tried again, she got nothing but dead air. Frowning, she stared at the phone. "What the hell?"

Lindsey leaned forward. "Whoever that was, you know they took the SIM card out when they didn't get Craig. And damn fast."

"No kidding. Listen. My antenna is wiggling like an earthworm. I want to call Noah about this and—no offense, Lindsey—I don't want to do it from here."

"No offense taken. But I'll be really hacked off if someone in this agency is into funny business."

"Starting with Craig. Come on. Let's get out of here and get some lunch. Get your purse and meet me by the elevator. I'll tell Sarah we're leaving for a while and to take messages."

Strangely—and as luck would have it— they were the only two in the elevator car.

"That call bothers the hell out of me," Lindsey said as they rode down.

Taylor nodded. "Me too. I'm going to reach out to Noah when we get out of the building. Give him a heads-up on it. Damn. I'd hate to think Craig was involved in something not quite kosher."

"Me too. Straight-arrow Craig? The thought of it boggles my mind. Still…"

"Right. You wonder how well you really know someone."

As they exited the building, Lindsey again tried to force back the uneasy feeling creeping through her. The fact that Taylor had the same feeling didn't help. Craig's death and the questions surrounding it were bad enough. The last thing they needed on top of that was another disaster in the making.

Chapter Three

Arianna was shaking with a mixture of nerves and excitement. How was it possible this wonderful chance had come out of the blue for her, a girl with nothing, who hardly knew anyone? A girl who had come to New York looking for success and excitement but who was reduced to working minimum wage jobs while she prayed for opportunities? And now one had popped into her life almost by accident. Chances like this didn't come along too often.

Drawing in a steadying breath, she waved at the man waiting for her in a booth in the high-end restaurant. Lips curving in a nervous smile, she slid into the seat opposite him. Although the man across from her gave her an answering smile, it did little to settle her shaky nerves. She had to make a good impression today. This could be her only chance.

"You look lovely, Arianna." His gaze rolled over her, taking in every detail of her appearance. "I knew you would make the perfect model."

"I've only done this for volunteer and fundraising events," she told the man. "I never expected anything to come of it."

"It's my business to spot real talent. We have a very particular clientele and they expect only the best from us." He paused. "And I believe you have that talent."

She wet her lips, a nervous habit, then stopped before she licked off all her lipstick. "I was so surprised when you called me."

And wasn't that just the understatement of the year. She had hoped but didn't believe that her appearance in the last charity fundraiser would get her some real honest-to-god jobs. Her savings had dwindled, her roommate was engaged and moving out and it seemed the market was flooded with restaurant hostesses.

She swallowed a sigh. Running off with Dwayne Goodlet right after her high-school graduation she was sure now had been one of the most stupid things she'd done, along with a whole host of others.

'New York, babe. We'll hit it big.'

Dwayne had hit it big all right. Falling in with a gang, ending up in prison and leaving her with no money and no skills to fend for herself. Lucky for her she'd met some nice people, or she'd be living on the streets. She shuddered at the thought.

But here she was, five years later, still unskilled, undereducated and her only saleable commodity seemed to be her looks.

A quirk of fate had gotten her into her first fashion show, where she'd heard girls saying how important it was to capitalize on their looks while they could. The girl who had brought her to the organizer had kept telling her if the right people saw her, the big money was waiting. Maybe she could catch on with a modeling agency and at last have some kind of stable income. When the man had approached her after the fashion show, she'd had all she could do to keep from screaming and throwing her arms around him. *Professional,* she kept reminding herself. *Cool and professional.*

She knew this was big money. The business card with raised lettering he'd given her bore the name of an agency several of the girls were familiar with.

"His models get to travel to very exotic places," Mari Wilde had told her. "They even get jobs in Europe and South America. Those pay big bucks, chickee."

Big bucks. That would certainly be nice.

A waiter approached their table.

"Would you like a drink?" the man across from her asked.

Alexander, she reminded herself. *His name's Keith Alexander.*

"No, thank you, Mr. Alexander. But some iced tea would be nice."

He looked at the waiter. "Iced tea for the lady and a scotch on the rocks for me. Now." He smiled again. "Let's get down to business. I have some important projects on the calendar and I want to discuss where you'd fit in. We'll need to get a portfolio done for you. Include you in the publicity package." He tilted his head, studying her. "You don't mind if clients might want to see a photo shoot, do you?"

"Oh no. No, not at all." Special observers were often invited to photo shoots. She didn't care as long as she got paid the amount he'd teased her with. Not to mention the travel to exotic places.

They ordered lunch, although Arianna wasn't sure she could eat all that much. Nerves had stifled her appetite. Alexander chatted at her all through lunch, his voice warm and pleasing as if he knew her nerves were strung tight and needed soothing. When the waiter had cleared away their plates, he pulled an envelope from his inside jacket pocket and handed it to her.

"This is just a simple letter of agreement," he explained. "It gives us permission to represent you exclusively. It explains your hourly rate and sets out which of your expenses we cover. If you could read it and sign both it and the copy, we can move forward. Bella Donna Models has been asked to provide the models for some major upcoming advertising campaigns."

Bella Donna. Arianna had to control herself. Several of the girls in the show had mentioned them. Said they did photo shoots in exotic places and their models got top exposure. One girl had warned her when Alexander approached her that the word was their models didn't last long. That Bella Donna was always looking for fresh faces.

Arianna didn't mind. As far as she was concerned, if there was a lot of turnover, it created opportunities for more people. For however long it lasted, it would establish her and give her the credentials to seek other representation. She read the letter through, but it seemed pretty straightforward to her. The fees she would receive made her eyes pop.

"You could have someone look it over," Alexander pointed out, "but there are no hidden clauses, as you can see. And we should move forward on this as soon as possible."

Of course we should.

"The thing is," he went on, "we have a big contract with a bathing suit designer and we're doing a location shoot in the Caribbean. On an island." He grinned at her. "Ever been to the Caribbean, Arianna?"

Ever been to the Caribbean? He might as well have asked her if she'd been to Mars. With the pen he handed her, Arianna scrawled her signature at the bottom of both the letter and the copy. Alexander took the original.

"Most excellent," he told her. "Let's get out of here. I think I can get you squeezed into this afternoon's photo session for portfolios."

"Oh," she breathed. "That would be wonderful. Are we going right now?"

"No sense wasting time. We want to be ready for Elite. I have a car waiting that will take us right to the studio. If all goes well, we'll be on a plane for Miami tonight, then off to the location."

Is this moving too fast? Should I ask for time to think it over? Discuss it with someone? But then I might lose the opportunity. Lord knew there were dozens of females out there like her, hungry for something like this.

Swallowing her misgivings, she let Alexander take her arm and guide her out of the door.

Chapter Four

They managed to snag the last empty booth at the little Italian place right next to the office building. Just as they slid into their seats, Lindsey's cell rang and she glanced at the screen.

"It's the office," she told Taylor as she pressed the button to answer. "God. I just left there. What now? Yes, Leda, what is it?"

"We have the television on in the break room, Lindsey. Someone just told me Mr. Wainwright's death is on the noon news."

Lindsey blew out a breath. "I guess we should have expected it. He's a player in the business community and his wife is a big deal in social circles. Anything negative?"

"No. It's being called an unfortunate one-car accident."

"Okay. You know the drill, right?"

She could almost see Leda nodding.

"We have no further information and all questions should be directed to you."

"Good work. No wonder you're so valuable. Listen. Set it up to record the next broadcast. If anything else pops up, text me, but we should be back in about an hour."

She sighed as she put the phone on the table and looked at Taylor.

"I know this is only the beginning. I'll meet with everyone this afternoon to create a game plan. I'll see who I can hand off some of my clients to so I can take over some of Craig's. I know they'll need special handling."

"What about Jerry Ortiz? This morning you identified him as working on some of those clients with Craig."

Lindsey chewed her lip, trying to choose her words with great care. "Don't get me wrong, Jerry's as good as they come, but he also has a healthy dose of arrogance and he may not listen carefully enough to our hot-button clients. Or he may see this as a chance to put his own stamp on things without clearing it with me."

Taylor nodded her agreement. "I hear you. I trust your judgment, so I leave it all up to you."

"Have you heard from Noah again?"

"Yes. He messaged while you were on the phone with Leda. He's on his way back from the Wainwright house. I told him to meet us here. I want to give him that cell phone we found and have him check out both the phone and the call."

"But if the number is blocked, how will he find out who it belongs to?"

Taylor's mouth curved in a tiny smile. "Trust me. Noah can find out just about anything. And if he can't, he knows people who can."

The waiter filled water glasses and served coffee and the two women reviewed everything so far, which, sad to say, wasn't that much.

"Call me crazy," Taylor said, "but I just have this wild feeling there's more to Craig's accident than we see on the surface, and that in some way it's connected to Elite."

"God, let's hope not." But Lindsey had the same feeling dancing along her spine, even though she did her best to squash it.

By then Noah had arrived, easing onto the bench seat next to his wife.

"So how did it go with the ice queen?" Lindsey asked.

Noah gave a little snort. "At least I'm not frozen to death, although it was close. Was she like that with you, Lindsey?"

"Except when Craig was around. I'll tell you." She shook her head. "I could never quite see the two of them together, but it was obvious they had a tight connection." She shrugged. "I guess it takes all kinds."

Taylor nodded. "I met her for the first time when Noah and I came down here to talk to Craig about the merger. When we had dinner with them, she certainly put on a good performance. I'm sure becoming part of Arroyo was important to her. Craig said she came from South American high society and I believe it." She turned to her husband. "So how was your meeting with her?"

"About as you'd expect. It's obvious she's grieving but she's also one of these people who never lose control. She had a couple of people there, obviously friends, helping her with the arrangements. It seems they took care of all that ahead of time."

"As I would have expected," Taylor agreed. "I'm sure you let her know we're here to help if she needs it. That's just standard procedure."

"I did, although I wouldn't hold my breath waiting for a call." He paused to ask the waiter for some coffee. "I discussed the autopsy with her."

Taylor snorted. "I'll bet that was fun."

"She made this big deal about not wanting his body mutilated, especially since everything looked so cut and dried. I explained it all to her again, and while she's not too happy about it, she's decided it would not be in her best interest to raise a fuss."

"Thank the lord for that. Where does that leave things as far as the funeral is concerned? We definitely need to have a presence."

"The detective I spoke with said they should be finished with everything, including lab results, in a couple of days. Natalia said she'd have someone call or fax the funeral arrangements over to the office as soon as they were finalized. Or have someone call us. She hoped everyone would be able to attend." He shrugged. "Should give the cops plenty of time to complete the autopsy. They're probably trying to pin down how a healthy man would suddenly have some kind of episode that would cause an accident like this." He shook his head. "I saw the pictures of the accident. The car was all smashed to hell against the concrete of the overpass. It doesn't look like he tried to stop at all."

Taylor's forehead creased in a frown. "You think it was suicide?"

"Not necessarily. The autopsy may give us some answers. I spoke to the medical examiner and he said they were waiting for his medical records to arrive, plus the lab analysis of his blood. They aren't sitting on it, believe me."

"If it was suicide," Taylor said slowly, "we may have more problems than we think."

"Let's not borrow trouble if we don't have to," Noah told her. "Wait for the facts."

"I agree. It's bad enough handling the flood of calls as the word of Craig's death spreads." Lindsey explained to him how they were dealing with things.

"She's got it taken care of," Taylor told her husband. "Elite's in good hands. Did Natalia say anything about Craig's ownership share of the agency?"

Noah shook his head. "She knew the setup. Craig told her when we first approached him. Right now she's the grieving widow, but once we get past that you can bet she'll be all over us asking questions. Too bad. She provided the startup capital for Elite and when we bought into the firm, she got a healthy payday. I'll remind her of that if need be. We have enough to do without going head to head with her."

"Speaking of paydays and the accounting," Taylor interjected, "I don't know if Craig was cooking the books here or not. That's the first thing I always think of when something strange pops up. It's just the way my mind works. Noah, we should bring in John Martino if he's available. If anyone can find something, it's John. He's the best forensic accountant around." She turned to Lindsey. "You remember John, right? You met him four years ago. What do you think? He's the best we can get for this."

Every muscle in Lindsey's body tightened and for a moment she stopped breathing. Shock ran through her system. She did her best not to show her reaction to Taylor. She just hoped her face didn't give away the thoughts racing through her mind. She remembered John Martino, all right. In hot, vivid, erotic detail. Probably in greater detail than she wanted.

Too many nights she still dreamed of his hands on her body, his mouth sucking on a nipple, his teeth scraping it. His touch everywhere, his fingers inside her, his lips pulling on her clit. And her stupidity where he was concerned. She hadn't seen the man for four years, but she still had to work hard to push him to the very back of her consciousness. But at Taylor's words, just like that, the current crisis faded into the background and sensual images swirled in her mind. She had to cross her legs and send her body signals that this was no time to be thinking about the things she and John Martino had done naked in her bed.

Four years ago Taylor and Noah had come to Miami, where she was working at the time, to talk to her about taking the job at Elite. John Martino, their close friend, had been in town digging through the books and accounts of a major land developer. He had joined them for dinner twice and it had been instant fireworks between the two of them.

Lindsey had never been the kind to fall into bed with anyone after just a hello. But John, with his dark good looks and incredible personality, his total sexiness and hands that did magical things to her body, swept all her rules and good intentions aside. For four days and nights they'd lit up the atmosphere with the air sizzling between them, something the Cantrells knew nothing about. Four days of intense emotion and even more intense erotic pleasure.

When he'd left her, the last thing he'd said was, "I'll call you. Count on it. We aren't even close to finished here."

She'd thought he meant it. When a couple of weeks had passed and she'd heard nothing from him, not even an email, she'd toyed with the idea of contacting him, but something had held her back. It wasn't as if he'd made her an actual promise. She reminded herself over and over that it was a common expression, a friendly way of saying *so long and it was nice.*

Finally, on one of the Cantrell visits to Elite, she'd managed to bring him up in a conversation with Taylor in what she'd hoped was a casual manner.

"How's John? Where is he now? What's his latest project like?"

It seemed John was in Bermuda for a special client and no one knew how long it would take. The man traveled all over the world. *Okay*, she'd thought, *I'm a big girl. John's a nationally sought-after expert in his field who probably never has a spare moment.* He was in great demand, and why not? He was the best at what he did.

So she'd waited some more, doing her best to push him to the back of her mind. Weeks then months had gone by without any contact. She needed to get over herself. It did sadden her that she'd been so sure the connection they'd made was strong, only to have nothing come of it. Or maybe she'd been the only one who'd felt that way and she'd misunderstood the whole thing.

She was still waiting for that call, anger and hurt and disappointment a ball of emotions she'd buried as deep as possible. Now she'd have to face him again, and she wondered what that would be like. How would she handle it? How would he? Would he act as if nothing had ever happened between them?

I have to stop driving myself crazy. I'm thirty-five years old, a mature, adult businesswoman, for god's sake, not some sex-crazy idiot.

"I think it's a great idea," she agreed, hoping her voice gave nothing away. "He's exactly what we need."

"Good. I wanted to get everything else set before I bring up our next challenge."

"Challenge?" Noah lifted an eyebrow.

"Yes."

As soon as the waiter had taken their orders, Taylor pulled the cell phone out of her purse and handed it to Noah.

"What's this?" He turned it over in his hands.

"A puzzle," Taylor said.

"This rang in a drawer of Craig's desk while your wife and I were meeting in there," Lindsey told him.

"Yeah?" One eyebrow arched. "It was in a drawer?"

"Yes." She looked at Taylor. "Startled both of us, me especially. I had no idea he kept some kind of secret phone hidden away. Noah, caller ID is blocked on the phone so you have no idea who's calling."

"When we tried to call back," Taylor added, "we got nothing. As if the phone itself was dead."

"Whoever had the phone on the other end probably pulled the SIM card."

"And in just seconds the phone locked and we don't have the password. I want to know who this guy is and who else called Wainwright on this phone."

Noah turned it over in his hands, studying it. "I'll call Liam Benedict. He's hired a data specialist who might be able to help us."

Taylor turned to Lindsey. "Liam owns a company in Tampa that creates specifically tailored security software for companies like defense contractors. Lately they've branched out and gotten into digital forensics, and hired on a couple of experts."

"The theory is," Noah added, "to find out how the codes on the SIM cards can be broken then write software that prevents that."

Lindsey's jaw dropped. "Wow. I thought I was up to date on this stuff."

"It's a whole new field," Taylor explained. "It's flourished since the government has refused to allow phone companies to release the lock codes on phones."

"But it's also come up," Noah added, "because people running illegal enterprises have hired people to write their own lock codes and change them regularly. I'd be happy to explain to you how it all works if I understood it more."

Taylor laughed. "Don't let him fool you. He's hooked on this stuff like a kid."

Noah laughed, an unusual sound from him. Lindsey was used to his implacable, stolid expression, one that softened only when he looked at his wife.

"We're still planning to be here for a few more days, right?"

"Yes." Taylor nodded. "Until we find out what the hell Craig was into and what position it leaves Elite in. I want to give Lindsey all the help she needs to make sure things are running to her satisfaction. And hopefully not find any more surprises."

"Then I'm going to call Liam and ask him if we can borrow his expert for a couple of days. I can send the plane for him."

Taylor nodded. "Do it. And call John while you're at it. Find out where he is right now and if he can free himself up."

Noah pushed his chair back from the table and walked away, holding his cell phone to his ear.

"All set," he told them when he returned to his seat. "He's tied up this afternoon, but he can be here for a late dinner. I arranged to send the plane for him."

"Good."

"I'm picking him up at the airport myself and I reserved a suite for him at our hotel. I'll order a second car for you, so I don't leave you stranded."

"That's not necessary," Lindsey told him. "I have my car here. I can take Taylor any place she needs to go before tonight or she can just borrow my car. We're all meeting for dinner, anyway."

Taylor nodded. "That works. Okay, back to the office and the client files."

"Nothing jumped out when you went through things this morning?" Noah asked.

"No." Taylor shook her head. "I checked them carefully, both the paper files and the electronic ones."

Noah looked from one to the other. "Why don't the two of you take another crack at them this afternoon?"

"I was going to suggest that exact thing," Lindsey said. "I want to go over the client files and ledgers one by one with you. Between the two of us we should catch anything out of the ordinary. Or just something that looks or sounds hinky."

"Let's do it," Taylor agreed. "After that phone call, I want to see if we missed something. Lindsey, I'd like a half-hour with each of the account managers to see where they are after this morning. Then I'm all yours."

Lindsey took a sip of water. "If Craig was into something I knew nothing about, I damn well want to find out what it is. And how it is I never even got a sniff of it. The two of us met every Monday morning to review the previous week and make sure everyone had their ducks in a row for the coming week."

"And he never acted weird?" Taylor asked. "You know, as if he had something on his mind? Although I don't know why I'm even asking. You're sharp enough you would have spotted it."

"I hope." Lindsey blew out a breath. "I'm sorry if I missed something — "

Taylor held up a hand. "Please. Don't apologize. Some people are masters at hiding things. You're far from stupid, Lindsey. Believe me, I had both Craig and Elite checked thoroughly before approaching him with the offer, so he had to be an expert at this. But now, I'm damned determined to find out."

"As am I," Noah added.

She looked at Noah. "I'd be very happy if we could get the autopsy results sooner rather than later. Who did you connect with at the police station?"

"Ron Vacca. He's the traffic-homicide detective in charge of the case. He seems like a straight-up guy. No bullshit. We got along okay."

"Is he going to see if he can move things along?"

Noah gave her a lopsided grin. "As much as possible. Some of this stuff takes a certain amount of time. You know that."

"I know. I just have this itchy feeling that if we had the autopsy results, we might have some answers about the accident."

"Of course," Lindsey pointed out, "it still doesn't tell us why he was where he was. He told me he was going directly home after he finished up what he was doing."

"And what exactly *was* he doing?" Noah asked. "Did he mention it to you?"

She shook her head. "He may have been working on last-minute stuff for a couple of shoots coming up in the Caribbean. He had some pictures of models on his desk and they looked like his usual type for these."

Noah lifted an eyebrow. "Usual type?"

"The clients that ordered these particular layouts — usually fashion designers — had specific types they wanted. No redheads, for example. No light-brown hair."

"What?" Taylor smoothed her hand over her auburn hair in an exaggerated gesture and grinned. "I think I'm insulted."

Noah laughed. "Doesn't matter. I don't want you posing for anyone other than me."

Lindsey looked from one to the other. She had always been fascinated by the chemistry and silent communication between these two. It wasn't that they shut other people out. In Taylor's situation, she had to be able to establish instant rapport with people. No, it was more the feeling that their chemistry went way beyond the physical. She wondered if she'd ever meet anyone she could have that with. And why the hell was she thinking of this in the middle of a building crisis?

"Maybe I should have taken a closer look at the schedule for them." She shook her head. "But, truthfully, there didn't seem to be any problems."

"And I may be creating something where there's nothing," Taylor pointed out. "That would make me feel a lot better. But right now, with that phone call and the unanswered questions about Craig's death, I think we need to be suspicious of everything."

"Then we should meet with Jerry Ortiz this afternoon," Lindsey told her. "Sooner rather than later is best, since he worked closely with Craig on a lot of his clients."

"We'll do it right after the staff briefing. Noah, we may need to bring in some experts to take this thing apart."

"You may be right. This could be nothing, or it could be one of those things where if there's smoke, there's fire."

"There may be nothing," she began, "but..."

"But you have good instincts. We should talk about it at dinner." He looked at his watch. "I want to take a look at that scene myself and talk to the cop who took the accident call. Taylor, I'll touch base with you when I have our expert in hand."

"Go ahead," she told him. "I'll get the check. Then we'll be at the office."

Lindsey tried to ignore the knots in her stomach as they took the elevator back up to the offices. What could have been going on at Elite that she knew nothing about? And why didn't she know? She'd been in this profession a long time and with Elite for four years. She wasn't a novice, either in marketing or in the business world at large. Whatever this turned out to be, she was going to fix it. She couldn't live with herself if there was something illegal going on at the agency and she'd missed it, and let the Cantrells down.

If only she could get rid of that uneasy feeling rippling through her.

The atmosphere in the meeting with the staff was subdued.

"I'll make this short," Taylor said. "Lindsey will be taking over the running of Elite Marketing, so everything goes through her."

"This morning our focus was on letting clients know what had happened and assuring them that they would still be taken care of. Taylor also needed the time to go through all the files, but I really need an in-depth study if we're going to move on smoothly. Please take time before you get involved in anything this afternoon to write a brief report listing your clients, and what you have going on with them."

Jerry Ortiz leaned forward.

"Do you have a plan for how to handle Craig's clients? Most of them were pretty high-dollar."

Lindsey bit back her retort. Jerry had always irritated her, but he had worked well with Craig and produced for Elite, so she swallowed her personal dislike.

"Taylor and I have some ideas, but we'll want to meet with you sometime today to go over everything, as soon as we get everything lined up the way it should be. If I'm going to take over Craig's responsibilities, I have to be sure I know what I'm stepping into."

He studied her for a moment before he dipped his head in acknowledgment. "Fine. I'm ready whenever you are."

Lindsey hoped the slight prickle of unease she got only had to do with the fact Jerry had a slight chip on his shoulder, and not that he might be hiding something.

"Give us an hour," Taylor told him. "We should be ready by then."

Chapter Five

They had just settled into Craig's office and were waiting for Jerry when Taylor's cell phone rang.

"Noah? We just left each other. What's up? Good. Will you take care of all the arrangements? Thanks. See you at eight." She disconnected and looked at Lindsey. "We're all set with John Martino. He'll be here later today, as a matter of fact. The plane will pick him up in Atlanta, where he just wrapped up a case. Then a stop in Tampa for Liam's man and both of them will arrive here in time for a late dinner. Thank the lord he's available."

So he's definitely coming here. It would take every bit of Lindsey's self-control not to give away her feelings, including her anger and sense of betrayal.

"Lindsey?"

She jerked herself out of her unexpected reverie to see Taylor giving her a searching look.

"Lindsey, did I lose you? Everything okay? Is there a problem with John?"

She unstuck her tongue from the roof of her mouth and pulled herself together.

"Not at all. This is a good idea. It will be nice working with him again. I'd like to be sure myself that everything's okay in that area, before I take full control. If there's anything to be found, John's the one to find it. I think we'll both feel better when John tells us whatever's going on has nothing to do with company finances." She took out her tablet and pulled up a file. "I'm ready."

They had just begun when a tap on the door frame had her looking up. Jerry Ortiz stood there, a half-smile on his face.

"You're busy. Should I come back later?"

"No." Lindsey put her work aside. "Please come in."

"Yes." Taylor smiled. "No problem."

Jerry settled himself in one of the chairs, his tablet on his lap.

"I brought information in case you need it," he told them. "I'm glad we're meeting, because I want to be sure everything is okay with the accounts I worked with Craig."

"Good." Taylor wore her best CEO smile. "I like the direct approach. And I don't know if everything's okay until I ask you."

"The first thing I'd like to know," Lindsey told him, "since I'll be taking over for Craig, is why the large number of offshore location shoots."

Jerry's mouth turned up in what Lindsey thought of as his patented public relations smile. "That's easy. The clients ate it up and we have a good place to use for it."

"A good place." Lindsey looked at her notes. "Was this Ruben Madea a close friend of Craig's? He didn't charge that much for using his island, but there were still costs involved, including transportation."

"We have a helicopter charter service that we do marketing for. We worked out a deal with them, so the trips cost next to nothing."

Lindsey had more questions, and Taylor inserted a couple of hers, until at last Lindsey called a halt.

"Okay. I think I've got what I need. We'll talk about this again, after I've had a chance to study it more."

"It's a good thing, Lindsey. Really. I'd hate to see it canceled. Señor Madea really enjoys them."

"That's nice, but we really aren't doing this for his pleasure. As I said, I need to go over it in detail. I promise I won't keep you waiting too long."

"There's something screwy there," Taylor said the minute the man walked out of the office."

Lindsey nodded. "I agree. Ruben Madea is an extremely generous host. Why? I think we need to look into him."

"Agreed." She made a note on her tablet. "I'll get with Noah on it. We use a firm in Tampa that's the best of the best."

* * * *

If the morning had been chaotic, the afternoon was even more so. She and Taylor spent the afternoon together, going over all the accounts with the account managers, then digging into Craig's. Once again they held brief review meetings with the account managers, but now they were fishing for other things. *Too bad we don't know exactly what we're looking for.* Most of the conversations had been straightforward, even the one with Jerry Ortiz. Still, both Lindsey and Taylor had a feeling someone was hiding something. If only they could figure out who and what.

She was glad of the activity, though. It gave her little time to think about seeing John Martino face-to-face again. She'd need all her wits about her to make sure he had no idea of the emotions she was doing her best to control.

At six o'clock, people began filtering out, checking with Lindsey to make sure it was okay to leave. She knew everyone suspected things were bubbling beneath the surface, filling the air with a sense of unease. She herself had an unsettled feeling, and was doing her best to remain calm for the staff.

By the time the last person had left the office, she had a dull headache and a gnawing feeling in the pit of her stomach that had nothing to do with hunger. She leaned back in her chair, stretched and rubbed her temples.

"Taylor, I'm sure I owe you and Noah an apology, but I haven't figured out for what yet. We've gone over everything here and it looks one hundred percent clean. Maybe I should have paid more attention to Craig's accounts, but damn! He was the head honcho. There was no reason to suspect him of anything. So why do I think we're missing something?"

"You don't owe me anything. I'm damn sure the excellent quarterly reports we got were your doing. Along, of course, with the fact that things seemed to be running smoothly. Craig was a rainmaker. We needed someone who could juggle all the balls and keep everything on an even keel, which is where you came in."

"Maybe I'm edgy because of the nature of Craig's accident, and that strange phone call didn't help, but I keep having the feeling I missed something."

"Don't beat yourself up, Lindsey. I had Craig checked out from top to bottom before we made him the offer to join Arroyo. If anyone missed something, it was me." She frowned at her notes. "Accident aside, if it hadn't been for that damn call today, and on a hidden phone no less, we probably wouldn't be questioning ourselves. That's enough to make anyone have second thoughts."

"Well, where do we go from here? I've taken Craig's high-profile accounts for myself, to Jerry Ortiz's irritation. This has nothing to do with him, but I don't trust anyone with them at this point except me."

"Good decision." Taylor looked at her watch. "I didn't realize how late it is. We need to get going."

"Give me a minute to freshen up and we'll be on our way."

Lindsey took a long moment to check herself out in the restroom mirror, determined that John Martino wouldn't find any indication of the emotions seething beneath the surface. She'd never had this reaction to a man before. Any man. What was the matter with her? She needed to pull herself together.

As she drove them to the hotel where the Cantrells were staying, she couldn't help wondering what John's reaction would be when he saw her. She did her best to maintain an outward calm, determined to keep this professional no matter what. This was business, and she would do well to remember it. Craig's death, the manner of it, the phone call, everything, meant she needed to be at the top of her game if the Cantrells were to continue to have faith in her. There was no room for a schoolgirl crush or wacky hormones.

She just hoped Taylor didn't sense anything.

By the time they pulled up to the hotel and headed inside, she was sure she had control of herself.

"We're having dinner in the suite," Taylor said as they stepped into the elevator. "I much prefer the privacy there over the public exposure of restaurants. Besides." She grinned. "If you remember, Noah is addicted to steaks, especially the ones from the cattle we raise. We always bring a freezer stocked with them to hand over to the hotel kitchen. Then we can order dinner whenever we want to."

Lindsey knew Arroyo Ranch, which Taylor had inherited from her father, was one of the largest in Texas and ran a very big herd of cattle. And she knew the bare bones of the story regarding the inheritance. She was still amazed at the way Taylor had stepped from her job as a financial adviser to head up one of the world's largest conglomerates.

"I remember. And they're excellent steaks."

"Everyone should already be here, so we can call down our order as soon as we get to the suite."

With a tiny bump, the elevator car stopped on the penthouse floor and the doors slid open. Lindsey followed Taylor down the hall to the suite at the end. The hum of conversation she heard as Taylor opened the door was a signal that Noah and the two men were indeed here. As she stepped into the living room of the suite, she spotted Noah in a large armchair talking to a man she didn't know who was sitting on the couch, fiddling with a cell phone.

But it was the man lounging against the bar who pulled her attention as if drawn by a homing beacon. In an instant every silent order she'd given herself, every vow not to be affected by the sight of him, disappeared like smoke. Her breath caught in her throat, her pulse suddenly throbbed between her thighs and her nipples popped to rigid attention. She was glad she'd worn a black dress today that concealed much of her body's reaction.

He was just as tall and lean as she remembered, with broad shoulders and long legs. Thick, coal-black hair that she'd run her fingers through, feeling the silkiness. A strong, masculine face highlighted by high cheekbones and a square jaw. Lips that could do wicked things to her body. Muscles that she itched to run her hands over and a broad chest she wanted to caress with her palms. Eyes the color of ebony looked out at her from beneath unexpectedly thick black lashes. Eyes that flashed with heat and desire and hunger.

Oh, hell.

She felt like a horny teenager instead of an intelligent, polished executive.

"Lindsey?"

She blinked at the sound of Taylor's voice, happy as it broke into her forbidden thoughts.

"Yes? Sorry, must be desk fatigue."

"I understand. Meet Aiden Colby, our excellent forensic data analyst."

Lindsey dug out her best professional smile and held out her hand. "Happy to meet you. Thanks for coming on such short notice."

He chuckled. "Thank Liam. He knows how much I love a challenge like this." He shook her hand, his grip firm. "Pleased to meet you."

"And of course," Taylor went on, "you remember John Martino, right?"

"I do." Lindsey was proud that she managed to keep her voice steady. "It's nice to see you again."

"I think the pleasure's all mine." His hand was warm as he took hers, and strong as he closed his fingers around it.

And oh, god, that deep voice just vibrated through her body. Her nerve endings ignored all the warnings she was sending them and vibrated beneath the surface of her skin. She sincerely hoped her nipples weren't pointing straight at him, but there wasn't much she could do about the pulse pounding like a jungle drum between her thighs.

She had to concentrate hard to fight back the memories of other ways those hands had touched her and the sensations they'd drawn from her body. She eased her hand from his with as much courtesy as she could muster and took a step back.

Taylor turned to her husband. "How long have you been here?"

"Just a few minutes. Aiden's anxious to get started on that phone, so let's feed everyone and get on with it."

"Perfect," Taylor agreed. "How about fixing drinks for Lindsey and me while I get everyone's orders and call room service?"

"Steak as usual?" John grinned. "I already warned Aiden on the plane."

"It's okay." The other man chuckled. "I'm a beef man myself, anyway."

In a few moments room service had been called and Lindsey found herself with a drink in her hand, doing her best not to keep staring at John. Thank heavens, Taylor launched right into business so her brain was occupied. Before long they were seated at the round table in front of the window, dinner had been served by the room service waiter and they were deep in discussion about the phone.

Dinner was excellent, as Lindsey had expected, but she was distracted because John had chosen to sit next to her. Whether by design or accident, his knee kept brushing against hers, sending a tiny shower of sparks straight along her leg to the hot well of her sex. Little quivers vibrated in her inner walls and her clit throbbed as if he was touching it.

Aiden looked at Taylor. "Tell me more about this phone and the man who had it."

Taylor gave him a quick overview of how Craig Wainwright had come to her attention and how Arroyo came to bring Elite into the corporate fold.

"We checked him out thoroughly before we made him the offer," she assured Aiden. "I'm very particular about who we add to the corporate family. The business had nothing that gave off warning signs and Craig never hinted he had something to hide. In fact, he was excited about tapping into Arroyo's international situation to branch out Elite's client base. If there's something off here, he did a good job of hiding it. Lindsey, you worked with him for four years. Any thoughts about this?"

She forced herself to ignore the now constant press of John's leg against hers and concentrate on the conversation. "I'm as shocked as you are. I never saw anything suspicious, either. Craig and I had different styles of operation, but they never clashed. Sometimes he'd be a little more uptight than usual, but that was typically when he was getting ready for another photo shoot. Traveling with high-maintenance models would give anyone a headache. I never had a sniff of something wrong."

"Someone has to be very good to fool you," Noah told her. "That means we're either letting our imaginations run away with us — which I don't for a minute believe — or Craig Wainwright was a master of deception and disguise."

"Whatever's going on," Aiden put in, "I guarantee you this phone is part of it. Any time a phone has that much protection, it makes me suspicious." He rose, picked up the phone and studied it again.

"Me too," Taylor agreed. "The fact that he even had it disturbs me. This situation has so much about it that smacks of trouble. We've got to get this thing unlocked, Aiden. Any idea how long it will take you?"

He snorted a laugh. "Anywhere from five minutes to five days, depending on how sophisticated the software is. From what Noah explained, I'm sure whoever made the call and got you instead of Craig pulled the SIM card as soon as he hung up."

"I immediately tried to call back," Taylor assured him, "and got nothing."

"That's the only way you could have gotten dead air. Just turning it off won't do that. The phone locked when you tried to call the number back earlier, so I can't even get into it to search for the call history. I'd better get going on this."

Taylor frowned. "If it's nothing but some weird personal stuff, I'm going to be very embarrassed."

"You aren't given to false alarms," Noah said. "Go ahead, Aiden. Ring us the second you get something. Anything."

"I'm on it."

As soon as he left, Lindsey refilled everyone's coffee cups and grabbed her tablet.

"I made some notes today." She tapped the screen. "I always worry when everything looks too perfect yet doesn't feel quite right. Anyway, I figured you'd want to me go over everything again with you before John gets into it. We could see if anything jumps out at us."

Taylor nodded. "Thanks."

Lindsey tried to figure out a way to shift to the chair Aiden had vacated, but there was no way to do it without looking awkward. John glanced at her, a tiny smile playing at the corners of his mouth as if he knew what she was thinking. Then both Taylor and Noah were seated again and she forced her brain into the conversation.

She was proud of her self-control, her professionalism, even as she was well aware of John's leg pressing against hers again, of the heat radiating from his body. It took everything she had not to remember him naked in her bed, the smooth muscles of his ass flexing, the hard length of his magnificent cock pressing into her. *Focus,* she told herself. *This brainstorming session is important.* Years of self-discipline would help her to focus on it entirely.

But two hours and multiple cups of coffee later, the only thing they had was an overload of caffeine and a mental nudge that they couldn't seem to find the cause for. On the surface, everything looked clean and shiny. Lots of high-value clients. A nice supply of medium buyers. A staff that racked up a lot of good visibility for those clients. Successful marketing campaigns. Magazine ads that blew everyone's socks off.

Noah leaned back in his chair. "You can't knock results."

"No," John agreed. "You can't. I need to start following the money trail. Often something very innocuous is exactly what someone's trying to hide."

Lindsey pushed her chair back and stood. She needed to make her exit as fast as she could within reason, before she did something that embarrassed her.

She rose from the table, grateful to get away from the hot contact with John and her body's inevitable response.

"Taylor, thank you very much for dinner. Best steak I ever had." She grinned. "Since the last one, anyway."

"You're certainly welcome. John, you know what we're looking for. I want every account and every financial record of any kind taken apart piece by piece. Lindsey, in the morning, could you please have someone print out a list for him of all the Elite clients? And be sure to give him whatever passwords he'll need so he can get started as soon as he gets to the Elite offices."

He'll be at the office. In the morning. Probably working all day. Damn, Lindsey. Get your act together. This is business. What makes you think he can be trusted any more now than four years ago? Don't blow this great opportunity Taylor has handed to you. Be professional. Yes, professional.

"Of course. Not a problem. I'll take care of it as soon as I get in."

"Be sure to give him whatever he needs."

Lindsey bit her lips at the look on his face when Taylor said that. His mouth quirked in a tiny smile, and she wanted to tell him not to get his hopes up. Or anything else.

"Well." She picked up her purse from the little table where she'd dropped it, proud that she'd remained so self-contained and controlled. She hoped no one noticed that her hands were shaking just the tiniest bit. "I'll say goodnight to everyone. See you tomorrow, John."

"Sounds good to me." The look he gave her scorched the air.

She wondered how Noah and Taylor could miss it. She could do this. She had to. She didn't exactly have a choice, and they needed John's expertise. This was business, after all—and some very serious business, it now seemed. But she wasn't going to put herself in that situation again. *Let him work his magic on some other unsuspecting woman and run off and leave her.*

She managed a smile. "Then I'll be going. Thanks for dinner."

Noah lifted the house phone. "I'll call down for your car."

"Thank you."

Casual goodnight, she told herself. When she got home, she'd give herself a pep talk on how to behave while John was working at Elite. She could do this.

But John, it seemed, had other ideas.

"Let me walk you down to the lobby." John set his coffee cup down and pushed away from the table.

"That's not necessary. I—"

But he already had his hand at her elbow, guiding her to the door, looking over his shoulder at the Cantrells. "See you both in a few minutes."

They were out of the room before she could protest again.

"John, this isn't at all necessary," she repeated as he guided her down the hallway to the elevator. She was doing her best to ignore the electric heat where his hand touched her arm, or the unwanted flash of hunger that just his touch elicited.

"I'm sure you can tip the valet and get your car yourself. I wanted a few minutes alone with you. I owe you an apology."

The last thing she wanted was for him to explain why he hadn't reached out to her again. How he didn't feel he should mix business and pleasure. How he hoped that wouldn't interfere with their working together. After all, they were both adults, right?

"It's fine, John. You don't owe me any explanation at all. We're good. Really." She hoped her smile didn't look as false as it felt.

He shook his head. "We have to talk."

The elevator car arrived and they stepped into it, the only occupants from the high-dollar floor. As soon as the door closed, he pressed the button to hold the elevator car in place.

"John, we can't do this now. People will be looking for the elevator. And I think a warning sounds if it doesn't move for a certain amount of time."

"Then I'd better talk fast." He leaned forward, caging her with his arms. "Any excuse I can give for not calling you all this time is going to sound lame. Business crowded my schedule, time got away from me, all of that is true. But that's not the whole story."

"Oh? Then what is?"

"We need more time than five minutes for me to tell you. I was a first-class jackass and I suffered for it. I'm not going to let that happen again. I've spent four years kicking myself for being such an asshole. When Taylor called, I pushed another job off on my partner so I could take this one. So I could see you."

Lindsey stood there, holding her breath. Her heart was beating hard and her throat was so dry she didn't think she could swallow.

"John." She wet her lips. "I don't think — "

"Don't think. Listen. Like I said, I'm an asshole. I'll be the first one to admit it. And any other names you want to add. When I left you four years ago, I had every intention of calling you within the month. Hopping on a plane to Miami or wherever you were by that time. Following up on what had started between us. Having a fun weekend."

"A fun weekend," she repeated.

"Because whatever it was, everything else aside, it was fucking good. Agreed?"

She just stared at him, unable to say a word.

"Okay. Don't say anything. I don't blame you. I got caught up in some international finance shit, used it as an excuse and time just kept passing. I've been single a long time, Lindsey. I told myself I wasn't interested in anything more than a good time. I kept myself busy and, after a while, too much time had gone by. It suddenly hit me I'd tossed away what could be the best thing that ever happened to me. When Noah called and asked me to come here, told me who I'd be working with, I jumped at it. Saw a chance to make up for being such a jerk, even if I had to get down on my knees and beg you. Because that's what I'm ready to do." He blew out a breath. "Listen. You have no reason to believe anything I say after what I did. Or didn't do. But I'm asking you for another chance, Lindsey. Begging you. Please. At least listen to what I have to say."

While she was still trying to figure out how to answer him, lips pressed against hers, warm and smooth. He traced the seam of her mouth with the tip of his tongue, back and forth, urging her to open for him. Without thinking, she did and he thrust his tongue inside.

And she went up in flames. Everything she'd spent four years burying surged to the surface and she welcomed him with an eagerness that embarrassed her. Tongues danced, sliding over each other, and his hot breath mingled with hers.

She didn't know how long it would have gone on if the warning buzzer in the elevator hadn't gone off. With great effort, she managed to tear her mouth away and push against him.

"We have to put the elevator in service again," she whispered.

"I know. Damn it."

In what seemed like seconds, they were gliding downward again. The car made several stops along the way, and Lindsey hoped neither of them gave a hint of what they'd been doing. She hurried ahead of John through the lobby to the outside valet area, but he was right with her.

"My car is here," she told him. "John, I have to go."

"I'm desperate to talk to you. Without anyone else around. We're working together all day tomorrow. How about a quiet dinner, just the two of us, so we can talk? Please, Lindsey, we really need to talk."

She sighed. *Better to get it over with. Whatever it is.*

"Fine. We can leave right from the office. Someplace quiet, okay?"

"Works for me."

He had his hand on her arm again as he guided her to the driver's side of the car. When she was seated, he leaned in and gave her a quick but hot kiss.

"See you tomorrow."

"Yes. Tomorrow."

As she pulled away from the hotel and eased into traffic, she couldn't help wondering if she'd just made a huge, huge mistake.

Chapter Six

How did I get myself into this mess?

Daisy kept asking herself that question as she eased to the edge of the big deck at the rear of the McMansion where she and the others had been taken two nights ago. Music filled the air from the outdoor speakers and the other girls, bikini-clad and damp from their frequent dips in the pool, were rocking it out, dancing with abandon. Excitement simmered beneath the surface. Tomorrow was going to be an exciting day and they were all stoked.

"Last chance to let loose," the man told them. "Tomorrow, we begin the real work."

Boss. That was what he'd told them to call him. A little joke, he'd said. It was his nickname, he'd added. Now she wondered if he did that so no one knew his real name.

A large limo had ferried them to Black Swan Island, just across from Miami Beach. Before that they'd spent a day being pampered and 'beautified', as her friend

Elise liked to say. Then the fittings for the bathing suits and other beachwear they'd be modeling. And then, after that, recreation. Tonight. The other girls were so excited they were almost drooling all over themselves. She had been, too, until she'd heard those pieces of conversation.

God, I am so stupid. What's that old saying? If something seems too good to be true, it usually is. A modeling job. Who was I kidding? An appearance at a fundraiser doesn't make me a professional. I can't believe I was such a fool. I should have listened when Daphne told me about the short shelf life of their models. Now I know why.

But the man who had approached her and taken her to lunch had had a real contract for her to sign. Then he'd set up a photo shoot for her, just as he'd promised. For prospective clients, they'd told her, before taking her to the lush tropical setting where the final pictures would be shot.

But they forgot to tell me what kind of clients they meant. Or what I'd be doing. Or where I'd be going. What if I hadn't overheard that conversation? I'd be getting ready for a trip to paradise that would actually be the trip to hell.

Please, god, get me out of this. I promise I'll never be so stupid again. Ever.

With slow, tiny steps, she continued edging around the deck, using the huge plants and trees as cover. The houses on this exclusive island just off the shore of Miami Beach were enormous and had security fences and other privacy barriers. But for whatever reason, the barrier wall with the house to the left stopped about six feet short of the water. That spot was her goal.

The men who had promised her fame and paradise knew little about her except she had no family and she was excited by the prospect of celebrity and money.

Now she knew it had all been planned. She shuddered as she recalled the conversation she'd overheard by accident. She'd been looking for the bathroom and had heard two men talking in the den across from it. She didn't understand all of it, but enough that she knew this was no modeling job, except after a fashion.

She'd thought about trying to tell the others, but she had a strong sense they either would not believe her or, worse, one or more of them might rat her out. She couldn't take that chance. Instead she had worked her way at once around to where she could step off onto the grass and out of the light.

She heard Boss' raised voice and strained to hear what he was saying. Was he looking for her? Asking about her? Had he missed her already? No, he was laughing. He wouldn't be doing that if he was looking for her.

She took a deep breath to calm her racing heart and continued her slow progress to the adjacent lawn and down to the water. She wondered if the people who lived here had sensors in the lawn. People this rich had all kinds of security. They were paranoid about it. She had to be careful not to trip anything. She was just damn lucky that none of them were outside on their huge patio. *God.* Could she be lucky enough that they were out for the evening? She didn't even know how many people lived in the house.

She had gotten a quick glimpse of it when the limos had brought all of them here. A limo! Stars in her eyes from that one. And from the opulent McMansion on this exclusive piece of land.

She crouched low, moving slow so she didn't call attention to herself. *There!* She was at the dock where their big boat was moored. No one knew that she had lived the first fifteen years of her life in a shack on the water on Florida's east coast. The water had become her friend and by the age of ten she could outswim anyone around. She hoped she could still make the distance to the shores of Miami Beach, a cascade of light in the distance.

Miami! The pinnacle of dreams. She'd thought for sure when she managed to make it there her life was about to change. She just hadn't known the change would be far from what she'd dreamed.

Just as she eased herself into the water, she heard a shout from the house where she'd been. The one they called Boss. She recognized his voice. Then another one, probably the bodyguard he usually had with him. Her stomach cramped, but she forced herself to remain still beneath the dock. Waiting. Would they invade their neighbor's property to look for her? Would they knock on the door and ask them? Not if what Daisy had determined about the real purpose of this outing were true.

She waited, shivering as much from the water as from fear, rubbing her arms to keep warm. Her fingers stroked the tattoo that the man said had attracted him to begin with.

"Designers love body art that shows off their clothes," he'd told her.

Now, as she touched it, she tried to draw strength from it, a cluster of vines reaching down from her shoulder and circling one breast, with a nightingale perched on the shoulder itself.

Please be my good luck piece.

Suddenly lights came on at the back of the neighbor's house, flooding the area, and Daisy had to back way up so she was hidden by the bulk of the big boat tied up there. Hugging herself, she submerged as much as possible and waited.

The couple she guessed were the owners were out on their back patio, talking with Boss. The man kept shaking his head until at last they walked down to the dock together.

"...not here," the man said. "She's not on the boat, or the alarm would have sounded. What kind of party do you have going on over there to lose one of your guests?"

"A very friendly one," Boss soothed. "She just had a little too much to drink and we wanted to make sure she didn't decide to go for a late-night swim. She probably went to lie down somewhere in the house and sleep it off." His chuckle sounded forced. "That's what I get for building a house so big I can lose my guests. Sorry for bothering you."

Would these owners wonder about being questioned?

God! Please don't let them come way down here looking for me.

After what seemed like an eternity, the couple were back in their house and Boss and the man with him headed back to his house.

"Take Felix and search every area of the grounds around the house," Boss told the man. "She's somewhere. We'd better make fucking sure she didn't get away."

"Your property is surrounded, Boss," the other man said. "And we know she's not down here at the water. She's hiding somewhere. We'll find her."

"We'd better or we'll all have bigger problems to deal with."

Daisy waited a few minutes more, just to be sure it was safe to leave the shelter of the dock. She could see the sudden commotion at the house she'd escaped from — the girls gathered in a group — and hear the high pitch of their voices. Whatever he was saying as he herded them inside, they weren't too happy with it.

Good. Maybe some of them will find a way to leave, too.

She waited longer while Boss came back outside with two other men and they searched wherever they could, checking behind the bushes and trees and down on their dock and boats. She was waterlogged and chilled by the time she determined it was safe to leave. Then, with slow, silent strokes, she began to glide through the water, heading toward the opposite shore. She hadn't done this for a long time and wasn't sure how her endurance would hold up. The shoreline seemed very far away and sudden fatigue gripped her.

Did they put something in one of our drinks? Oh, god, please let me make it.

She did her best to pace herself, propelled by the knowledge of what awaited her if she failed, and prayed that she didn't die before she got to the far shore.

Chapter Seven

For the second night in a row, Lindsey had gotten very little sleep. Only this time, instead of a dead body invading her dreams, it was a naked body. *John's.* The last time she'd seen it was in her shower the morning he'd left.

"I have to fuck you one more time." He'd sounded so desperate. "It could be days before we see each other again and I need something to hold me over."

She remembered it as if it had happened yesterday. The two of them in her big tile and glass shower, water from the rain showerheads sluicing down on them and making their skin slick. Their hands on each other's bodies rubbing, caressing. His large ones palming her breasts and squeezing her nipples. Her smaller ones stroking his rock-hard cock, treating him to light little squeezes, her hand slippery with soap as she moved it up and down. His strong hands lifting her and sliding her onto his swollen shaft as she wound her arms and legs around him.

Damn!

At five-thirty she gave up the attempt, indulged in a less than satisfying session with her vibrator, then jumped into the shower to clear all the erotic images from her brain and try to think about the day ahead of her. She arrived at Elite, carrying another box of pastries, at the same time as Taylor and John.

They all exchanged polite smiles, but she could feel the heat of John's eyes boring into her as she fumbled with her keys and unlocked the big glass doors. The pulse in her sex jumped into a steady beat and she fought the need to clench her thighs together. She told herself that she had both her emotions and her hormones under control. She was a professional and needed to behave like one.

"Morning, everyone. It looks like we're all ready for an early start."

Taylor nodded. "That's a fact. There's a lot to do. Lindsey, one of the things I want to discuss with you is restructuring how the accounts are set up so you have more oversight on all of them."

"I never would have expected to need it," she sighed. "But then, I didn't expect all this, either."

"I don't think any of us did." She studied Lindsey for a moment. "This is going to mean more work for you, gathering the reins of Craig's clients and checking to make sure there isn't something going on somewhere else."

"I can do it." She'd damn well better. She kept pushing back on the feeling that whatever was going on was somehow her fault. "Elite is an excellent agency with a great client list. If part of it is somehow damaged, I want to fix it immediately."

"Okay, then. Noah has some business to take care of, so he's out for the day. But he's going to check on both the autopsy and the lab results and see if there's a firm date for the funeral."

"Good." Lindsey jotted a reminder to herself in her Notes on her phone. "I want to make sure everyone has that information. Elite needs to make a good showing."

"Why don't you set John up? Then we can all get to work."

"Yes, of course." She avoided looking at him. If only she could forget the scorching heat of the kiss the previous night, or the erotic dreams it had produced that had robbed her of sleep.

"I don't expect you have an empty office," John said, "so anywhere will do."

"We actually have an empty space —" Lindsey started to say, but Taylor broke in.

"As a matter of fact, John, I'd like you to work in Craig's office. You need to be able to access anything on his computer more than I do, even things not on the LAN. I noticed Craig had his hard drive partitioned so he could do both. Let's hope if anything is password protected, we can get Aiden over here to crack it."

"By the way, how is he doing with the phone?" Lindsey asked.

Taylor grimaced. "Not as well as he'd like. He said whoever set up the codes on the SIM card is probably someone Arroyo should hire."

"Damn." Lindsey rubbed her forehead. "This just keeps getting more complicated."

Taylor nodded. "And we don't even have a clue as to what's being hidden and why. We can be damn sure, however, that it's illegal and probably involves a very large amount of money. The telephone is a good indicator."

"That's kind of what I'm hoping we'll start learning about today."

"Don't get ahead of yourself," John warned her. "We've been through this before. If someone has something to hide, most times they are either very clever about it or hire people who are." He grinned. "Otherwise you wouldn't need me."

"I have a feeling you'll really earn your fee this time. Lindsey, were you saying you had an empty office?"

"Yes. One of our account managers left a couple of weeks ago. Health problems. I have a workspace with all the electronics you need. I'll set it up so you have full access to everything on the system. Will that work for you?"

"Definitely. I'm rearranging my schedule so I can work from here for a few days, or however long it takes. I can't in good conscience get on with my calendar until we have answers on Craig's death and what the hell he was mixed up in."

"I hate that this is screwing things up for you," Lindsey told her. "I know what kind of responsibilities you have."

"And an excellent staff to handle things for me. Right now, I think this is more important. I just need a desk where I can hook up remotely to my office in San Antonio."

"What about Noah? Will he need space also?"

Taylor grinned. "Noah's office is his cell phone and a tablet, a specially designed one that I think cost as much as an office building. He's good to go. Why don't I get Sarah to help me? I'll be needing her to do some things for me, anyway. You can go ahead and get John set up."

"No problem."

She pushed away the vestiges of the dream with ruthless discipline. This was business and she'd keep it that way. Based on what he'd intimated, quick hookups were a pattern with him. Maybe he was just looking to get something going for the duration of this job. He hadn't impressed her that way in the beginning, but it was pretty obvious she'd misread him.

She was going to write the situation with John off as a lapse in judgment and let it go at that. *Just pretend none of it ever happened.* He could do the job he'd been brought in for and find another playmate on his own time.

The look he gave her was strange, as if he was trying to get a fix on her attitude. *Too bad.* She wasn't going to let personal feelings interfere again. One mistake was enough and that wasn't who she was, anyway. In all the years she'd been working, she'd never had an office romance or a relationship with any of the other people she worked with. Maybe his not calling her was a blessing, a lesson learned.

"John, would you like me to have Leda fix a cup of coffee for you?"

One corner of his mouth tilted up. "I can get my own coffee, Lindsey." His voice was low and soft. "Thanks for the offer, but I don't expect to be waited on."

He still had that quizzical look on his face, but now it was colored by something flashing in his eyes that she couldn't exactly name. *No problem.* She'd just put it out of her mind.

Right.

"Who handles your accounting on a regular basis?" he asked while he filled his mug.

"We have an in-house bookkeeper who handles the day-to-day financial activities. An accounting firm does the quarterlies and year-end reports and tax returns. With twelve client account managers at Elite, you can imagine there's a lot going on involving money." She pasted on another of her professional smiles. "But I'm sure you're familiar with procedures in marketing firms. Anyway, I'll have Leda get you the information."

She led John out of her office and into what had been Craig's. In her best executive manner, she made sure he had everything he needed, including all the passwords to access protected files.

"We may have to get Aiden in to decipher Craig's password for the stand-alone part of his drive. Just let me know. If you need anything at all, press seven on the phone. That connects you to Leda, my admin. She can get you whatever you need."

She started to leave the office, but he closed his hand around her wrist, holding her in place.

"And if what I want is you? Can she get me that or are you going to spend the day avoiding me?"

"John," she began. She wasn't going there. *Uh-uh.* She still had lingering feelings of rejection from the last time.

"That kiss last night," he interrupted. "I didn't imagine how affected we both were by it."

"That kiss was a mistake. I'm past it."

When she tugged her hand, he released his hold on her, but she could still feel the press of his fingers as if they were burned into her skin.

"I'm not. We both know this isn't the time or place to discuss it, but trust me, we will, and sooner rather than later." A muscle twitched in his jaw. "I made a big mistake four years ago, Lindsey. I used the work as an excuse for not calling you, when the truth was I didn't want more than what we had. Never did. Permanent relationships were messy and time-consuming, or so I'd always told myself. I was actually glad the job took so long, but I plan to rectify my mistake."

"Don't say anything you'll regret." She paused. "I'm sure Taylor will check with you about lunch."

Lindsey was proud of herself for keeping it together. When she walked out of John's office, no one would have known that inside her emotions were like the Atlantic Ocean in a perfect storm. How on earth was she going to get through whatever time he was here for? Four years ago, she'd been stupid, mesmerized by him. Now she was paying for it and it was a lot harder than she'd expected.

She thanked god for her hard-earned discipline that allowed her to focus on her work all morning. The business of Elite could not grind to a halt, despite Craig's death. She had deadlines to review, ad layouts to approve, photo shoots to check on. She had a conference call with one of the modeling agencies they used who insisted they were being shut out of some of the best assignments. It took several minutes to soothe them and assure them they were mistaken. She even promised to scout the particular site chosen for this shoot herself and make sure everything was in order. She'd double-check the date and location they'd given her and get back to them.

Taylor buzzed her late morning to ask if she was available and also to say she was thinking about ordering lunch to be delivered.

"I could go for that," Lindsey told her. "I'd rather spend the time in my office than a restaurant. I can do that on my own time."

"Good. How about asking Leda to take everyone's orders? You pick the best place."

"There's a great deli in the next block that delivers. I'll have her email each of you the menu." She paused. Swallowed. "What about John?"

"Of course. Have her find out what he wants. Arroyo will pick up the tab. No arguments, please."

Lindsey had been creating an outline of the promotional activities scheduled, the clients affected by them and which agent was handling them. She was putting the finishing touches on it to discuss with Taylor when Leda buzzed her to say Jerry Ortiz wanted a word with her.

"Sure. Send him in." She had an idea of what he wanted and had some questions of her own. Two events were highlighted on Craig's online calendar. She had mentioned them to Taylor and voiced her concerns.

"You handle it," Taylor had said. "I'll be backup if you need it."

"Knock knock."

She looked up to see Jerry in her doorway.

"Leda said this was a good time."

"Sure. Come on in. I wanted to chat with you, anyway."

Lindsey leaned back in her chair and waved Jerry in. As he sat in the chair in front of her desk, she studied him. Medium height, good-looking in a Latin-lover way with thick dark hair and a slightly olive complexion — she could see why he'd fit in with the Caribbean environment. Was that why Craig had chosen him to assist on these assignments?

"Oh? About what?"

"Since I'll be taking over the reins of Elite, I'll also be moving Craig's clients to my desk. I'll want to discuss with you exactly what you did for him and with which clients, and evaluate the situation."

Was it her imagination or did his face pale a degree or so? There was a definite twitch in a muscle in his cheek.

Hmmmm.

"Anyway," she continued, "we'll set some time aside for that in a day or so. But what's on your mind?"

"I guess this goes along with what you just said. Did you actually cancel the next two shoots or did I misread the memo from you?"

Lindsey nodded. "I did. I haven't studied the full list yet, but I wanted to give myself some breathing room."

"You mentioned touching base on them, but I didn't think you'd cancel any without talking to me. I worked with him on all of those and I don't think canceling them is the right thing to do."

"Trust me when I say we need some space here with these." She looked down at her notes. "I see there's one about to start right now. Please get hold of them and have them bring everyone back to Miami. Now," she snapped when he frowned.

Jerry looked as if he'd swallowed something bitter. "I don't think I can do that. The photographers and models just arrived and the host is all set up for them. Everyone will be pissed off if I do this, including the client. And before you ask, the guys we use are the best in the business. But they know it and like to throw their weight around."

"I'll take care of the client, but I want that shoot canceled ASAP and everyone back in the States."

"That could be complicated."

"Then uncomplicate it. Apologize to our host and offer everyone double their fee. That should soothe a lot of people. But bring them back." She paused to take a sip of her coffee. "Now, how about filling me in on the details? I've been trying to put some kind of outline together. They vary in length from two days to six. And we seem to be doing a large number of them offshore."

Jerry shrugged. "It depends what the client wants. If we're doing a one-page layout, that takes less time. A magazine article more. A series of ads, even longer. I usually went on the longer shoots with him."

"I'm curious." Lindsey kept her tone as even as possible. There might be nothing wrong here except Craig taking every opportunity for expenses-paid Caribbean vacations. And Jerry, of course. How had she not kept track of this before?

Because it wasn't my business. Not on my list of responsibilities and I had other things to handle.

"About?"

"We live in pretty much a tropical paradise here. Surely there's someplace on the mainland where these things could take place?"

An expression flashed across his face that looked like a mixture of anger and distress, or it could have been her imagination. Lindsey kept her own expression bland but interested.

"The clients liked the secluded environment of Parrot Cay and the flavor of the Caribbean. It was completely surrounded by water with only the one estate on the entire small island. Craig said it worked because there were no distractions, and the models could relax in privacy when they weren't working."

"Partying," she guessed.

"Not at all." He shrugged. "They worked hard in the hot sun then relaxed at the pool with drinks and food."

Lindsey looked at her computer screen. "But some of the trips that only took two days—surely they could have been handled locally?"

"Craig was all about giving clients what they want, and they wanted to be portrayed as international businesses. Things always went off without a problem, I can tell you that."

She took a deep breath and forced herself to relax. "Look. It's less than forty-eight hours after Craig's death. As I said earlier, Taylor has handed the reins for Elite over to me. I feel a responsibility to reassess the offshore events and look for alternatives in South Florida. I'm not saying do away with them altogether, but I'm putting them on hold for the moment. Meanwhile, get the people back who just arrived there before they start setting up."

"Fine." He pushed himself out of the chair. "But a lot of people are going to be pissed off."

"I'll deal with it."

As he strode from her office, something about his attitude rubbed her the wrong way. The more he reacted the way he did, the more certain she was there was something weird about the whole thing. She needed to sit down with John and ask him to track every bit of money involved in them on both sides of the ledger. Her pulse accelerated a tiny bit at the thought and she reminded herself she was professional. *A businesswoman.* She needed to get those damn four days out of her mind and pretend they never happened.

Right.

She shut down her computer, locked it to make sure no one could get into it and headed for the spare office where Taylor was working. She stopped at the doorway, noting that the woman was studying something on her computer screen.

"Is this a good time?"

Taylor looked up, pushed her reading glasses up on her head and smiled. "Why do I think this is not a coffee break?"

"Maybe with a shot of something in it. I need to run something by you." She gave Taylor a short overview of her suspicions regarding Jerry, including canceling the current shoot before it could start. "Something there tickles my radar, but I can't say exactly what. I just feel something's wrong, especially the way he objected to it. As if it would be an insurmountable problem."

Taylor nodded. "Go with your gut. If we have some unhappy people because of the current one being canceled, I'll be your backstop. Could be." She sighed. "I have this feeling, like you, there's something we're not seeing here. I hope we're wrong, but if something else was going on and Craig went to all the obvious trouble to mask it, it might be more than just padding expense accounts or getting freebies from people. Of course, since I took over Arroyo, you'd be amazed at all the ways I've discovered people figure out to screw the world."

Lindsey sighed. "Yeah, it gets depressing. Okay, then. I'll make sure everyone is up to date on their assignments, but I'm putting anything more in-depth on hold until we go over all of Craig's records with a microscope."

"Good. And, Lindsey? Let John know about this. He can trace the expenditures and match them to income from clients. His priority is Craig's accounts and any others connected to him. He'll need to get as much input from you as he can, on this and other accounts. It will help him know where to focus."

She'd known this was going to happen. No way would he be able to do a proper forensic audit without having as many pieces of the puzzle as possible. And who else would be in a position to give them to him, right? She'd just shoved it to the back of her mind and hoped.

She spent the afternoon analyzing the offshore trips, checking the contracts with the clients and doing some price comparisons with locations she found in South Florida that had the same ambience. She wanted to see if the Cantrells had contacts they would be willing to utilize for this. But that could wait until things settled down. With everything in an uproar, trips to tropical islands were the last thing to deal with.

She also went over the master list Leda had put together for her, checking how the other agents were handling their clients and what their needs were. Not all of them required photo layouts. For many of them Elite's graphics people created what was needed. Marketing a person or product could be much more complicated than many people realized.

"I know you had lunch because we ate together, but have you thought about dinner?"

She looked up to see John lounging in her doorway. And damn it. She got that funny little feeling in her misbehaving pussy again, along with the tiny snap and sizzle that danced unwanted through her body. She wondered if there was a rehab and cure for this, like alcoholism or drug addiction.

"Is it that late already?" She glanced at her watch. "Wow. Time sure flies when you're having all this fun."

He grinned at her and her stomach did tiny flip-flops. Maybe she could lock herself in the closet until they passed.

"Noah's huddled in with Taylor, going over some things he took care of this afternoon. Then they want a minute with us. He's got information on the autopsy and the plans for the funeral. After that, I believe they have a dinner meeting."

She leaned back and ran her hands through her hair. "Let's do it."

They congregated in Craig's office, where John had been working.

"I think everyone's pretty coffee'd out," Noah began, "so I'll just get right to it. I met with Natalia Wainwright this morning. I know she realizes she can't disconnect Elite from what's going on, so she's doing the proper thing. Funeral's in three days. She gave me the name and address of the funeral home, which I'll text to make sure we all have it."

"I'll have Leda memo it to everyone on staff, too," Lindsey told him.

Taylor looked at everyone. "Lindsey, I think we should plan to go together. Noah and I have some other business to handle while we're in the area. I'm trying to put it off for a couple of days but if not, why don't we all just meet here?"

"That works," Lindsey said at the same time as John nodded.

"About the autopsy. This isn't usual procedure, but I convinced the police to email me the results." Noah took out his cell phone and tapped the screen, bringing up an email.

"You must have done some heavy convincing, because those aren't public knowledge."

"Helps to have friends in high places. The actual cause of death was injuries caused by the crash. His neck was broken on impact."

"God." Lindsey blew out a breath. "How awful. Do they know what caused the accident?"

"They're pretty sure it was a heavy dose of an erectile dysfunction drug. There was a huge amount in his system. Something else." Noah tapped the screen again. "It seems Craig was taking prescription medicine for severe tension headaches. The police found the prescription bottle in his pocket. The directions said he was supposed to take them twice a day, and more if the pain was severe. But there was no trace of them in his system."

Lindsey stared, mouth open. "Are you kidding me?"

"I wish. They think it's possible someone substituted the dysfunction meds for the pain meds. It caused an attack of some kind that made him lose control of the car and crash."

Taylor frowned. "What did his wife have to say? I know she loved Craig and she was very nice to everyone here, but, I don't know, there was something…?"

"I got the same impression. However, she's either very stunned or doing a great acting job. She'd already received the information by the time I got there, so I asked her how long he'd been taking the pain meds."

"And?"

"Again she was either shocked or doing another great acting job. Said she didn't even know about his headaches. That he'd never told her about them. Then she burst into tears."

Lindsey heaved a sigh. "It's hard to know what's real and what's acting with her. Do you think maybe he went off the meds to take the other pills for whatever reason? What did she have to say about that?"

Noah's face was always set in an implacable expression so it was hard for Lindsey to tell if he was reporting information or commenting on his impression. "She wondered if he started taking them as a surprise for her, and shed a few more tears."

"You think she was faking it?" Taylor asked.

He shrugged. "Like we both said, with her, it's hard to tell. I think she's one of these people who's so busy making sure she's doing and saying the right thing that you can't tell what's real and what isn't. Lindsey, would you know anything about their marriage? Were they okay as a couple? Were they having any problems in the bedroom?"

"Lord, no." She blew out a breath. "We never had that kind of relationship, nor would I have wanted it. At all. I can tell you she was always the loving wife when they were together, or whenever she dropped into the office. She liked to tell people what a great investment it had been for her to fund Elite. But she was also quick to tell people it was strictly Craig's baby. She had no part in the operation."

"Is that true?"

"As far as I can tell." Lindsey spread her hands. "But who knows the truth, at this point."

"Do you think he might have been having an affair?" Noah persisted.

Lindsey thought for a minute, then shook her head. "No. He'd been a little preoccupied lately, but when I asked him about it he said it was nothing. Just juggling demanding clients, which I could certainly understand.

And more of those damn trips. The couple of times I mentioned them, he said that's what the clients paid for."

"Let's not write anything off just yet. I'll bet we know people we could make discreet inquiries to. About that and everything else. Let me jot something down in my Notes section." Taylor picked up her phone and tapped something on the screen. "We have a lot of contacts here. I'll figure out the best people to approach."

"Wouldn't he have noticed an extreme difference in his, um, anatomy?" Lindsey asked. Then her lips curved in a tiny grin. "Not something we'd know about, right, Noah?"

Lindsay wanted to laugh, watching the stone-faced man fight the smile teasing at his mouth.

"You'd think. The lab says there was so much of the dysfunction meds in his system it's a wonder he didn't walk around with a permanent hard-on." He tapped the screen again. "The real kicker is both pills looked exactly alike." He looked at the others. "Anyone get the same feeling I did?"

John nodded. "Someone could have switched his pills and he'd never have known the difference. If the dysfunction pills ramped up his blood pressure and heart rate, and that escalated the tension headache because, hello — no pain pills — together that could have caused the accident."

Taylor turned to him, a questioning look on her face. "But who would have exchanged them? That's the real question, isn't it? And when?"

"It's the question of the day," Noah agreed. "The prescription says to take one in the morning, the other twelve hours later. If he worked late or at least into the dinner hours, it makes sense he'd carry them with him.

Theoretically it could have been anyone, either at home or at the office."

"I can't think who at the office would even have an interest in harming him," Lindsey said in a slow voice. "I have a good feel for what goes on at Elite and if there was anyone here who fit that bill, I promise I'd know it. What has Natalia said about it?"

"Very little." Noah rubbed his jaw. "I wish I knew if she was really so wrapped up in grief or just doing a good job playing a part."

Taylor laughed. "Forgive him. He's suspicious of everyone."

"And with good reason," he reminded her.

"Is it possible whoever switched the pills expected a different ending?" Lindsey asked. "Maybe what they hoped for was just to incapacitate him and sideline him for a while."

"That's what the medical examiner said." Noah shoved his phone back into his shirt pocket. "But why? That's the big question. I spoke to the detective assigned to the case. The police are opening a full investigation. I hate to be the bearer of bad news, Lindsey, but they'll probably be around here more than you'd like. They'll want to question everyone on the staff."

She tensed, her first thought being the staff and how they would react.

"Oh, joy. Although I am surprised they weren't here the next day, talking to people."

"They had no reason to until the autopsy," Noah pointed out. "Up until then it was classified as just a single-car accident."

Lindsey raked her fingers through her hair. "I'm going to ask people to reschedule client appointments or hold them at their offices until this is over. I don't need people who pay us a lot of money in the midst of a police investigation. That's a surefire way to kill business."

"I'm sorry." Taylor leaned forward in her chair. "Word of his death is going to be bad enough, especially if details of the autopsy get out. I know gossip spreads like the flu in this industry. Well, any industry really. But marketing is like an overgrown family with too many busybodies and too many people willing to do anything for business. Anyway, I'm not going to dump the agency and all of this in your lap and take off. If you're okay with it, I'm going to set myself up in Craig's office to handle my business until the worst of this is over. I don't want to leave you with this whole mess in your hands."

Lindsey wondered how Taylor would react if she jumped up and hugged her. She was sure she could handle it all, but having the head of Arroyo ride shotgun for this was a real blessing.

"Thank you. I would never ask you to inconvenience yourself like that, but I can't tell you how grateful I am. I promise you both the staff and our clients will feel a lot better if they know this is important enough to you to do this."

"Happy to do it. And John will be here for as long as it takes to get his part of the job done."

Lindsey was afraid to look at him, worried at what he might see on her face. She had to get past this or she'd be in a big mess.

John cleared his throat. "As a matter of fact," he said, "I'm wondering, Lindsey, if you'd mind working a little later tonight to walk me through the basics on some of these projects and clients. Having more information helps me interpret the numbers better."

"Of course. Whatever you need."

As soon as the words were out, she wished them back. She was sure she could have found a different way to phrase her response. John looked at her with both a question and hunger swirling in his eyes. *Damn.*

Taylor pushed away from her desk and rose, breaking the charged moment.

"We're having dinner with some people tonight. John, are you good to Uber back to the hotel when you're finished? Or maybe Lindsey could drop you off? Is it out of your way?"

It's out of my sphere of self-control, but what can I say?

"It's no problem at all," she answered in a smooth voice. She could certainly manage to control herself for a short ride. "I'm happy to. John, I thought I'd order in some sandwiches for us. Does that work for you?"

"Anything is fine."

"Get whatever you want and charge it to Elite," Noah told them.

"I really don't like to do that," Lindsey began.

"That's an order." Taylor winked. "One of the perks of being the big boss."

The Cantrells left for their appointment, Lindsey ordered a sandwich tray from the deli and fifteen minutes later, one was delivered.

"Let's take the food into Craig's office," Lindsey suggested. "That way we can work and eat at the same time."

John rested the fingers of one hand on her arm, then ran them gently from her elbow to her wrist, sending tiny shivers through her. "This isn't what I had in mind when I asked you to dinner, you know."

"But this is important," she insisted.

"It is, which is why I'm not arguing. But, Lindsey, I'm not letting you off the hook here. You're going to listen to what I have to say if I have to tie you to the bed."

His words sent a rush of heat through her and she had to dig her fingernails into her palms to stay calm. She had such control over every other area of her life. How was it she turned so stupid the minute she saw this man or he touched her? If any other man had walked out of her life without any contact the way he had, she wouldn't give him more than a frosty hello. She had to find that control where John Martino was concerned. *Somehow.*

It helped that the moment they started working, he was all business.

"I want to review the profits and expenses from each client. The first thing I always do is take a pass at the electronic ledgers and the bank accounts. I did that today and found nothing. Not unusual, but that in itself always makes me look twice. The books look almost too good. Not even one penny out of place. That's rare, if not impossible."

"And that means?"

"That somebody didn't want the accounting questioned," he told her. "They wanted your accounting firm to get to the point where they only did a cursory look at everything. Know what I mean? Either your in-house bookkeeper is better than any I've ever worked with or someone is going to a lot of trouble to make sure no one has a reason to question anything."

She nodded. "As if no one wants you to look beneath that surface."

"Right. A good accountant would look at these, reconcile everything and say good job."

"And that's exactly what happens every quarter."

"But I've been doing this long enough to know that nothing is perfect. Someone always makes a stupid mistake that tells you they're human. I have some notes here about certain expenses and certain client fees and maybe you can clarify things for me. Between the crazy cell phone call and Craig's weird, sudden death, Taylor's convinced there's something going on here that's being well concealed."

"I hate to say it," Lindsey sighed, "but I have to agree with both of you. I just wish I knew what."

"Tracing the money — both income and expense — is the first step to finding out. Sometimes you have to be looking for something to find it out of place."

They began with the individual client accounts, comparing expenses and income to bank deposits and withdrawals. John had done a cursory review to familiarize himself with them, but Lindsey was able to answer questions about specific expenses and income. At the end of two hours, nothing weird had shown up and she was pretty sure they were both getting eyestrain.

John leaned back in his chair and rubbed his eyes, confirming her thoughts. "I've only been through one year so far, going in reverse, but everything looks good. Like I said before, almost too good."

"The business does very well," she reminded him. "When you chart it, you'll see we've continued to grow at a steady rate."

John was silent for a moment.

"But that's not the problem. No one is saying it out loud. Yet. But someone wanted to get rid of Craig Wainwright. That same someone swapped his heart medicine for sexual stimulants. That made him a ticking bomb, set to go off at any moment. Which is exactly what happened."

"But who?" She rubbed her forehead. "Noah had a full check run on him. He wasn't cheating, no one on the side. He didn't gamble. He and his wife had what I would call a strong relationship."

"Well, we're damn sure missing something. The problem is, I haven't been able to find any money that's missing to trace. It's the weirdest thing." He saved everything on the screen and closed it out. "I've never missed yet and I sure don't intend to this time."

"But in all your other jobs, you knew money was being hidden. You just had to find where."

He nodded. "Because the books were cooked to reduce the amount of capital. But when I analyzed the business, I could figure out how much to look for and start searching. So far I can't find one thing out of sync. The growth percentage is right. The income per client fits. Fuck. I'm missing something and I hate this. I say we call it a night and start fresh tomorrow."

"Works for me. Let me just shut down everything in my office and we'll get going."

He was waiting in the reception area when she'd finished. She flipped off all the switches but one night-light, locked the doors behind them and headed for the elevator. They were in her car and she had just cranked the engine when he touched her arm.

"Lindsey."

His voice had that soft-rough sound that had turned her on so much. Still did, damn it.

"Don't, John. I'm not falling for this line again." And she wouldn't. Her trust meter as far as he was concerned was off the charts.

"It's not a line. I swear to you. Since the last time we were together I have not been with a single woman. Not even for five minutes, except for business."

She gave a short laugh. "In four years? You expect me to believe that?"

"I miss you, Linds. A lot." He stroked her cheek with the backs of his fingers.

She shuddered at the sensations it awoke in her.

I can't do this.

"It's hard enough working with you and keeping this professional. What do you want from me?"

He lifted her hand from the steering wheel and brought it to his lips, pressing his mouth to her knuckles. "I want you to take me home with you tonight, let me explain my life and how I screwed up, make a fresh start with you. I want you, Lindsey, and not just for a couple of nights. Not this time. Please give us another chance."

Her body was definitely not listening to her brain. But maybe, she thought, she could be the one to walk away this time. Maybe she could get her fill of him, satisfy that unfinished feeling and be done with it. This time she'd be in control.

Chapter Eight

They rode from the office to Lindsey's home in silence for much of the way. For a long time, he just sat next to her, looking his fill. She was just as he remembered her, except maybe better. Her hair, like thick, honey-colored silk, she still wore just brushing her shoulders and framing a heart-shaped face. Her body had just the right amount of curves, and he could not wait to get his hands on them. He wanted to look into her eyes, the same rich, dark green he remembered framed by the thickest of lashes, and read what was going on behind them. But the flash of headlights and streetlamps didn't give him enough light to see what he wanted.

Finally, needing to fill the silence with something, John turned on the car radio and found a station with Top 40 music. He slid a glance sideways, watching for any reaction, but all he could see was how tightly strung she was. How she gripped the steering wheel until her knuckles were white.

He hoped this was a good idea, but he'd figured it was the only chance he'd have. One more day and she'd have such an effective barrier erected between them that he'd never be able to crack it. He'd berated himself a million times over for the way he'd handled things. He shouldn't have been so cavalier about the way he'd said goodbye, but he'd figured it would only be a couple of weeks at the most before he could contact her again. They'd come together like thunder and lightning and he'd wanted to give her some space to make sure she was sure about seeing him again.

Once before he'd met someone like her. The electricity between them had been so powerful it consumed them. His career had just taken off and he'd had clients coming out of the woodwork, but he was obsessed with her. He'd called. Sent flowers. Sent gifts. Offered to fly her to Atlanta to be with him since at that moment he couldn't leave.

He realized now he hadn't given her any breathing room, but he'd been younger and more stupid. It had ended in a big flash when she'd told him he was choking her. That she felt claustrophobic, hadn't known if she was ready for a permanent relationship at that time.

It had taken him a long time to get past that. He'd always kept his relationships brief and superficial. When he'd met Lindsey, he'd been so afraid of a repeat performance that it seemed he'd backed away too much. Then he'd gotten caught up in two complex projects that had taken every waking moment of his time. By then he'd figured that if he'd called, she'd have hung up on him.

He should have taken the chance.

Lucky for him, Taylor Cantrell had needed him for a job where he'd be working as a team with the woman he couldn't get out of his mind or his dreams. So here he was, shocked that she had in fact agreed to take him home with her and hoping he didn't fuck it up six ways from Sunday.

He was surprised when they turned into an older residential neighborhood with stucco houses, flourishing plant life and mature palm trees. She'd told him she'd moved but he'd expected something more modern. Upscale. *No*, he corrected himself, *that's not Lindsey at all.* The driveway she pulled into belonged to a cream-colored stucco house with dark blue shutters, thick shrubbery giving it a tropical look, and two very large palm trees in her front yard. It looked like a house lived in and loved and well cared for. Another side of her identity he hadn't taken the time to know.

"Not what I expected at all," he told her. Then he wondered if he'd made a mistake saying anything.

"Shows how little you know about me." Her voice was flat, but edged with something he couldn't quite identify.

"I realize that, and I hope it's not too late to admit it." When Lindsey turned off the engine, John sat for a moment, gathering his thoughts. "Do you by any chance have any wine? I should have thought to ask you to stop so I could get some."

A tiny smile played at the corner of her lips. The first sign that there might be some hope here for him. For them.

"Need some liquid courage, John?"

"Believe it." He let out his breath.

"Come on. I have a really nice white chilling in the fridge."

He followed her into the house, which had an open-floor plan with the kitchen, living room and dining room all part of one great room. He stood there, hands in his pockets, looking around and taking careful note of how she'd furnished and decorated it. Hardwood floors gleamed as if just polished, and scatter rugs picked up the colors of the fabrics on the furniture. It was obvious everything had been chosen for comfort but with an eye for design. Tasteful pictures of the Gulf of Mexico and of Spanish architecture hung on the walls. It was a home designed to be welcoming and John had felt it almost as soon as he stepped inside.

"You've done a nice job with the house. I'm sure you love living here."

"I do." She dropped her keys into a bowl on a little table by the front door and kicked off her shoes. "Have a seat. I'll get the wine."

He wanted to sit on the long couch with its colorful throw pillows and padded arms, hoping she would sit next to him, but he figured that was too much to hope for. Instead he chose the matching armchair, resting his feet on the ottoman in front of it. He would have to take it very slow here. The couch looked comfortable, but he didn't want to find himself sleeping on it.

It was time accept he'd been a real asshole, and maybe for much longer than he cared to admit. He supposed being as successful as he was in a sought-after profession, he'd gotten way too full of himself. Taken people for granted. Women, anyway. How had he let that happen?

And now the woman he wanted to hold and keep forever was no doubt about to pitch him out of her life—and deservedly so—unless he could turn things around.

"Here you go."

Lindsey handed him a graceful wine goblet filled with a crisp white wine. He took a sip of it, the flavor exploding on his tongue. He'd have to watch himself not to drink too much of this and forget what he was trying to do.

Lindsey took her own goblet and sat at one end of the couch, lounging into the corner, legs tucked up under her. She also took a tiny swallow, and licked a stray drop from her lip. The gentle sweep of her tongue made his cock harden so fast that he was afraid it would push through his fly and embarrass him.

"Okay, John." She studied him over the rim of her glass. "The floor is yours. I can hardly wait to hear what you have to say."

His lips twisted in a self-deprecating smile. "You aren't making this easy for me, are you?"

"Any reason why I should?"

He swallowed a sigh. "Probably not. Okay. Well. I confess to my everlasting shame that I have never taken a relationship seriously. No reason to. I had sudden and unbelievable success in my career and women were constantly available. I had a reputation for short-term relationships—*very* short-term—and I wasn't looking for anything else." He took a healthy swallow of his wine, hating to admit he needed the boost it gave him. "I liked my freedom and lack of responsibility for anything except my work."

"I wouldn't say that's a sterling recommendation, John." The smile on her face had little humor in it. "In fact, it's no recommendation at all."

"You're right. It's not. And there isn't even a way I can apologize for it without sounding like an insufferable ass. But when I met you, for the first time I had feelings I couldn't control. It was only a couple of days, and when I thought of what might happen if we were together longer, it scared the shit out of me. When I left you and went off to my next assignment, I figured I'd bury myself in work the way I usually did. Put some distance between you and what I felt. After a while I'd text or call you and, as soon as I got free again, see if we could get together."

"But that didn't happen," she pointed out.

"No. It didn't."

"I can hardly wait to hear why."

He took another healthy slug of the wine. He'd better slow down or he'd be shitfaced and thrown out on his ass.

"At first, I really was busy. That's god's honest truth. The new client had a complicated situation that was taking far more time than I expected. Then, every time I reached for my phone, something stopped me."

"You'd lost interest," she guessed. "Why am I not surprised? Then what are you doing here?"

"No." He shook his head. "I hadn't lost interest. Quite the opposite. I had such an intense, immediate craving for you that, like I said, it scared the shit out of me. Instead of fading as I'd expected, it just got stronger. The only thing I could do was not reach out at all."

"Thank you for that enlightening explanation." She unfolded her legs and rose from the couch. "I think we've had enough wine for tonight. And if you don't mind, I'd like to call a cab or an Uber for you. Get you back to the hotel. This was a huge mistake."

He set down his wine, stood and grabbed her arms, pulling her toward him.

"I'm trying to tell you I'm the one who made the mistake. I was scared to accept my feelings for you.

Worried I'd lose, I don't know, freedom or whatever the hell I thought I had. Have to adjust my well-ordered life. But then, when weeks had passed and I hadn't reached out to you, I had such an empty feeling growing inside me. And the sense that in my own stupidity I'd thrown away something very special."

"But you still didn't call," she pointed out.

"No. I was confused because I'd never felt anything this strong for anyone before. Not a good recommendation for a man my age. And by then I was embarrassed. And scared. Worried that you'd act exactly the way you did last night, and want nothing to do with me outside of business. For which, by the way, you're totally justified." He studied her face for a long moment, trying to see if there was a little hope there for him. There had to be, or she wouldn't have brought him home with her, right?

He took a deep breath, cupped her face and pressed his mouth to hers. Gently, at first, just touching the softness of her lips. It was like kissing velvet. He licked the surface, a gentle swipe of his tongue before nudging her mouth open and sliding that tongue inside.

Easy, John. Take it slow.

But exerting that kind of control was very hard, because all the pent-up need for her was ready to explode. She tasted so damn good. So fucking good. He'd forgotten how just the flavor of her worked its way into every corner of his being. Holding himself back, he licked the silky softness inside her mouth, a slow, languorous movement of his tongue coaxing hers to dance with his.

It was only when they both ran out of breath that he lifted his lips from hers, but he didn't relinquish his hold on her. For the first time since he'd seen her again, he felt there might be hope for them. For him. He was still shocked at the intensity of his feelings for her, but he wanted to see where this would go. He'd managed to convince her to bring him home with her. He wasn't about to do anything now to fuck it up again until he found out what they had.

She wrapped her slim fingers around his wrists but didn't pull his hands away. Instead she studied his eyes, her own swirling with emotion.

"Please give us a chance, Lindsey. I swear I won't disappoint you again."

She took so long to answer him he was sure she was going to tell him to forget it. But when she spoke, her words shocked him.

"I am probably the dumbest woman alive," she said at last. "If you hurt me again, I'll dismember you and scatter the body parts over seven states."

He laughed softly. "And you'd have the right to." He touched her mouth with his, a light brushing movement. "It seems I have my work cut out for me, a job I look forward to with everything I have to give. Thank you, Lindsey, for giving me a second chance. I promise you won't be sorry."

He lowered his mouth to hers again, wanting to ravish it but restraining himself. Slow at first, because he didn't want to scare her away. Or, worse yet, make her think this was all he was after, because it wasn't. He didn't want her to think this was just about sex, because it was a lot more. She was a smart, savvy, complex woman and he wanted her in his life. He had one chance to get it right and he wasn't going to blow it.

This time he nibbled at her soft lips, running the tip of his tongue over the sensitive flesh in a gentle tease. Threading his fingers through the silk of her hair, he tilted her head this way and that. Her fragrance filled his nostrils, something with a trace of honeysuckle combined with the outdoors. Then he trailed his lips down the slender column of her neck, taking a nip here and there.

She moaned at the tiny erotic caresses and pressed herself against him. He felt the soft roundness of her breasts against the hard muscle of his chest. Sliding his tongue between her lips again, gliding it over the slickness of her own, he eased his hand down to cup the curve of her ass and squeezed.

Tentative at first, then with greater determination, Lindsey traced the lines of his face with her fingers, along his cheekbone and down his neck. Just that barest touch set his nerves dancing and an ache of need settled in his balls. Going slow was going to take every ounce of effort he had, but he was determined to show her this was more than just hot sex for him.

When they broke the kiss, they were both breathing hard. Her face was flushed, her eyes slumberous and the visible pulse at the hollow of her throat beat like a jungle drum. He reached behind her, found the tab on the zipper of the dress and eased it all the way down. It stopped just at the curve of her ass, and he couldn't stop himself from sliding the tips of his fingers beneath the flimsy silk of her bikini panties and caressing the hot flesh beneath.

She moaned again, a tiny, erotic sound that sizzled through his body.

How was I so stupid as to walk away from her? Cut her out of my life?

With careful movements, he slipped her dress from her shoulders, down her arms and past her hips. When it pooled at her feet, she stepped out of it and kicked it away.

John took a moment to drink in her entire body with his eyes, remembering the seductive swell of her breasts with their ruby tips, cupped now by a pale blue bra with flowers. The slight curve of her stomach and the flare of her hips, highlighted by panties that matched her bra. The flowers on her panties sat temptingly on the little swell of her mound, tempting him.

Not too fast, he kept reminding himself. *Slow. Make it good. Make it last.*

This was important. He wanted more than just tonight with her, more than a short fling then goodbye. He had this one chance and he wasn't going to blow it.

He lowered his head and traced the swell of her breasts with the tip of his tongue, a gentle lick before taking one taut nipple into his mouth, fabric and all. He closed his teeth around the hard flesh, eliciting a cry of pleasure from her, so he bit a little harder.

"John." The word came out as a whimper. "Oh, god."

He wanted to yank off his own clothes and press against her, flesh to flesh, but he was so close to coming just from touching her that he needed all the protection and restraint he could get.

When he'd tormented one nipple until it was hot and swollen, he moved his mouth to the other one and gave it the same treatment. Lindsey slid her hands down to his arms and dug her fingers into his hard muscles to balance herself. He lifted his head to take her mouth again, sucking hard on her tongue while he eased his hands between the fabric of her panties and her warm skin and squeezed the supple muscles of her ass.

Jesus!

His thick shaft was so hard he was afraid it would break off, an indication of how great his need for her was.

He slid his middle finger into the hot crevice between the cheeks of her ass and stroked it up and down in a very slow tempo. She clenched against it, little sounds of pleasure drifting from her.

John tore his mouth away from her and stared hard into her eyes. He saw in them the same need, the same smoldering heat that rushed through his own body, and lifted her into his arms.

"Which way is your bedroom?"

"There." She pointed. "On the left. The one with the lamp on."

He was glad she'd left a light burning because he didn't want to stumble around in the dark while he was holding her. The amber glow from the bedside lamp cast a warm blanket over bedroom furniture that was designed with a distinctive Florida look. The floral spread and throw pillows in pastel colors added to it, but John was only interested how soft the bed was and how much room they'd have.

He yanked the covers back on the bed and placed her with precision on the sweet-scented sheets, letting her legs dangle over the edge.

"I've been dreaming about this for way too long." His voice was thick and guttural with need.

He knelt between her legs and eased her bikini panties down over her hips and her legs, dropping them on the floor. His throat went desert-dry at the sight of her gorgeous cunt—waxed with meticulous care, leaving just a narrow strip of hair on either side. He stared so long that she smiled at him.

"No," she said, "there isn't."

"What? Isn't what?"

"Anyone that I've been waxing for. Isn't that what you wanted to ask me?"

"Yes." He gritted his teeth. "But I don't believe I have the right."

"I'd tell you that you made such an indelible impression on me that no one else seemed to pique my interest, but then I'd be feeding that enormous ego of yours."

"It isn't my ego that's enormous right now," he growled.

He run his thumbs in a gentle movement along the trimmed hair then pressed enough to open her lips and expose her gorgeous cunt. Pink and slick with her moisture, it made his mouth water and his pulse ratchet up. Leaning forward, he ran the tip of his tongue the length of each delicious expanse of wet skin. Her breath hitched, her hands fisting to help her maintain control.

He took his time, lapping with slow, unhurried strokes, pressing her more open each time his tongue traveled from top to bottom and back again, moving ever closer to her clit that had flushed a dark red. When he couldn't deny himself any longer, he took her tiny swollen flesh into his mouth and drew on it hard, clamping his teeth at the tip.

"Oh, god!" she cried out, her head thrown back.

"Not god," he murmured against her hot flesh. "Just me, but I'm going to take you to heaven."

He moved one hand to slide two fingers inside her slick sheath, sucking in his breath when he felt her wet heat. Taking her clit between his teeth, he tugged it back and forth in cadence with the movement of his fingers in and out of her. Her sexy little moans were driving him crazy, even as he wanted to hear more of them. Feel more of her.

Lindsey bent her knees and braced her heels on the edge of the bed, using the leverage to push herself against his hand and ride his fingers. He added a third one, stretching her flesh just a little but sucking in his breath at the tight feel of it. He wrapped his lips around her clit and flicked his tongue back and forth in a steady rhythm, looking up just enough to watch her as he drove her higher and higher.

Her orgasm hit with sudden force. Her body arched, her heels dug deeper into the mattress and she clenched around his fingers so hard he wondered if she'd break them. She spasmed again and again, delicious little noises coming from her mouth. He rode her through it, licking and nibbling and thrusting his fingers in and out, until at last her body was limp and she lay there, spent.

When her breathing had evened out and all the spasms had stopped, he eased his fingers from her and, seeing her watching him, slowly and carefully licked each one.

"That's the best meal I've had since the last time we were together. You taste so damn fucking sweet." He rose from his knees and leaned over her, stroking her cheek with gentle caresses.

Fresh from an orgasm, her face was flushed, her eyes sparkling — he loved seeing her like this. Her lips curved in the sexy smile that turned him on.

"I think one of us is overdressed. Don't you?"

"I'm about to take care of that right now. But first, let's get you more comfortable."

He lifted her in his arms and rearranged her on the bed so she was lying with her head on the pillows.

Taking a moment, he brushed his mouth over hers, enjoying her little hum of satisfaction when he shared her taste with her. Then with quick efficiency he stripped off his clothes and tossed them on the chair in the corner. Before he added his slacks to the pile, he took out his wallet and retrieved a string of three condoms. When he dropped them on the nightstand, Lindsey laughed, a low, sensual sound.

"I see you came prepared, but aren't you a little overly ambitious?"

"Let's call it hopeful."

He climbed into bed and stretched out full length beside her, loving the sight of her naked body, sure he'd never get tired of looking at her.

"I want to touch you," she murmured, her voice husky.

"Please do." He wanted her hands on him, her mouth, her tongue. Jesus, he'd been dreaming about this for longer than he cared to remember.

Lindsey rose to her knees and took a long moment to drift her gaze over his body from his chest to his feet, before letting it come to rest on his swollen cock. Without thinking, he reached down to wrap his fingers around it, hoping to ease the ache, but she brushed his hand away, replacing his touch with her own. The contact was electric, sending bolts of heat straight to his balls. When she stroked them up and down, with just a light caress, he couldn't help but groan.

Her lips tilted in a playful smile and she leaned over, giving a gentle swipe with the tip of her tongue over the head of his shaft. Heat flushed through his body, fueled by the desire he'd tried to ignore for so long.

Lindsey opened her mouth wider and slid her lips down the length of his shaft, splaying her fingers against its base before reaching down to cup and squeeze his balls. She set up a slow rhythm, gliding her mouth from root to tip in a steady cadence, sweeping her tongue over the sensitive head. Her silken hair fell forward like a curtain as she bent her neck and he brushed it back behind her ear, wanting to see her face as she pleasured him.

He loved the feel of her touch and wanted it to go on forever. But he was already so primed he was afraid his self-control would disappear too soon. Closing his eyes, he gave himself over to the pleasure of her lips, her tongue, her fingers. When she slid her free hand between his thighs to cup his balls, he had to bite back the cries of pleasure that bubbled up in his throat.

"Let go, John," she murmured against his hot flesh. "Let me feel and taste you."

He was so close to coming. *So close. Closer.*

Then his control fractured and he let go, filling her mouth, his cock pulsing, her hands and fingers working him, getting the last drop of pleasure from him. At last, spent, he heaved a huge sigh.

"I hate to tell you," he said in a strangled voice, "but I don't think I'm up for round two for a few minutes."

Her low, throaty laugh brushed his nerve endings.

"No problem, I'm in no hurry. I've waited a long time for this, wondering if it would ever happen again." She leaned over so her face was a scant inch away from his, studying him as she searched for the right words.

"You don't have to say it again," he told her, wrapping his arms around her and holding her close to his chest. "Trust me. You have nothing to worry about ever again. I'm only stupid once."

He stroked his hand down her body, following the curve of her hip and thigh, before drifting to her center.

Her pussy was still wet from her earlier orgasm so he slid his fingers easily between the plump pink lips.

He moved his head to take a soft bite of her earlobe before whispering, "Let me show you just how smart I am."

Chapter Nine

Detective Marco Dania stood next to his partner, Detective Dean Alpert, looking down at the body of the young woman on the beach in front of the hotel. The officers in the radio patrol cars, the ones who had received the 'person down' nine-one-one call, had set up a perimeter around her. Considering it was on a beach, however, with an early morning breeze blowing, no one held out much hope for forensic evidence in the vicinity. When the officers had then called their sergeant at the command, he'd assigned Alpert and Dania then rousted out the rest of the personnel they'd need.

The woman — *more like a girl,* Dania thought — was clad only in the tiniest bikini he had ever seen. Her hair was wet and matted from the salt water, and she wore no jewelry. Identifying her would be a bitch. His anger rushed to the surface as he tried to think what had driven her to this. She had to have come from quite a distance to collapse here like this. Something had scared the shit out of her.

There didn't seem to be any boats close by and if she'd fallen from one, and no one had reported her, asking questions wouldn't bring any results. Oh, they'd do it, because it was routine, just like they'd canvass the hotels and condos in the immediate vicinity, a long and tedious job. But he didn't hold out much hope.

The lab would test her blood for drugs and alcohol. Forensics would take her fingerprints, but if she didn't have any on record, it would be a Herculean task. Maybe if they didn't get any answers right away they'd get lucky and she'd be in the Missing Persons database.

Of course, she might not be missing, but he'd make a wild-ass guess that a girl this age who'd been swimming for her life had gotten herself into something over her head. That meant the odds were pretty good she was missing and, if he was lucky, someone had reported her. He hoped so. It would make his job a lot simpler. Otherwise identifying her could be near impossible.

What bothered him was she looked so much like several young women — girls — her age who had been reported missing over the past three years. Girls who'd just vanished without a trace. They had a whole collection of them in the database. In some cases, their parents had filed the Missing Persons reports, but in many of them, it had been a roommate or close friend. As a matter of fact, he had just been looking at the file a week ago, checking on the status of another missing girl, when a friend of his, a detective with the Fort Lauderdale police department, had called about the same thing. He, too, had a file of missing girls, all the same age and type. He wanted to know if it was just confined to his area or if it had spread farther, like into Fort Lauderdale.

They had discussed the situation and both decided to do some additional digging when they could. They hated to think someone was snatching these girls off the street, killing them, or maybe worse. *Yes*, he thought, *in some instances there are worse things than death.* He'd make every effort to find out where this girl came from, if she'd been reported missing, who reported her. Maybe they'd get lucky with a hit on the tattoo. He sure hoped so.

He tried to ignore the sick feeling creeping through him.

He swallowed a sigh and looked at the man standing beside them, an early morning jogger named Morgan Hazlitt, who'd found her when he came out a few minutes after dawn to run on the beach. The man was staring at the sight of the dead woman, a sad expression on his face.

"Tell me again how you found her," Dania ordered him.

"She was lying at the edge of the water when I came out to run on the beach," Hazlitt said. "I thought maybe she was... I don't know what I thought. I waded in and pulled her out, thinking at first she'd just fainted or something. But she didn't have a pulse. I tried chest compressions and got nothing. Lucky I always have my cell with me."

"You always run at this hour?" Dania asked.

The man nodded. "Every day if I can. When my wife and I vacation here, we both get up early, but she's not a runner. She goes to the exercise room while I'm out here. Not too many people around at this time."

Alpert snorted. "No kidding. It's barely sun-up. You've never seen her before?"

"No. Never. We've been here for a week and I'm out on the beach every morning."

"Okay, give me your name, your room number and your cell phone number. We'll get in touch with you if we need you but I'm pretty sure that won't be necessary."

Dean Alpert, who had been talking to some gawkers on the beach, walked over to him. "The coroner texted that she's on her way, with a forensics team, although there really isn't anything to find. Get out your cell and snap pictures of the body and the surrounding area, and take a couple of shots that show the distance to the hotel."

"You think that Hazlitt guy was telling the truth when he said he'd never seen her before?"

Dania nodded. "In this case, yes. If he's the one who killed her, he'd never have called it in."

Alpert shrugged. "You never know. Maybe a late-night rendezvous gone bad. He's married and didn't want the wife to know."

Dania laughed. "You've been watching too many bad movies. He never would have left her on the beach in front of his hotel, if that were the case. Or if he did, he wouldn't have called it in himself. He wouldn't want his name tagged with it in any way."

"Yeah, you're right." Alpert sighed. "It's never that easy."

"Let's see if we can put a name to her and see what we can find out about her."

He didn't think the girl was more than twenty-one, if that. Although she was pale, her features set in lines of fatigue, she was still beautiful. Thick black lashes lay against the pale skin of her cheeks. Thick hair, the same color as her lashes, hung from her head in wet clumps, although he'd bet it had been beautiful when it was dry and combed. Her full lips were so bloodless they were almost white. She lay on her back where Hazlitt had found her, arms crossed in front. Probably the way he'd arranged her after realizing he couldn't resuscitate her.

He shook his head. *What a waste.* Where the hell had she come from? What had been so terrible that her only course for escape was to swim in the Gulf of Mexico to get to someplace safe?

He took out his own cell, snapped a few shots of her face and texted them back to command. Then he added a message.

Get Riley to run this through facial recognition and see if anything pops.

Then he stood there, looking out at the expanse of water in case by some remote chance something out there tripped a switch in his brain. Pleasure boats were beginning to dot the water, people out for a day on the water. Scattered in among the bowrunners, cabin cruisers, jet boats and fishing boats now setting off for the day were a fair number of sailboats and a couple of very large yachts, no doubt heading for the marina a mile down the coast.

Could she have come from one of them? Slipped overboard in the middle of the night to escape from…what? But even as he thought it, he realized how ludicrous the idea was. Any of these boats would have been anchored either at the public marina or at a private dock at someone's house. She'd have been able to escape on land. Right? And if she'd fallen overboard, someone would have reported her. Unless, of course, they had something to hide. Then they'd make doubly sure there was no trace of her.

Fuck.

Well, he'd get people doing a canvass of the houses on the water and the boats in the marinas, see if by some miracle something turned up.

But his instincts told him she'd been running from something. Just a feeling he had, but he'd learned after ten years as a detective to trust his gut.

Damn, but he hated shit like this. Too many bad things happened to young women — girls, to be honest — these days. He wanted to find the bastards and strangle them with his bare hands.

Shoving those hands in his pockets, he stared across the blue-green expanse of salt water he was facing. There were a couple of private islands out there reachable by private causeways. The residents counted their wealth in the millions. Many millions. The thought of going door to door and asking them if anyone was missing a young woman flooded his mouth with a sour taste.

He sure hoped to hell Riley came up with some identification. Maybe then they'd have a place to start.

Chapter Ten

It was just after seven when Lindsey dropped John at
the hotel so he could shower and change before
heading to the office.

"I want to get there before everyone else," she told
him when she let him out. "And don't take this the
wrong way, but I'd like to keep this under the radar as
much as possible."

He nodded. "I understand." Then he grinned. "But
you have to go a long way to put anything over on
either Taylor or Noah."

"I know." She bit her lower lip. "I just don't want
them to think—"

He cupped her chin and turned her face so he could
look into her eyes.

"Trust me to be circumspect and discreet, Lindsey.
Especially in the office. Okay?"

"Okay." She let out a little breath. "I'll do my best to
trust you on this."

"You can. And I'll keep doing my best to earn that trust." He stroked his thumb over her chin.

"How will you get to Elite?"

"I'll take a cab, but I'm also thinking about renting a car. You won't always be able to chauffeur me, and I like having my own wheels."

"Makes sense."

He paused. "Lindsey, I know it was just the one night, but there was something special about it. Something deep. If you didn't feel the same connection I did, tell me now."

For a moment she hesitated. She'd given this a lot of thought before taking him home with her last night and she'd come to a decision. Two could play at this game. She was getting too old to let men dangle her on a string. Make false promises. Disappear from her life and show up much later as if nothing had happened. She wanted this time with John because, hell! The sex was unbelievable. But this time she'd be the one to walk away when it was over.

She slowly let out a breath. "I did. Feel the same. "

His sensuous mouth curved in a smile. "Good. Very good. Please trust me, Lindsey. I won't make the same mistake again. I'm in it for the long haul, and I hope you are, too." He ducked his head for a swift kiss, just a brush of lips. "Okay, I'd better get the hell inside."

"I'll have pastries at the office," she called as he closed the door.

He nodded, winked and walked into the hotel.

She allowed herself a moment to admire his very fine ass before pulling out into the street. Yes, she'd enjoy the hell out of this because she deserved it. But she wasn't putting her emotions out there again. She'd learned a painful lesson the last time.

She was running much later than she wanted so she headed straight to Elite, and was glad the offices were empty when she arrived.

Leda arrived a few minutes after she'd finished turning on the lights and got her office going.

"Would you please call down to my favorite bakery and ask them to send up a pastry tray?" Lindsey asked her. "Make it enough for everyone."

"They'll earn it." She looked at the sticky note on her telephone. "You want today's client meetings rescheduled? Can I ask why? I'd think right now we need to be hand-holding more than ever."

"Don't freak, but the police will probably be around here today asking questions. We don't need them in the mix with our clients."

"Police?" Leda's eyebrows shot up nearly to her hairline. "Holy crap. What for?"

Lindsey explained to her about the autopsy and that everyone on the staff would be questioned.

Leda's eyes were like saucers. "Do they really think someone here did this? Switched his pills?"

"I don't think so, but they can't leave anything to chance. As soon as everyone's here, get them in the conference room for a few minutes and I'll lay it out. I don't want them to freak any more than I know they will."

Sarah walked in five minutes later, stowed her things and stuck her head into Lindsey's office.

"Taylor's not here yet, but —"

"Yes, she is," a musical voice floated behind Sarah.

The admin jumped. "Holy cow, Taylor. You've got super stealth skills."

Taylor laughed. "I had to learn them when I inherited Arroyo and found some of my executive staff were trying to kill me off."

Sarah's eyes widened. "You're kidding."

"Not even a little. If not for Noah, they probably would have succeeded." She turned back to Lindsey. "Anyway, that's later in the day. The big news is Aiden Colby called early this morning to tell us he's cracked the SIM card." She glanced at her watch. "He should be here in the next fifteen minutes and he said what he found is not going to make us happy at all. Lindsey, I want to make sure you sit in with us when he gives us the information. It's important for you to know everything."

Lindsey forced herself to remain calm, but what on earth could he have found? How could something relate to Elite and she knew nothing about it? She wondered how many other things she might have missed, and how. Things it seemed she was just not paying attention to.

"Thank you, Taylor. I want you to know I'm as surprised as you are about this—"

"Stop right there." Taylor held up a hand. "Whatever he found, I don't blame you for any of it. People can be very devious and deceiving when they want to. Let's wait until we have the information before we start pointing fingers or shouldering blame, okay?"

Lindsey nodded, breathed a sigh of relief as Taylor left the office and had just booted up her computer when her phone buzzed.

"Yes, Leda?"

"Aiden Colby is here along with Mr. Martino and Mr. Cantrell. Mrs. Cantrell wants everyone in Craig's office, and I'm to hold all calls." Leda's voice had an uncertain edge to it.

"That's fine," Lindsey assured her. "If anyone wants to see any of us, just tell them emergencies only until this meeting is over. Then I need all the staff together for a very brief meeting."

"Got it."

She made sure to fill her coffee mug before walking into the office. She didn't think her stomach could hold any pastry, as tense as she was.

"I'll still be working in the other office," Taylor said, "but this one has more room and gives us a better meeting setup. Let's get to it."

When everyone was seated around the table where John and Lindsey had been doing some of their work, Aiden cleared his throat.

"Taylor, you told me you had Craig Wainwright investigated with your usual thoroughness before you made him the offer to join Arroyo. Am I correct?"

She drew her brows together. "Of course. Why? Did I miss something?"

"If she did," Noah interjected, "it's an anomaly. She usually uncovers everything right down to their choice of underwear."

"Even the best miss something now and then," Aiden told them.

"Come on, Aiden," Taylor said. "Give. What have you uncovered?"

"This guy had to be either a master of secrecy or he's closely connected to someone who is. To be able to keep a link like this hidden so no one had a sniff of it, and discovered it in an investigation, takes a lot of skill and practice. Or a connection to someone who can tell him what to do."

"A link like what?" Noah's voice was deep and edged with impatience. "And how did you find it? Let's have it, Aiden."

Aiden pulled a tablet from his briefcase.

"How I found it is how I find everything. I break down the encryptions and follow the codes. Even with burner phones, there is a way to trace things, if you know how. People who write programs for phones and other electronics usually build on a code word. The important thing is finding it. I did, and with less trouble than I expected." He looked at Lindsey. "Taylor and Noah have heard this before, but I wanted to give you the simplest explanation of what I do and how I find what I'm looking for."

"Thank you." She folded her hands in her lap, reaching for a calm she was far from feeling. She was sure whatever was coming was going to be bad. "I appreciate it. This is a brand-new area for me. Plus, I worked with Craig for four years, fairly closely. I can't believe I would miss something as bad as whatever you found."

"People more used to dealing with this stuff have missed it, so don't beat yourself up. So you already know this is a burner phone and what that means. No official carrier, plus the calls will be going to another burner phone."

Lindsey frowned. "But how do they activate it without a carrier?"

"Aahhh." He smiled. "That's like putting nickels in an anonymous piggy bank. You buy SIM cards already activated by an anonymous provider with a specified number of minutes. Or you can buy a Dark Web card that only routes your calls to other users in that same system. It bypasses all the usual carriers."

"Then how do you trace the calls? And find out who has the cards? And the phone?"

He grinned, like a kid who was just been given the biggest Christmas present.

"What's that old saying? I could tell you, but I'd have to kill you?" He winked. "Just joking. Once I have the code word, I break down the data into little pieces then go out into places I shouldn't be to match them up. That's the simplest explanation."

"Okay." She nodded. "Simple is good for me."

"So, cutting right to the chase, here's what I found." He looked at Taylor. "The call came from a man named Alex Enescu. I'm sure you've never heard of him and you should be plenty glad of that. I dug around for information on him and let me tell you, he's not someone you'd want to share a drink with."

"Who is he?" Noah demanded. "How does he fit in here?"

"He's Romanian, and if he was a Mafioso, they'd call him the *capo de capo*. The boss of all bosses. He came to the States a few years ago and has a big estate in Miami Beach. He's probably running his organization from there. It's a sad fact that too many men like him have come over to this country and set up shop here. Miami's one of their hotspots. International port, lots of activity, lots of ways to disguise what they're doing.

"According to what I read," Aiden went on, "he has his finger in whatever makes money, legal or not. Everything from clothing factories to nightclubs to illegal drugs to illegal arms to you name it. If it makes money, he's into it."

Noah stared at him. "Are you fucking kidding us? What the hell was Craig Wainwright doing hanging out with someone like this?"

"I think I need to have another chat with our investigators." Taylor looked at Noah. "If Craig really was involved with this man, we could be looking at serious trouble here." She let out a slow breath. "International trouble. Arroyo is, after all, an international conglomerate, and we go out of our way to avoid any kind of problems in the countries where we do business. All right, Aiden. Go on. So this guy is the head of some big criminal network?"

"Oh, yeah. And he stays untouched because he pays all the right people. And, by the way, makes sure everyone knows if they come after him, they're dead. He's not only the boss of all the bosses — he's the worst of the worst."

"I can't believe this." Taylor rubbed her hand over her face. "How did this happen? How did they hook up? Did he reach out to Craig? Did someone connect them?"

"That's the question we need to find the answer for," Noah growled.

Taylor shook her head. "I know this is far-fetched, but do you think he has any connection to Ruben Madea, our oh-so-generous host who owns the island in the Caribbean that Elite uses for photo shoots?"

"Anything is possible." Noah's face was a hard mask. "But let me point something out to you. If we're dealing with both Hispanics and Eastern Europeans, what's the first thing that comes to mind?"

Lindsey frowned. "A wide network of criminals? More extensive dope trade? Illegal arms? What makes this so different?"

A muscle twitched in Noah's jaw. "Sex trafficking."

Lindsey felt as if every drop of blood was draining from her body. "Are you kidding me?"

Noah shook his head. "The sex trade has really gone international in the past few years. Plus, this could be a joint operation between two international organizations covering the whole gamut."

"We need to find out if there's a connection," Taylor insisted. "Hispanic criminal? Island in the Caribbean? Romanian crime boss? Not only would this be a disaster for Elite, it also presents a danger to the models Craig took there. By the way, which agency does he get the models from anyway?"

"That I can tell you." Lindsey tapped the screen of her tablet, where she'd ben transferring all her notes for easy access. "Something called Bella Donna."

"Pretty Woman," Taylor translated.

"Yes," Lindsey agreed. "Appropriate, I guess. They have offices in New York and Miami."

"Noah, could you put someone on it ASAP? I want to know who the owners are and the names of their other clients. And don't use our usual people. They fell down on the job where Craig is concerned so I'm not inclined to trust them at the moment," Taylor said.

"I'll get hold of Charley Graham again. I'm going to send both names — Ruben Madea and Alex Enescu — to him." He looked up at Lindsey. "Charley runs a top-shelf security agency based in Tampa that we use for a lot of things. He can turn over rocks other people can't even find."

"The agency is actually part of Arroyo," Taylor added. "Noah put it together when he became vice-president of security for the entire conglomerate and hired Charley, who is the best of the best, to run it."

"I can give you a couple of names, Taylor," John broke in. "For the future. Several of my other clients use them to vet people."

"Text them to both of us," Noah told him, his face a rigid mask of anger. He shook his head. "Fuck. If Wainwright was still alive, I might have to kill him myself. Was he that money-hungry that he was willing to get in bed with someone like Enescu?"

"Uh, I hate to throw this into the mix but—" John looked around at everyone. "What if the sex trade came first and Elite was created as a vehicle for finding girls and processing them?"

There was dead silence for a moment, then Noah exploded.

"Fucking son of a bitch. God damn it to hell. John, you take those books apart inch by inch. And I'm putting Charley Graham on everyone and everything. Fuck. Just fuck."

Lindsey thought Taylor looked as if she was about to faint.

"I thought we were past finding sham companies in Arroyo." Her voice was strained when she spoke. "That we'd know the signs."

"Some people are very, very good at it," John told her in a soft voice. "When you originally told me about Elite, I checked them out and they looked perfect."

"I'm calling Charley now." Noah stepped out of the room with his phone to make the call. When he returned, he gave them one sharp nod, an indication Charley's people were already on it. On everything.

Lindsey felt nauseated. How was it possible all this was going on almost right under her nose and she didn't even have a hint of it? She was an experienced executive, with credentials in this business. She was supposed to have her shit together. How did this happen?

"Taylor. Noah." She set her coffee cup down, convinced that if she drank any more, she'd throw it up. "First of all, I hope you believe I had nothing to do with this. And secondly, you must think I'm pretty damn stupid not to know this was going on practically under my nose. I feel sick about it. I can't—"

"Stop." Noah's voice cut her off. "We don't think any such thing. I guarantee you Enescu is very sharp to continue to operate at the level he does, and he's used to hiding things. Second, Craig was no idiot. If he got himself involved in this, he knew from the beginning what he was doing and how to hide it so there was never a smell of anything wrong. So, let's get past that, okay? We do not blame you for a bit of this."

"All right." She blew out a breath. "I— Thank you."

"Go ahead, Aiden. Let's hear the rest of it."

"There were a number of calls on that phone between Enescu and Craig. Very cryptic ones. There were also some between Craig and Madea. Basically, they used the phone to arrange meetings, shipment, although of what I can't figure out. They just referred to merchandise. It could be any one of a number of things."

Noah nodded his head. "We brought that up before. Guns. Drugs. And our latest idea, the sex trade. But how in the absolute fuck would Craig get involved with someone like Enescu?"

Lindsey was sure if Craig was standing in front of them Noah would have beaten him to a bloody pulp.

"The first question to answer," Taylor said, "is how he met him. Does Enescu travel in the same social circles as the Wainwrights and others? Would they embrace a criminal like that?"

"The social circle thing is totally possible," Aiden pointed out. "That's how it happens to a lot of people. A sniff of the money to tease, then a little more and a little more, not caring how and where it came from and boom! You're right in the middle of a crooked mess. Craig could have gotten involved in conversation, heard the big numbers flying around. Decided he wanted in on it."

"Unfortunately," Noah said, "totally possible. Or…" He leaned forward. "Think about this. What if Ruben Madea was the one who introduced them? What if Madea created this relationship with Craig, let him use the island for the photo shoots, then brought in Enescu to meet him? Dangled big, big money in front of him?"

"But Craig's wife supposedly has plenty," Lindsey reminded them.

"He could have wanted to build his own fortune," Taylor suggested. "A lot of men are threatened by a very rich wife." She looked at Noah and smiled. "I'm lucky my husband isn't one of them, but…"

"Are you kidding me?" Noah winked at his wife. "Didn't you know I married you for your money?"

But Lindsey saw the look that passed between them and knew that was as far from the truth as it was possible to get. Everything else aside, Noah Cantrell was one of the most self-confident men she'd ever met.

"Okay, everyone." Taylor rapped her knuckles on the table. "Time to focus on fixing this. John, if this is true, Craig had to have been making a shitload of money on whatever it was they were doing. Have you been able to trace any of it yet? Where it came from? Where it went?"

"Not yet. I told Lindsey the books for Elite are so clean they squeak and that makes me very suspicious.

Even the most honest person in the world makes an error now and then. That's why they have accountants. But that's only a first pass. A view of what's out there in the public eye, so to speak."

"And now?" Lindsey asked.

"Now I have to do the real work. Digging into accounts, looking for anomalies, comparing billings to deposits and so on and looking for inconsistencies. I pride myself on being able to find anyone's hidden money anywhere, any time. Lindsey, are you able to work with me for the rest of the day? Are you needed on something else?"

"Whatever it is, we'll clear you," Noah answered for her. "This takes precedence. That okay with you?"

"Yes," she agreed. "I just need a few minutes with the staff to prep them for the police. Then I'm good to go."

She'd do whatever it took to get to the bottom of this. She couldn't get rid of the feeling of nausea gripping her. How had she never caught on to any of this? How had she trusted Craig, worked side by side with him and been so oblivious to so many things?

"Good. Taylor, have Sarah pull together everything on every visit to the Caribbean that Craig took where Jerry accompanied him. You and I will discuss this with him together and see just how much he does or doesn't know. Then we'll plan our strategy on how to handle the current situation with the few clients we've got on the calendar for this afternoon."

"I agree. Give me an hour to see what's going on with everyone else and if the departments like art and graphics are up to date on their projects and what needs approval."

"I can do that."

"John, go way back in the books to when Craig began using that place for photo shoots. No," she corrected herself. "Further than that. Right to where Elite began. Track every bit of money. Every single penny in and out. Then go on to his personal accounts."

"You know I have no information prior to when I joined Elite four years ago," Lindsey reminded the Cantrells.

"Doesn't matter," Taylor said. "It's your brain we want. Plus, you have enough knowledge of how this business works to spot something out of whack even if you weren't here."

"Thank you for your confidence in me."

More than I have in myself right now.

"One last thing." Noah looked around at all of them. "You can correct me if I'm wrong, Lindsey. You probably knew Craig better than the rest of us. Whatever he was involved in, I don't see him as taking the lead on it."

"You're right." She wrinkled her forehead in thought. "He did great with Elite, especially after I came on board, but I don't see him as someone who could pull together all the strings of a complex international operation."

For a second there was heavy silence in the room.

"That means we have a lot of digging to do," Taylor acknowledged. "Noah, that's probably something else we should bring Charley in on. Meanwhile, John, anything at all you can find in his financials, business and personal, might give us a thread to tug."

"I'm on it."

"One more thing," Taylor added. "Lindsey, we need to talk to Jerry Ortiz and find out what he knows about Madea, what this situation is, and see if he's involved in this, too. He could be the one who's been helping cover this stuff up. But when we talk to him, let's be as casual as we can. If he is involved, we don't want to send off any warning signals. And I want to wait and see what John finds today, also."

"Let me know whenever you want to do it. I might just message him and ask him what his schedule is like for the rest of the day."

"Sounds good. All right, people." Taylor rose. "We have a lot to do. Let's get to work. We'll get together again at the end of the day, unless of course someone finds something before then."

Lindsey didn't want to tell her she wasn't too optimistic about that. If Craig Wainwright had hidden what he was doing so well all this time, nothing would be easy to find. But one thing she did know. When they found it, the effect would be like a bomb going off.

Chapter Eleven

Lindsey drained the last of the coffee from her mug, debated about getting up to refill it and decided against it. She'd already had so much today that she was close to a caffeine high and afraid her nerves would get the better of her. But there was no doubt she'd needed it.

First there'd been the meeting with the staff. To say they'd been appalled about the results of the autopsy and unhappy that the police would be swarming over them was an understatement. At last they'd managed to get past the initial shock and questions, and said of course they'd do whatever they could. Lindsey had kept a careful eye on Jerry while she spoke, watching his reaction. Of course, while he might have been involved with what Craig was into, it didn't mean he knew anything about the man's death.

She had to say, the two detectives who arrived to question everyone were professional and respectful. Leda helped her monitor the questioning while she worked with John and let her know everyone was cooperating. However, she was sure this was a dead end for them. At least she hoped.

The work with John was tense and nerve-racking, especially since she had to control her body's unwanted reaction to him triggered by their close proximity. She considered herself a disciplined person, and it was a damn good thing, because the air between them was so charged with electricity she wondered they got any work done at all. But she had to do it.

The work was tedious and draining, but there was a lot at stake here. The knowledge of how important this was, how devastating what they found could be, had to override everything else.

Yesterday, they'd started working at Craig's desk, the two of them sharing his computer, but that was too restricting, so they used the passwords to access the mainframe from their laptops. That way they could work at the big round table and be more comfortable. But every time she looked at an electronic ledger sheet or a report, her mind kept going back to what they'd learned about the man who had called Craig.

"You've been staring at that same screen for five minutes." John's voice held a note of amusement.

"What? Oh!" She leaned back and raised her arms to stretch. "Sorry. I was just—"

"Wondering if Craig got into this before or after Elite?" He rubbed a hand over his face. "That's the big question, or one of them. There are plenty more."

"No kidding." She shook her head, hoping to clear her brain. "I know it's right in front of us. I just can't figure out what it is."

"Obviously new clients were added after the Arroyo deal, but you've checked each of them and there's nothing hinky about any of them. Right?"

She nodded. "Right. And you can't find anything in Craig's finances or the agency's that sends up an alarm. At least so far. Also right?"

He nodded. "It's frustrating, because usually after the first pass through everything, I have some clue as to what I should be looking for and where. But here? Nothing. Damn it." He went back to looking at the page on his laptop. "So I started at the beginning and went over these accounts again, knowing I was missing something. Sure enough, there it was, but so innocuous I missed it before. Something that's been sitting right in front of us, but so cleverly disguised we passed right over it."

She peered at his laptop. "Right over what?"

He leaned back in his chair. "I've done a brief profile on each Elite client, just so I could have a complete picture of the agency operations. The billings on almost every client fall within certain parameters, except for one."

"Which one? I know some are larger than others, but they basically all fit the same profile."

"What about Masquerade?" He pointed to his screen. "They're a stand-alone day spa that show an incredible amount of money moving in and out. I'm surprised no one noticed before."

Lindsey glanced at the laptop screen. "Masquerade? I'm embarrassed to say I've really had nothing to do with them, so I can't tell you much about them. I guess if I looked at the figures, I just thought they were very expensive. They were Craig's client, so I had little to do with them. And the financials were his responsibility, as the owner. He handled the oversight of all the accounting. Why? What's the problem with them?"

"They seem to be okay at first glance, but I don't know. Something makes the back of my neck itch. A lot of money is spent on Masquerade. Usually, for that kind of bucks, you're advertising an entire chain of spas."

Lindsey shook her head. "I know for a fact that it's just the one facility. They've been on the books for a long time. It was Craig's account. The spa was a client before I came on board. Whenever I asked about them at the client review meetings, he brushed off the questions. Said the owner was a longtime friend and he kept them as clients as a favor. Although for the money they paid us and the amounts we spent on them, we should have been reviewing them on a regular basis. But when Craig called them old friends, I just let it go. He handled it himself and they always paid their bill on time."

He rubbed his jaw, his brow creased in thought. "Maybe I'm seeing something when nothing's there. There's two ways you can look at this. It is exactly what it appears and nothing more, or it's one of what could turn out to be many places where money was being washed. And the more I look at it, the more I think there's too much financial action for a facility like this. Plus, every other client this size had been purged, and most likely referred to an agency that handles entities more that size."

"I never really thought about it."

"I kept coming back to it because it's the only thing that's the least bit out of whack. I need to start checking the bank accounts, looking at expenses and deposits. Can you pull up the billing history for Masquerade and we can make comparisons?"

"Sure. Not a problem." She typed the password into her computer for the accounts receivable. "Okay, I've got it." She caught her bottom lip between her teeth. "Regardless of the billing, warning bells should have gone off when a man as busy as he was didn't just hand this off to one of the junior agents. Truthfully, though, at the time I was so busy getting up to speed on everything else and bringing in major clients myself that I just didn't pay much attention to it."

"Maybe they were just trying to be competitive with all the other larger spas in the area. This whole area is filled with spas, both the day-only ones and those that have facilities for overnight guests. Does your information list what Elite did for them?"

"Yes." She began reading from her screen, scrolling through invoice after invoice. "Damn, John. We did stuff for them the same size as businesses five times their size. Why didn't anyone ever catch this?"

"Who would that be? You already said Craig handled all of this himself. He was the head man. Did he ever present you with a complete spreadsheet of income and expenses for all clients?"

"Only sort of. Those sheets wouldn't include what we did for them as compared to others. And, truth be told, Craig was very proprietary about his personal clients."

"We're going to have to look at each one of those, too. Unless he read you in on every detail, all you ever had was his word for anything."

"And no reason to question it." The possibilities were making her sick.

"I hear you." He studied his screen again. "Something else here. All of Elite's financial records are incredibly neat. I know you said your bookkeeper is manic about it, but, Lindsey? Listen to me. Nobody—and I mean *nobody* — has financial records that never have so much as one digit out of place. One decimal point. One...anything. And I've examined financials of corporations that pay many thousands of dollars for accountants to handle this stuff."

"I don't know what to say."

"Let me pull up the list I created of each client and the annual expenditures. I'm not saying Craig was cleaning money but if — repeat, if — he was in some kind of business with Ruben Madea and Alex Enescu, you know he was washing the money through Elite."

Lindsey clicked through the reports on her laptop. "Here's something else. Their clientele is pretty static. They always report at capacity, but what is capacity for a spa? Do you limit the number of facials? Mani-pedis? Wax jobs? Tell me I'm wrong, John, but doesn't every business have a fairly uneven graph line? Some months are busier than others. And Christmas? Hold on a second." She typed in some commands, pulled up what she wanted and turned her laptop so he could see the screen. "For December they spent barely more than the other months. Their income is finite for their size, yet they're spending huge amounts on marketing every month."

John began typing on his laptop again. "Let's see the rest of Craig's accounts and read me the names. I'm going to look at the accounts receivable and the bank deposits."

"Wait." Lindsey jumped up and hurried over to Craig's desk. "Taylor asked Aiden to crack the password on Craig's computer for the part not connected to the server. If this is what we think, the regular accounts won't tell the story, right?"

"Very good." He grinned at her. "Want to be my assistant?"

She just smiled as her fingers flew over the keys. The password worked, but even then she had to work through layers to find what she wanted. The more she dug, the sicker she got. *How was I so stupid as to miss all of this?*

At last, when she'd completed her search, she pushed back from the desk.

"Okay, come take a look."

On the screen were transactions she'd never seen before, with banks she'd never heard of, for huge amounts of money. She moved so John could sit down and work his magic, the sick feeling getting worse as he pulled up more and more information.

"He was doing it, wasn't he?" she said at last.

John nodded. "All of this is off the books, but he's covered because he lists them as legitimate clients. But he's moving three times as much or more to these offshore accounts, then back through something called Litton Industries. Sure as hell that's a shell corporation. Then it's moved from Litton to numbered accounts that he can access."

"Hiding money. Accumulating it. And a fucking hell of a lot."

"Bingo!"

"They must have a website," Lindsey said at last. "That would tell us something about the business. I mean, everyone has a website these days, right?" She typed the name into the search bar and, in moments, images filled her screen. "Here it is. Take a look."

The screen showed a low adobe building, Spanish in architecture with a red barrel tile roof. To Lindsey it looked more like a large home than a day spa, except for the parking lot that had about ten cars parked in it. But again, considering Elite's client list, it was not what she would have expected the firm to be spending time on.

She clicked on each of the pictures one at a time. They were all professional photos of a typical day spa operation. Then she opened the screen with all the information.

"According to this," she said, "on paper it's owned by a woman named Madeleine Cross."

"Let me see what I can find out about her." John's fingers danced over his keyboard. Lindsey slid her chair over so she could watch his screen, but the images changed so fast she almost got a headache.

"How do you even know what you're looking at?" She blinked. "Are you even reading any of this stuff?"

He nodded. "It doesn't take more than a glance to know if I'm on the right page or not. Okay. Here we are. Not that it tells us anything."

"Where?" Lindsey studied the screen. "Oh, okay. I see. The corporate papers for Masquerade. Damn! How did you do that?"

"It's all in the magic touch," he teased, flexing his fingers. Then his face sobered. "But as you can see, all it gives us is a place to start. See? It just shows it being owned by another corporation, which is the way a lot of these things work. Shit."

He went to work on the keys again, Lindsey watching as he moved from one website to another. At last he sat back, frowning.

"What?" Lindsey stared at the screen. "What's the problem?"

"I'm going to need more time to do this, and even then I have to figure out how it's connected to Craig.

Whoever set this up knows his stuff—or hers—and has layers on top of layers."

Lindsey sat back in her chair, discouraged. "I don't know which upsets me more, the fact that we need a shovel to dig up this information or that Craig was involved in something like this. I'm telling you, John, if you'd met him, you'd never have expected this of him. He was bright, funny, great with clients. Creative. Popular in the community. He and Natalia traveled at the top level of area society."

"You'd be surprised how many times people like that make their money in the muck and mud."

Anger surged through her. "Everything about him was a lie."

"Not everything," John corrected. "Part of him was just as you described, or you never would have stayed with Elite."

"I guess you're right. So where does everything stand now?"

He pointed to the document up on the screen. "Since Natalia provided the startup capital for Elite, I want to find out where her money came from. It could be something simple like family money, or it could be illegal funds washed through so many shell corporations it would be difficult to define the source. And if the shell corporations were all based in Delaware, like Litton, that makes it even more difficult. That state is a breeding ground for paper companies. Do you know that almost three hundred shell corporations list one address in Delaware as their corporate address?"

Lindsey stared at him. "I knew that companies used Delaware because of their secrecy rules, tax incentives and business-friendly case law. But holy shit, John, none of that applies to Elite."

"No, but it could apply to Natalia. The money came from her, so I'm not so convinced she's uninvolved in all this. And maybe Litton is the lynchpin to move the money in and out."

Lindsey's eyebrows rose almost to her hairline. "Natalia? The perfect wife? The society queen? I can't even."

"Don't be fooled by appearance," he warned her. "The best people in the dirty money business are those who appear to be the least likely. You'd be amazed what I find when I start digging like this. It will take some time, but I've never not found the trail." He winked. "That's what I do, kiddo."

"And he does it well." Taylor stood in the doorway. "I didn't mean to interrupt you, but Sarah just let me know that Natalia had someone call here to remind us the funeral is tomorrow at two. The message is she hopes we will all be there for Craig's final farewell."

"As we will," Lindsey told her.

"All their closest friends will be there. I'm not saying any of them are involved, but it never hurts to scope things out. We probably won't be lucky enough to overhear incriminating conversations, but we might at least get a feel if anyone might be involved in whatever this is."

John looked up at her. "Absolutely. If in fact Craig was involved in some nasty business, and if he was using Elite to clean money, you know he wasn't doing this alone."

Taylor fiddled with her pen. "I agree there have to be more people involved in this. I'd say someone—either one or both of the Wainwrights—has known a long time. This didn't just start yesterday and Craig wouldn't go into whatever this is with complete strangers. He didn't trust easily. That much I know about him."

Lindsey drew her eyebrows together. "Do you think Natalia knew what was going on? And obviously still is?"

"I don't know. Hard to tell. She could be just what she seems to be on the surface—a rich woman who bankrolled her husband." She sighed. "Sometimes I just hate being so suspicious of people, though."

"Being doubtful can save a lot of anguish later on," John pointed out. "Anyway, our skepticism may be overboard, but Lindsey and I think one of Craig's clients, a spa called Masquerade, might not be what it seems."

Lindsey turned her laptop so Taylor could see the screen. "First of all, take a look at the place. Here."

"Pretty building," Taylor remarked. "But not quite the usual client these days for Elite."

"That's what Lindsey and I both think," John told her. "And for a place that size, unless they charge up the yin yang and then some, there's an unrealistic amount of money moving in and out."

"Not that Masquerade isn't an attractive place," Lindsey added, "but it is so much smaller than the other Elite clients."

"You won't be too happy with what I'm finding in Craig's bank accounts, either," John added.

Taylor's smile disappeared. "What do you mean?"

He gave her a rundown on what he'd discovered. "I'm going to look further into Litton and into Natalia's trust. Because the money to start Elite came from there, there is a connecting financial thread. And it also means

I need to check the financials on every other one of Craig's clients."

"Which is why I have Lindsey working with you."

John nodded. "I hate to say this, but Elite is the kind of structure that is ripe for money laundering because of the nature of the business."

Lindsey grimaced. "Lucky us."

"Another thing, over and above the ridiculous sums of money," John went on. "The more I look at Masquerade, the more it sticks out like a sore thumb."

"It's out of whack with the norm and we want to know why." Lindsey glanced at him. "Right?"

"Exactly," Taylor agreed.

"What other reason would it have for being on the books as a client?" Lindsey asked. "If it's not a phony enterprise used to launder money, and it's not a big legitimate client like all the others, then what? I'll tell you, the words 'laundering money' give me the shivers."

John snorted. "No kidding."

"It's strange they haven't even called here yet," Taylor pointed out, "when everyone else has. You know, someone is going to have to take over that account. Make contact with them."

"And that makes this the perfect opportunity to check them out." Lindsey looked from John to Taylor and back again. "Why don't I do a little more research about them first, just so I can make sure we aren't getting false alarms before we do anything else? I can make a list of similar spas around the country and dig up the kind of promotions that have been done for them. You know, for comparison. I'll bet we'll find a lot more activity than we've got here."

Taylor nodded in agreement. "I think it's important to take the time to do that."

"Yes, it is," Lindsey agreed. "If Craig was into something illegal, he'd want to disguise it, right? And look here." She clicked over to another page. "Do you know what the word masquerade means? To go about under false pretenses. To disguise oneself. Maybe it's just that simple."

"Very smart." John smiled at her. "Whatever Craig was into with Ruben Madea, you can be sure he wasn't doing it for free. He'd need a conduit for the money and a way to hide it. A spa would be perfect for that."

Lindsey sat back in her chair and raked her hair back from her face, tucking it behind her ears. "What if this isn't just about the money?"

John frowned. "What do you mean?"

"What if the spa is not just a money pipeline? What better place to use to smuggle drugs? A good accountant can build a pyramid of accounts so it takes someone like me to trace its origin and disbursal."

Taylor stared at her. "You're right. What if that's all true?"

"And something else." Lindsey swallowed. "We thought of this yesterday. What if this isn't just drugs or guns? What if Craig was also involved in sex trafficking, like you brought up, Noah? They could run the girls through Masquerade to beautify them" — she used her fingers to make air quotes — "before shipping them off to the next stop."

John's face darkened. "That's not uncommon. And if that's true, it's no wonder he wanted to keep it all to himself and not discuss it."

"We don't really even know anything about their operation," Lindsey pointed out, "except what's on Elite's books and their website."

Taylor nodded. "Someone needs to go take a look at the place. Lindsey, I'd say a day at the spa is just what you need after the funeral. You've been under a lot of pressure and shouldering a lot of responsibility. And where better to relax than at a client's business?"

Lindsey chuffed a laugh. "Me?" She pointed at herself. "You want me to be a spy?"

Taylor shook her head. "No. I want you to treat yourself to a day of pampering, courtesy of Arroyo. Of course you wouldn't think of going to someplace that isn't a client. I know when I go to a spa or a salon, I always gossip with the staff, so I'm sure it wouldn't be out of line for you to do the same thing."

"You want me to pump them?"

"In a way that's not obvious. And take a good look at everything. Scope out their operation. Call them and get an appointment. You're clever, Lindsey. I know you can do this."

Lindsey gave an unladylike snort. "Thanks for the vote of confidence. I'm still trying to absorb the fact that Craig was involved with people like Madea and—" Then she sobered. "You don't think this agency was funded with money from that source, do you?"

"Not as far as I've been able to tell. He told us Natalia had covered the startup costs. We checked her out, and she comes from a very wealthy family in South America. Her money is all inherited, comes out of a trust and, as far as we can tell, it's squeaky clean."

"If Natalia has all that money and Elite has been doing so well, why would Craig get involved with people like that?" Lindsey rubbed her forehead. "Doesn't make sense."

Taylor shrugged. "There's no understanding some people. I've learned that."

"I just can't believe I misread him so badly. I worked with him for four years and none of this ever showed up." She spread her hands. "I guess some people have a hunger for money and power that overtakes them. I've been questioning my own intuition since this all came out, wondering if I read people as well as I think I do."

"He fooled us all," Noah said. "And that's not easy for any of us to admit. Especially since it's more and more evident he was already involved in this before we brought Elite into the Arroyo fold."

"Damn, Noah." Taylor blew out a breath. "You can bet the next company we look at for a subsidiary is going to be put under a virtual X-ray machine. Meanwhile, let's move on. John, you need to get out your biggest shovel when you go back to digging."

"Okay." John swallowed the last of the coffee in his mug. "Let me get a refill and go back to work. I have to cast a much wider net. If Craig indeed was washing the money through Elite, there are a number of ways he could be doing it. I may dig into some things that piss people off."

"No problem," she assured him. "The majority owner of this agency died in an unusual manner and Arroyo needs to protect its interests. I'll get one of our lawyers on it right away." She pulled her cell phone out of her pocket and was already punching in numbers as she walked out of the room.

Lindsey glanced at John. "Must be nice to have an army of legal eagles on speed dial."

He grinned. "You ain't seen nothing yet. You didn't know Taylor before she inherited Arroyo, did you?"

"No. I met her when she did some business with the firm I was with in Miami."

"She's always been smart. More than smart. She was a hotshot financial manager in Tampa when she discovered that the father she'd been told was dead was actually alive and head of a multinational conglomerate."

Lindsey's eyes widened. "You're kidding."

John crossed his heart and held up his hand. "Scout's honor."

"So how did all this happen, then?"

"She went to San Antonio to tell him who she was. He figured she was just some cheap money-grubber trying to scam him and threw her out. She went home madder than a hornet."

Lindsey laughed. "I'll bet. But…didn't she try to see him again?"

"Are you kidding? Not her. She was once and done. But the old man had her investigated, found out she was the real deal and was about to reach out to her when he was killed. Shocked the hell out of everyone when his will was read and he'd left everything to her."

"So what happened?"

"She wanted no part of it. She's got a boatload of pride, you know. She ignored every letter they sent her and refused all phone calls. Noah finally went to Tampa and practically dragged her back to Texas. She gave him hell and told him in no uncertain terms she made her own decisions."

"But she went?"

"Oh, yeah." John chuckled. "Bitching at him the entire time. There was some nasty business with the executives at first. You can ask her about it sometime. But she stepped into the head role at Arroyo liked she'd been born to it. Old Josiah Gaines must be grinning from ear to ear at how she handles everything."

"She certainly does it well," Lindsey agreed. "And it's obvious she and Noah got past their initial animosity."

"That's quite a story, too. Maybe someday you can get her to tell you all about it."

"Oh." Lindsey flapped a hand in the air. "I'm not sure we'll ever be that close. Besides, half the time she terrifies me — she's so knowledgeable and efficient and in command."

"That she is. A lot of people have underestimated her, to their eternal sorrow. That only happens once, though."

"Let me call Masquerade and see if I can make an appointment for a day of coddling." She dialed the number on the computer screen.

"Masquerade." The voice was low and musical.

"Yes, your place was recommended to me by a friend. I'd like to make an appointment for a full day…massage, facial, the works." She named the day.

"Of course. Who did you say recommended us?"

"Oh, I don't remember. It was at a luncheon with a lot of women."

Pause. "I see. Well, I'm sorry but we are fully booked with our regulars for the moment. If you'd like to leave your name and a phone number, I can call you when we have an opening."

"Booked?" Lindsey glanced at John. "I'm sorry to hear that. You came highly recommended. Are you sure you can't squeeze me in?"

"Perhaps if you told me who referred you," she said again.

"No, that's all right. Thank you, anyway." She disconnected and stared at John. "That's very weird."

"Weird how?"

"I've been to a lot of spas, and they never turn away a client. If they're booked, they either figure out how to squeeze you in or convince you to take an alternate date. And the woman asked me twice who recommended me, as if that would make a difference. Legitimize me somehow. Like I said, weird."

"I agree." John closed out the screen on his laptop.

Lindsey studied her screen again. "I'd like to get a look at this place."

"You realize if you do, then you can't be the one from Elite who contacts them about a new agent for their account. You can't snoop then show up as their new account manager."

She curved her lips in a half-smile. "Then maybe I should just go and personally introduce myself. Tell them I'll be handling things for them and also make an appointment to try some of their services. Give me a chance to scope the place out and see if the so-called owners are there."

He frowned. "Lindsey, these aren't going to be nice people. They're dangerous, and so are the people who work for them. You'd have to be very, very careful."

"I know that. But it's natural for someone from Elite to come by and reassure them that their account is going to be handled in the same manner. Right?"

Lindsey looked at their worktable, notes strewn across the surface along with a stack of printouts.

"You think we can leave all this for a while?"

"I think for the moment we're at a standstill." He closed his laptop. "I'm with you. Something doesn't sound quite right here. My senses are telling me we may have stumbled on to something. I have no idea what it is but maybe taking a look at it will help."

"Let's do it." She closed her own computer and picked up her purse. "But first I want to make sure Jerry Ortiz canceled the current shoot and brought everyone home. They flew there in a private plane, so transportation shouldn't be a problem."

Jerry was behind his desk, his phone to his ear, feet up on the desk when she rapped on his door.

"Let me call you back," he told the person on the other end and disconnected. "Hey, Lindsey. What can I do for you?"

"Just making sure you called off the shoot and brought everyone back from Parrot Cay."

"Yeah. About that." He frowned. "It seems the plane they were using had to leave to ferry some friends of the owner someplace. But they should be back soon. I told him how important this is."

"What did he say?"

He grimaced. "He wasn't too happy, I can assure you. Gave me a whole spiel about how good he's been to Arroyo. How he likes to invite his friends over the last day to meet everyone." His laugh sounded forced. "Said he wasn't the least bit happy about this."

"I imagine. So when is the plane due back?"

"Uh, today I think. I can call him back and double check." He tried for another smile. "But he did say they got part of the shoot finished, so it's not a total wash."

Lindsey tamped down the wave of anger rising in her. She wanted to strangle him, but it wouldn't do her any good.

"Okay, here's the way it is. No more shoots of any kind. Kill it. I'll deal with the client. We'll gift him one free campaign if I need to. But Arroyo has three planes within an hour of that island. Either that plane gets back and unloads those people today or I'm sending my people in, and they'll have security with them. Understood?"

Jerry paled. "That's not necessary. I'll take care of it right away."

"Good. Anything else will make me very unhappy."

They left Jerry's office and John went to give Taylor a heads-up, while Lindsey told Leda where she was going.

"If anything urgent comes in, forward it to my cell. Otherwise I expect we'll be back before long."

It was a typical Florida spring day, warm but not hot, with a nice breeze scented with salt water and tropical flowers. They did a quick drive-through at Coffee Talk before Lindsey plugged the address of Masquerade into her phone and let the sexy voice give her directions. As they drove, Lindsey sipped her mocha latte and tried to run through everything in her mind. Neither of them said much, for which Lindsey was grateful. Last night was still too new for her. She was still sorting through the mixture of emotions she'd been able to put aside while focusing on work.

As if he was tuned into her brain, John reached over and squeezed her thigh.

"If you're quiet because you're thinking about Masquerade, good enough and keep thinking. But if it's about us, Lindsey, I hope those aren't bad thoughts because it's all good. More than good. I promise, no second thoughts this time at all. And I'm going to spend every spare minute proving it to you."

Lucky for her she was spared the necessity of responding, as her electronic guide told her they'd reached their destination. The Spanish villa-style building sat back from the road on a quiet side street. It was larger than she'd assumed from the pictures, with some parking in the front and a sign directing people to more space in the back. Hibiscus trees in large ceramic pots stood on either side of the carved, wooden front door.

There were four cars in the parking lot, all of them high-end luxury vehicles. A driveway to the right led to parking in the rear of the building.

"No windows in the front of the building," John commented.

"Privacy," she pointed out. "And a sense of exclusivity. I'm going to go in and introduce myself. I'm wondering if you should wait for me here in the parking lot or take a trip around the block." She tilted up her lips in a half-smile. "I'm not all that good at this secret-agent business."

"Me neither, but I'd say parking lot. If you drove alone, you'd leave your car here, right? So just tell them you're out with someone else from the agency stopping in to see various clients and assure them their service from Elite will not be interrupted in any way."

"Good thought. Okay, wish me luck."

"I know I don't have to tell you this, but get as good a look as you can. And watch yourself."

She smiled at him. "Believe me, I will."

She stopped, took a deep breath and let it out, centering herself before she pulled open the heavy door and walked into Masquerade. The first thing she noted was the quiet luxury of the place. Instead of the usual tiled floor in the foyer, she stepped onto thick carpeting that silenced footsteps. The receptionist sat behind an antique desk, her computer and other equipment in a matching breakfront behind her with doors that could close everything off at night. Delicate-looking but comfortable furniture was attractively arranged for people who might be waiting. A single-serving coffee maker and a crystal water pitcher sat on a sideboard. Soft instrumental music drifted from hidden speakers.

The woman behind the desk, who looked to be in her thirties, could have been a walking ad for the place. Her shoulder-length hair fell in a perfect cut, her makeup impeccable and her elegant suit screamed money. As Lindsey approached, the woman rose and pasted her practiced smile on her face.

"Good afternoon. My name is Ria. Welcome to Masquerade. May I help you?"

"Yes. My name is Lindsey Califaro." She handed the woman her card. "Executive vice-president of Elite Marketing. The spa is one of our clients."

Ria took the card and studied it, then looked at Lindsey. "I'm sorry, I don't handle any of this. Is there something I can do for you? A message I can relay?"

"Our president, the person who was in charge of this account, passed away suddenly. I'm trying to visit as many clients personally as I can, to assure them there will be no interruption in services. I'm wondering if by any chance the owner is here."

"I see. No, she's not usually on the premises."

"I'm sorry to hear that. I'd really like to speak with her. You know, give her my personal assurances."

The other woman studied Lindsey for a long moment. "Perhaps our manager could help you. Could you excuse me for a moment?"

"Of course." She looked at the expensive menu of services on the desk. "Mind if I look at one of these while I wait?"

"Of course not." She handed one to Lindsey. "I'll be right back."

The brochure was printed on pale blue vellum with navy ink and a design of ivy tracing the edges of each page. *Expensive*, Lindsey thought.

She took a seat in a small chair that was surprising in its comfort, and began to look over the list of offerings. The usual spa services were listed, the prices in line for what appeared to be a luxurious facility. Twice while she sat there looking it over, the door opened, both times admitting a woman who appeared to be about Lindsey's age, with a girl she was sure was just out of her teens. Without waiting to be checked in, the woman opened one of the doors to the interior of the spa and hustled the girl through it. Lindsey tried to see what it looked like, but the door was closed in a hurry.

In seconds Ria was back at her desk.

"I informed our manager that you were here, and she'll be right out to speak with you."

"Is there some kind of prom going on?" Lindsey asked.

"What?" The young woman looked startled. "Excuse me?"

"I noticed some very lovely young girls arriving with women I guessed were their mothers, so I wondered what the occasion was."

"Oh. Yes. Well. Not a dance. A private party. This is a special treat for them. We do this often." Her smile was smooth and practiced. "You can't introduce them to the delights of a spa early enough, right?"

"I suppose, although it seems a lot of money to spend on girls that age for one event."

"Oh, no, not at all." Ria spoke quickly. "As I said before, a very special occasion and their...parents...can well afford it."

Lindsey noted this was the second time the woman had hesitated at the use of the word "parents". She filed it away in her memory bank.

The front door opened again, and Ria excused herself to check in yet another young girl. This time when the door to the interior opened, Lindsey stood and followed them, craning her neck to look around them. What she saw was a day spa with the most luxurious appointments she'd ever seen, and she'd been to a lot of them.

"I'm sorry." Ria touched her arm. "Only clients are permitted in the spa proper." There was the trained smile again. "Privacy. I'm sure you understand."

"Oh. Of course."

Lindsey had barely nodded her thanks and moved to sit down again when a woman emerged from the interior. She was dressed in slacks and a collared silk blouse that Lindsey was sure didn't come off any rack, fitting as if they were tailored for her. Her ebony-black hair was swept back from her face and fell just to her shoulders. Her makeup was as flawless as any Lindsey had ever seen.

She approached Lindsey with her hand out and a practiced smile on her face.

"Noreen Chandler, manager of Masquerade. I'm happy to meet you, Miss Califaro. Craig always took very good care of us. His death saddens us all."

Her greeting was polished, her tone of voice pitched low and pleasing, but Lindsey got the distinct impression the woman wished she would vaporize. Disappear. Never come back. *What on earth is going on here? Is it possible we were right about the real purpose of the spa?*

"As it does us." She matched her tone to the other woman's. "We will miss him greatly, but I know he'd want us to keep things moving along. Be sure the clients were well taken care of."

"Yes. I'm sure he would." She glanced at her watch. "If you'll excuse me —"

"That said, I'd like to set up an appointment to review everything with you and plan out your promotions for the next six months. We want all our clients to know that, despite Craig's sudden death, Elite is still on top of things."

"I understand, and I appreciate it. I do have to contact the owner. She'll be the one making the decisions on everything."

"Of course." She handed Noreen a card. "I gave one of these to Ria, but you should have my contact information, also. I'll be in touch in a couple of days."

"Oh, that won't be necessary. They'll be contacting you, I'm sure. It was nice to meet you, but if you'll excuse me, we have a full house today. I need to make sure everything runs smoothly."

"Yes, about that. I noticed the young girls arriving. A special party, Ria said."

Noreen nodded. "At their social level, it's a common occurrence. Sort of a private debutante event."

"I see. Well, since you're so popular, before I leave I'd like to make an appointment for a full day for myself."

"Oh." An apologetic look washed over the manager's face. "I'm so sorry, but we aren't taking any new appointments for a while. Our calendar is completely full."

"It is? Well, you must be very good."

"We like to think so. Thank you for stopping by. We'll be in touch."

When she stepped out into the parking area, she noticed John had moved over to sit behind the steering wheel.

"Ready to make a getaway at a moment's notice?" she teased, opening the door.

"No. Just thought it would look a little better."

"Good thinking."

As soon as she climbed in and closed the door, he edged out of the parking lot and drove off.

"How did it go? You weren't in there very long."

"Yes. Two women showed up with young girls. I'll tell you about that in a minute. First let me give you directions back to the office. I want to tell Taylor and Noah about this."

"So what did you find out? Anything?"

"Not much at all, as a matter of fact. It's obviously a very high-end, very select spa. Luxuriously decorated and outfitted, with prices to match. But the interesting thing is, the clients who came in while I was there were young girls. I'd say neither of them was older than twenty. They were brought in by older women, who might or might not have been their mothers. No one my age came in."

"Did you find a way to ask about it?"

"Of course. Ria, the receptionist, said there's a posh private party they are all going to."

John shrugged. "You and I have both seen those parties. Been to them. Parents bring their kids when they get old enough."

"Yeah." She leaned back in her seat, running everything through her brain. "I met Noreen, the manager, and gave her the spiel about how sad Craig's death is for all of us but assured her that Elite was not going to let anything fall through the cracks. I told her I wanted to meet with the owner to discuss their upcoming marketing plans."

"And?"

"She gave me a polite brush-off. Said she'd have to have the owner get back to me, but she didn't sound like she was in a hurry to make that happen. Also, I tried to book a full day for myself, and she very nicely told me they were booked for the foreseeable future."

"And we already discussed how out of the ordinary that is."

"Right. Like I told you before, I have been going to spas for years and have never yet had one turn me away. No matter how full their schedule is, they always find a way to work you in. Maybe not on the day you want but close enough. Also, she told me they do a lot of these special groups like the girls I saw today."

John frowned. "So, if they're that busy, why do they even need a marketing plan at all? Sounds like they've almost got more business than they can handle."

"I agree. I'd say it's not even necessary." Lindsey rubbed her forehead. "John, are we making something out of nothing here?"

"Maybe, but I'd say no. This is one of those things that makes me want to turn over every virtual rock and find out what's beneath it." He turned into the parking garage for Elite's office building. "Let's see what emerges when I dig into Craig's bank accounts tomorrow." He grinned. "And while I'm at it, if I happen to slip into Masquerade's, who's to know?"

Lindsey chuckled. "I'm sure glad you're on our side, that's all I'm sayin'."

"You know if there's something there, I'll find it. No matter how smart they are, when people start hiding money, they always make a mistake."

"It's almost six o'clock," Lindsey told him, glancing at her watch as they rode up in the building's elevator. "Let's tell Taylor what we learned, which may be nothing, and see what she and Noah have on-going."

"Sounds good." He started to say something else, but just then the elevator doors opened.

"What?" she asked.

"Later. Let's take care of business first."

Chapter Twelve

Arianna stood with as much patience as she could muster while an assistant blotted the perspiration from her body and reapplied her makeup. She had been posing in this teeny-weeny bikini for three hours already and she was getting tired. And thirsty. It was hot as hell on the Caribbean island. The sun was unrelenting and today there wasn't even a whisper of a breeze.

The small plane had dropped them here three days ago and everything had been nonstop since then. At first she'd been over-the-top excited about this opportunity. The test shoot in New York had gone well, the photographer had praised her, and before she could blink, she'd been loaded onto this plane with the others and flown to this lush tropical island.

She'd never been to a place like this before. Face it, she'd never been anyplace besides Ohio and New York and the bus ride from point to point. And for sure not to a private island owned by one person. A house so big she was sure that without directions she could get lost in it. One with an indoor and an outdoor pool, as well as a private beach. A house so enormous, with enough bedrooms that each of them had their own.

If only she could share this. The agent had asked the girls to hand in their cell phones, promising to give them back after the shoot was finished.

"No distractions," he'd teased.

Still, she'd managed in the ladies' room at the office to call her roommate and tell her what was happening, with a promise to call later with more details.

Each day after they were finished, they'd been given the opportunity for a swim. Just swimming, no posing. Three of the girls had chosen a pool, but she'd never been to the beach before so she and Maya had indulged themselves, standing in the water and letting the waves roll in over them, basking in the Caribbean sun.

At night, a cook prepared dinner and they were served on what she was sure was the finest china and crystal. Then they went to sleep in beds big enough for four people with sheets like satin and fluffy pillows. The entire atmosphere was enough to seduce anyone into a world of pleasure. How would she handle it when she had to return to her fourth-floor walkup in New York? Chances were now she could afford to move, and maybe still be friends with some of these girls. The thought cheered her up.

If anything bothered her at all, it was the man introduced to her as the owner. Although he was middle-aged, he looked like he worked out every day. He was tan and fit and treated them with gracious cordiality. It did bother her that while he smiled a lot, that smile looked artificial. More than that, however, was the look in his eyes, like he was measuring her for something. It frightened her. Maybe that was the look he gave people he did business with, and it had become permanent.

She looked at the four other girls who were involved in this shoot with her and wondered if they felt that same way. She was afraid to ask them. What if they said something to the agent and he sent her home? And she never got paid?

She thought again about dinner and the rooms they'd been given. Such big rooms for each of them. At first Arianna thought it was to give them privacy but today, out of nowhere, she'd suddenly been struck with the feeling it was to keep them apart. And she had no idea why. They'd all eaten dinner together, but then the man in charge, the same one she'd met in New York, had ushered each of them to bed with a big smile and a bedtime glass of champagne.

"It's important each of you gets plenty of rest," he'd told them. "We want you to look perfect in the photos."

Get over yourself, idiot. This is your chance to make a lot of money and have a career. Stop being a ninny.

The agent had been sitting in a beach chair watching the shoot. Now he rose and headed over to where Arianna was standing, waiting to be called again.

"Getting tired?" He smiled at her, his teeth very white against his sun-darkened skin.

She nodded. "Just a little."

"We'll break for lunch in a few. The meal will be served in the house, where it's cooler, then you girls have the afternoon off."

"Oh? Are we finished with shooting all the pictures?"

He nodded. "We have an excellent collection to select from. I am happy with all of you. A very successful shoot." He rubbed his hands together.

"Can you tell me what magazines this is for? And when it will appear? I'd like to tell my friends."

Not that she had that many, but she didn't think it would be good for him to know she was all alone in the world.

"It's actually for several ad layouts. I'll be sure you have the information." He grinned. "Tonight, we celebrate with a small party. You'll have fun."

"Party?" Why did the thought frighten her? Who would be there except the crew, the girls and this man?

"Yes. Our host has invited a few close friends to help us celebrate the success of the shoot. They like to meet the models and brag to people when the ads come out that they know you."

She was surprised that people on this level of wealth were a bunch of groupies, but she just nodded.

"So tomorrow we go home?"

"That's the schedule, but we may have a little surprise trip for you all. You know, as a reward for good work."

"Trip to where?"

"Ah." He smiled "If I told you, it wouldn't be a surprise. Look. Here comes one of the gofers with iced water for you. Have a drink. It will cool you off. We are almost done here."

As he walked away, Arianna realized he hadn't given her a real answer to her question. The knot of fear in her stomach that had developed yesterday tightened at once into a big fist.

It didn't get any better when the 'visitors' arrived late that afternoon. No one had to tell her that posing for pictures wasn't the only thing she was expected to do. Then she had by accident overheard a phone conversation that reinforced her unfortunate belief that something was very wrong here and she'd made a huge mistake.

She excused herself to use the restroom, taking the hallway that passed the owner's den, where the door stood a tiny bit ajar. The man himself, their host, Señor Madea, was on the phone.

"Don't be an idiot. I can't just load them up and send them back. I've told you that every other time you've called. Arrangements have been made. By midnight tonight, they'll all be loaded on the boat and there will be no worries."

Loaded on the boat? What boat?

Arianna pressed herself hard against the wall, trying to hear the rest of the one-sided conversation, hoping no one else would come along.

"What? Fuck you. Craig would never have let this happen. If those people come storming onto this island, you and I might just as well be dead. What? Fine, but I don't guarantee that you or I will live to see next week. I'll go tell them to get the plane ready now."

Arianna scurried along the hallway to the little guest bathroom, closed and locked the door and leaned against it, trembling. Was it possible they were going to be rescued? That the plane would fly them home?

At last, composed, she made her way back to the pool, where a shouting match was in progress between Señor Madea and two of his guests. Three of the men she had assumed were his security guards on the island were rounding everyone up and telling them to pack their equipment *pronto*. People were scurrying in every direction and the Bella Donna agent was yelling at the girls to get their asses in gear, to gather what they could and hop into one of the long golf carts parked in the big paved area outside the front door.

She said a silent prayer as she ran for her little travel bag, which was all she'd been allowed to bring, and hurried outside, determined not to be left behind.

I'll never be this stupid again, if I can just get home safely.

Chapter Thirteen

Almost everyone had left the Elite offices by the time they walked in. Noah and Taylor were standing in the reception area, both texting on their cell phones.

"Oh, good," Taylor said. "You're back. I can hardly wait to hear what you've found out."

"Not much, but that in itself was interesting," Lindsey told her. "Masquerade is quite the place."

"Let's go ahead and close up and you can tell us all about it over dinner."

They decided to eat at the Italian restaurant across from the office building for the sake of convenience. For the first time today, Lindsey began to unwind a little. While they ate, Lindsey and John filled Noah and Taylor in on what they'd discovered and all about the visit to Masquerade.

"I completely missed this during the first pass at the accounts," John told them. "The first thing I look for is anything out of the ordinary, and this time, for whatever reason, I didn't find anything."

"Because it didn't stick out," Lindsey pointed out. "Why would you think anything unusual about a small client who didn't need much in the way of services? I certainly didn't. You were looking for big dollars and places to move them around. That's why, the first time around, it never tripped any signal wires."

"I just hate the thought of some fucker being cleverer than I am," John griped.

Lindsey gave a small laugh. "John, none of us is perfect. And Masquerade wasn't high on the list of anything we've been investigating. We had no reason to look there for irregularities. None. That's just the damn fact, so let it go and move forward."

Still, she already knew John well enough to be aware of the fact it wouldn't stop there. Even if it turned out they had nothing to do with Craig's death, there was definitely something wrong. He would make it his business to find a way to take it down and everyone connected with it. And now he would be even more intense about it. A tiger had been unleashed and someone had to pay for that.

"Lindsey." Noah looked at her across the table. "Do you think they could be moving drugs through there?"

"I have no idea what a situation like that would look like, but yes. It's possible. I know spas get deliveries of goods on a regular basis."

Taylor leaned forward. "So, a dealer, for example, could bring the dope to Fort Lauderdale, package it in boxes disguised as spa goods and have it delivered to Masquerade. But moving it out of there wouldn't be that easy to disguise."

"Don't kid yourself," Noah told her. "Kilos of heroin or whatever drug is on tap are not very big. But each container can be cut and repackaged hundreds of times and delivered to the dealers. Who's going to stop a woman with a big shopping bag from a spa?"

"You're right," she agreed. "Sorry. That was dumb of me."

"Not dumb. Just not something you'd think of off the top of your head. But it's a very real possibility." He took a swallow of coffee, set his cup down and looked around the table at everyone. "And if they are also using it as part of their sex trafficking ring, maybe a place to beautify the girls, then everything you saw is right on target."

"I think my warning lights blinked as much regarding the girls brought in by women who didn't act at all like their mothers as they did by the fact they don't have time to book an appointment for me. No place like that turns away business. You find a way to make it work."

"Okay, Lindsey and John. I think your assessment of Masquerade is right on the money. One of the Arroyo companies owns a chain of spas. Whenever we're in a city where one is located, we always check it out. If a customer wants an appointment, no matter how booked they are, they always manage to work you in. I'm sure they never tell anyone they can't go inside to where the main part of the spa is. That would set off warning bells right away."

"Well." Lindsey sighed. "On the one hand, I'm glad to know I wasn't wrong when my suspicious nature reared its head. On the other, however, it upsets me to learn that one of our clients may not be on the up and up and I never knew anything about it. Never even suspected."

"So, let's talk about tomorrow." Taylor looked at Lindsey. "First on your list will be full-out research on

Masquerade. Every tiny bit of info you can find. John can tell you how to access sites not even on your radar and you can follow through with that while he digs into Craig's finances. Are you good with that?"

"I can do it," Lindsey assured her. "No worries."

"Fine. If you have problems accessing anything, ask John. I swear, he can find one black grain of sand on the beach."

He grinned. "It's all in knowing where to look and how."

"All right. John, go ahead and access Craig's bank accounts. I've got the paperwork to cover you. I want to know where every penny came from and where it went. Go back as far as you possibly can, both of you."

John made a note. "You don't think Natalia will freak if she finds out we're going through Craig's bank records?"

Taylor shrugged. "His personal finances are tied to Elite, so she doesn't have a choice. In any event, John, I know you can do it without her even having a hint of what's going on."

He nodded. "My specialty."

"Don't forget we have the funeral tomorrow at two," Lindsey reminded everyone.

"Oh, I haven't forgotten," Taylor assured her. "Believe me. I'm actually looking forward to it so I can eyeball some of these people. I'll bet whoever owns Masquerade will be there."

"Yes, if he—or she—is such a good friend," Lindsey added, "I'm sure they'll show up for the funeral. It will be interesting to see the mixture of people."

Noah snorted. "You can bet Ruben Madea won't be one of them."

"I'm sure," Taylor agreed. "My money says he'll stay as far away from this as possible."

"But there's still the business he was in with Craig — what happens to that? Won't he want to follow through on something that's unfinished? Is he expecting money for drugs he facilitated? Anything else? Other merchandise? A payout?"

"What other kind of merchandise?" Lindsey asked.

Noah's features settled into a hard mask. "I hesitate to even say the words, but is there a possibility Craig was involved in the illegal sale of guns?"

"Guns?" For a minute Lindsey was afraid she would faint. She was a news junkie and knew about illegal arms dealt to rebel groups in other countries, to drug cartels, to terrorists. The thought made her ill.

"Here. Drink this." John handed her a glass of water.

She sipped it slowly, taking a minute to gather her thoughts.

"Sorry." She tried to smile. "I think I hate illegal guns worse than drugs."

"It's a very lucrative business," Noah pointed out. "I'm already pissed that Craig might have been dealing drugs right under our noses. Add the possibility of guns to that, and my blood pressure goes through the roof."

"Craig's lucky he's already dead," Taylor told them, "or Noah would be all over him. But let's not get ahead of ourselves here. We have no proof of anything. For all we know, Masquerade could simply be a conduit to wash money for drug cartels. Which, while far from a good thing, is better than the alternatives. Let's just hope all this turns out to be far-fetched."

"Amen to that," Lindsey agreed.

"I need to get into those accounts first thing tomorrow," John told them. "I'll plan on getting to the office very early and getting started."

"As I said earlier, I have the paperwork to cover us," Taylor said, "so you can dig into Craig Wainwright's bank accounts."

"Oh, I'm geared up for this all right. Have you ever known me not to be?"

"Good." Noah finished his coffee and signaled for the check. "We've all had a busy day. I say let's get some sleep because tomorrow will be even more intense."

By the time they left the restaurant, Lindsey was fighting both physical and mental exhaustion. She wanted nothing more than to go home and soak in her big tub. One of the first things she'd done when she bought the house was to have a luxurious spa tub installed. Every time she soaked in it, she counted it money well spent. Would John be sharing it with her tonight? Should she ask him? Wait for him to say something?

She was still trying to figure it out when Noah left to get their car. But as she stood in front of the restaurant, she wondered if the Cantrells felt as awkward as she did. John was still without wheels of his own. Would he catch a ride back to the hotel with the Cantrells? Ask to come home with her? In front of Noah and Taylor? Should she say something?

Was that a smile Taylor was doing her best to hide? Did she know about last night? Was the chemistry between Lindsey and John so strong it was almost visible?

When neither she nor John uttered a word, Taylor added, "I'll let the two of you figure out the best place to do it. Oh, here's our car. See you in the morning." As she got into the car, she looked back at them. "Don't stay up too late."

The car pulled away from the curb and Lindsey turned to stare at John.

"She knows."

He winked, swallowing a grin. "Yes, I'm afraid so. And probably she's always known. It's very difficult to hide anything from her."

"I don't know whether to laugh, cry or hide in embarrassment."

John pulled her into his arms against his hard body.

"A smile will do. We're working hard at this, Lindsey. Nothing we're doing has suffered and it won't. But be warned. I kicked myself for so long for being such a selfish, arrogant fool before. I always figured there'd be plenty of time if we got to it, then I almost ran out of time. I'm not going to miss this chance for us again. That's a promise. Trust me, and I mean that."

She wanted to, in the worst way. She was sure, also, that if either Taylor or Noah had felt this was a bad idea, they would have spoken out.

"Okay." She blew out a breath. "I believe you. But..."

He touched the tips of his fingers to her lips. "I hear you. No buts this time. How about taking me home with you again?"

"Will we be making another early morning run to the hotel?" she teased. "You know, so you can be presentable when you get to the office?"

"I took care of it for the moment, being hopeful. We need to go back to the office for my messenger bag, where I stashed some clean stuff and a shaving kit. I'm kind of hoping I can lose the hotel room after this."

Her heart did a little jitterbug. That would be taking a huge step forward and she wasn't sure she was ready for it.

"Or not," he said, forcing a smile. "I just want you to know I'm all in."

"Let's see how tonight goes, okay?"

She was encouraged when he didn't draw away from her. Instead, he pulled her against his body, letting her feel everything from his rigid abs to his thick, hard, swollen cock. He slid his lips in a light caress over hers before taking a step back.

"You're calling the shots, Lindsey. Whatever you want is what we'll do."

When he said that she almost told him they'd go get the rest of his stuff, but she stopped herself. She wanted this one more night to be sure she wasn't making a mistake.

"I want to go home and climb into my spa tub and forget about Masquerade and Craig Wainwright for tonight."

"I can get with that program, as long as there's room in there for me."

"I think we can manage that."

* * * *

A thread of excitement wiggled through her when they stepped into her house. John followed her into her bedroom, dropping his messenger bag next to her small tufted chair. When she walked into the bathroom, all she could think about was the two of them in the big tub that was the centerpiece of the room. Her breasts ached with heaviness and the pulse in her sex throbbed so hard it threatened to pound loud enough to be heard. She wanted to squeeze her thighs together. No, she wanted John's shaft inside her hot, slick channel, then she wanted to squeeze.

Get a grip, Lindsey. The night has hardly begun.

"That's some tub."

She startled when he slid his hands around her waist, unaware that he had moved up so close behind her. He tugged her back a little, so she leaned into his body.

"It was my treat to myself when I bought the house. You have no idea how many nights it's been my savior."

He nuzzled her neck then took a tiny nip of the lobe of her ear.

"You going to show me how it works?" His tongue drew a line down her neck. "Share it with me?"

"Um, yes. I mean, I will. Of course."

When he licked and nibbled at her like that her brains scattered and she couldn't put a decent sentence together if her life depended on it.

She slipped from his grasp and bent down to turn on the taps. A push of a button set the jets working, pushing bubbles through the warmed water. Lindsey lifted a bottle from the little table beside the tub, uncapped it and sprinkled the essence of hyacinth into the water. The scent filled the air, just a hint of it but enough to tantalize and arouse.

"I'm going to undress you," John said, tugging her silk top over her head, "one item at a time."

He tossed the garment to one side then strung light kisses up the length of her spine, from shoulder to shoulder. He coasted his mouth back to the nape of her neck and went to work again, teasing with light nibbles. Next came her bra, which followed her top. Still standing behind her, he eased his hands around to cup her breasts. When he pinched her nipples, she sucked in a breath at the spears of heat that lasered through her, right to her soaking-wet sex.

"I remember how much you liked that," he murmured. "I even made you come just by playing with your nipples. I made you lie back against me and braced your legs apart with mine. Then I worried and teased those nipples until that orgasm just burst from inside you. Remember?"

"Yes," she moaned. "I do. I do."

"You wanted to squeeze your thighs together so much. You begged for me to let you touch yourself. Play with your clit. I finally let you touch it and pinch it, but no fingers inside yourself. Remember that?"

"Oh, god. Yes."

"You know how hot that was? My cock was so hard and aching that one touch and I'd have gone off like a rocket."

John moved his hands to lower the zipper of her skirt and ease it down so it pooled at her feet.

Her sex was pulsing now with tiny spasms and her clit ached and throbbed. Then he slipped one hand into the front of her bikini thong and eased his finger between her swollen lips until he touched that sensitive bundle of flesh. When he began to stroke it, Lindsey sucked in her breath, her entire body quivering with the desire to come.

"Clasp your hands behind your head," he ordered.

When she did, it gave him even greater access to her. With one of his hands at her mound and the other cupping a breast, her entire body ached with need.

"The tub," she managed to say, "I need to turn off the water."

He looked over her shoulder. "So you do."

With that, he hooked his thumbs into the lace edging of her thong and tugged it down her legs, helping her to step out of both it and her shoes.

"Bend over and turn off the taps." His voice was hoarse with need and hunger.

She planted her feet on the floor and bent from the waist, reaching across to where the taps were. When she did he slipped one hand into the hot crevice between the cheeks of her ass and drew his thumb in a straight line down to her opening. She tightened her muscles around it, every bit of her straining to draw it in deeper.

But then, damn it, he backed away. When she turned, he was taking off his own clothes, hanging them with neat precision over the valet rack against the wall. God, she loved to look at him. She didn't think she'd ever get enough of it. With his sculpted abs, muscular thighs and arms and narrow hips, he had the body of a man fifteen years younger.

"I don't know when you find the time to work out." She ran the tip of her finger along the center of his flat chest, through the curls at his groin and down the length of his cock. She had to force herself to stop gripping that hot, hard shaft and stroking it to bring him to orgasm.

"Good genes," he teased.

Then he lifted her in his arms and stepped into the deep tub. With great care, he lowered himself into the water until he was seated, taking her with him and arranging her with precise movements between his thighs. His legs bracketed hers and he drew her back until she was leaning against his chest. She wanted to purr with satisfaction.

Cupping her breasts, he teased the nipples with his thumbs. He had placed her so the length of his cock was wedged between the cheeks of her ass, and every time she made a movement, her flesh rubbed against it. She was torn between wanting to come and never wanting to move.

She closed her eyes and leaned back against John's chest, just drifting. The friction of his thumbs on her nipples set up a fluttering in her sex, the inner walls rippling with tiny spasms. She tried to close her legs and squeeze hard against the sensation, but John had her legs spread on either side of his.

"You're mean," she whimpered, as she tried to shift her position.

His laugh was a low, rough sound in her ear, his breath a soft whisper.

"If I let you come too soon, where's the fun in that?"

"Lots of fun," she protested, shifting her hips. "I promise."

He chuckled again and closed his teeth on her earlobe in a gentle bite. "But even more doing it my way."

He pinched her nipples and gave them a light tug, setting off another chain reaction. With his lean, muscular arms circled around her she was captured and held in place while he teased her at his leisure. The aerating effects of the bubbling water soothed at the same time as they stimulated, pushing her to the edge and keeping her there no matter how much she tried. The press of his cock in the crevice of her ass didn't help either, the long, hard length so tempting and teasing.

They stayed like that for a long time, neither of them speaking. In truth, it seemed as if no words were needed. John spent a long time rubbing and squeezing and pinching her now ultrasensitive tips and kneading her breasts. Ever since he'd discovered that she responded so well to stimulation there, he'd made that a focus of his efforts.

A moan of pleasure tore from her as he pressed her legs even farther apart and slid one hand down past the gentle curve of her stomach to toy with her mound. Just the barest caress of a fingertip over her throbbing clit made her cry out with need. That sexy chuckle in her ear didn't help either, driving her even crazier.

Lindsey felt as if she'd been transported to a cloud, one where a steady hum of sexual desire vibrated through her, just enough to keep her on edge but not enough to break the spell. She wanted to come, wanted that climax, yet John played her body so skillfully she didn't want to lose the continuous surge of pleasure gripping her.

She blinked when she felt something warm and slick touch her arm, and when she looked she saw that John had poured some of the scented body wash she used into his hand and was slowly stroking it up and down her arms.

"Mmmm."

All she could do was lie there and hum with satisfaction as he applied it to every area of her body. Then he soaked the washcloth and let warm drops drizzle over her until all the soap had been washed away.

"I almost hate to get out of here," she murmured, putting her arms around his neck and leaning against him as the water drained from the tub and he lifted her onto the rug. She was still right on the edge of orgasm, just as she'd been when he began undressing her. Every touch of the towel as he moved it over her body was like the sensation of a vibrator against her humming nerves. And watching him dry himself off didn't do much to calm that down.

"No more teasing," she whispered when he carried her to the bed. "I want to feel you inside me."

The covers had been stripped back—she wondered when he had done that—and he placed her so her head rested on the pillow. In seconds he had dragged his toiletries kit from the messenger bag, pulled out a string of condoms that he dropped onto the nightstand, torn one off and sheathed himself.

Then he was there, over her, nudging her thighs apart and kneeling between them. Gripping his cock with one hand, he took a deep breath and pressed the dark purple head against her opening. Then, with a flex of his hips drove himself inside her.

Sweet Jesus! The man definitely has more than his share.

He filled her so completely the sensation made her catch her breath. Lindsey bent her knees and planted her feet on either side of his body, lifting herself to meet his thrust. *More,* she wanted to scream. *Faster.* She reached around him and dug her nails into the firm flesh of his ass, trying to make him increase the speed.

But he set the pace and rhythm, and despite her moans and pleas he didn't vary from it. Now slow, now a little faster, now faster yet. As his thrusts picked up speed, he drove in even deeper, again and again. Lindsey wrapped her legs around his hips, locking their bodies together and they moved as if they were one person. Faster. Harder. Until she lost all sense of self and surroundings. Until nothing existed but this man and his rock-hard shaft and the pleasure he was giving her.

"Open your eyes," he commanded.

When she did, she saw his eyes staring right at her, black onyx with a touch of amber. And, swirling in there, an explosive mixture of hunger and need.

"Now, Lindsey." He practically growled it. "Right now."

He drove into her, hard, three more times. Four. Then, as if someone had tripped a switch, they exploded together. Her inner walls gripped him, milking him, and her legs kept them locked to each other. There was nothing there except their bodies pulsing with need and hunger and incredible emotion. Again and again they spasmed, until there was no energy left in either of them, and at last they were limp, spent.

Lindsey let her legs fall to the side, bracketing their bodies, while she caught her breath. When she looked up, John was smiling at her, a tiny dimple winking in his cheek. He brushed her damp hair back from her forehead and dusted her lips with a kiss.

"There are no words," he told her.

She nodded, knowing what he meant.

"And just in case you think otherwise," he added, "this is about a lot more than sex. I can get just sex anywhere. But I can't get what's happening between us with anyone else. Believe it. Do not forget that, Lindsey. Promise me."

Even though she heard the intensity in his voice, she wasn't about to make a mistake again. She could lose herself in the sensual pleasures he coaxed from her body, but her heart was still locked away. *Once burned, twice shy*, she reminded herself.

"I—I'll try. That's the best I can do right now, okay?" And she would, even as she guarded her heart.

"I want to tell you something, Lindsey." John studied her face for a long time, his eyes dark again with emotion. "When Taylor called and asked me to come here and work on this project, at first I almost turned her down."

Lindsey frowned. "Why?"

"Like I said the other night, I was afraid to see you. Afraid of what you'd say after all this time. I did a shitty thing, Linds. And I was mad at myself for never getting back to you. When I finally realized what I'd thrown away because I was so afraid of commitment, I didn't know how to fix it. The worst thing for me would have been to show up and find you with someone else. I'm not sure how I would have handled that."

She thought for a minute, choosing her words with care. She reminded herself this could all still turn to garbage, and she didn't want to feel that hurt again.

"Lindsey?" He strung light kisses along her jawline.

"I'm not with anyone else, John. How could I be? Four days with you ruined me for anyone else."

As she spokes she was surprised to feel the tension easing from his body.

"Thank god for that." He let out a soft breath. "I swear to you, Lindsey, I'll never be that stupid again." He dusted a soft kiss on the tip of her nose. "I'm damn lucky to get a second chance with you. I don't intend to blow it."

At last he eased himself from her body, pinching the top of the condom to keep it closed. She lay there with her eyes shut while she waited for him. He was back in seconds, nudging her closer to the center of the bed, then climbing in and spooning her against him. His cock, now at rest, nestled between the cheeks of her ass and he banded one arm around her, cupping her breast in his large hand.

"When this is all over," he said in a low voice, "we're going to have a serious discussion about the future."

"John." Her voice was slurry with sleep. "We hardly know each other yet. We've spent all our time in bed."

"Not all of it," he disagreed. "And we've been together enough for me to know I'll do whatever it takes to keep you in my life."

A tiny thrill squiggled through her.

"How about we take care of business first? Then we can talk about the future."

"Count on it." He kissed the shell of her ear. "No bull here, Lindsey. You can fucking count on it."

Chapter Fourteen

John and Lindsey were at the office in the morning well ahead of everyone else. John was itching to get started taking apart Craig's financials and creating a money trail, and she had regular client work to take care of, along with more research into Masquerade.

When Noah and Taylor arrived at seven, John was already in the zone with his laptop and she had moved to her office to take care of current Elite work. There were graphics to be approved, client projects to be updated and a new schedule to be created to make it easier for her to track business. She tasked Leda with creating a master calendar and distributing it to everyone. She also requested a large printout to put on the board in her office, listing the schedule for each month including the one for the upcoming month. Now that she was in charge of everything, she needed to streamline her organizational method.

She didn't know what to make of the fact that both Cantrells stopped at her office to let her know they were there, but neither of them commented on the fact that she and John had arrived together or asked where he'd slept the previous night. She did her best to act as if nothing was out of the ordinary and just got her coffee along with everyone else, stopping John before he headed back to his work.

"If it's all the same to you," she said, "I'd like to have my staff meeting and get that out of the way before I dive back into Masquerade. Also, Taylor said right after I speak to the staff she wants us to meet with Jerry." She made a face. "That ought to be a lot of fun."

"Whatever you need to do. Elite's all on your shoulders now, so that has to come first. You know where I'll be. Just join me whenever you can."

"Thanks. I'll go have Leda set it up for me."

It would be important to bring herself up to speed on everything until Elite settled into its new routine. She didn't want anything to fall into a crack because she wasn't paying attention. She also wanted to assure them yet again that nothing was changing as far as they were concerned.

The biggest problem would be Jerry. The day before yesterday, after discussing it with Taylor, she'd had him cancel all the location shoots scheduled for Parrot Cay, including the current one. He had not been pleased at all. She was sure he'd been stewing about it and wouldn't wait for the staff meeting to bring it up. Sure enough, when she buzzed him to come to her office, he showed up with a chip on his shoulder that was almost visible.

When he walked into the office, he frowned when he saw Taylor sitting there, as well.

"Am I in trouble because I didn't think we should cancel the shoots?" he asked.

Taylor shook her head. "I'm just getting myself up to speed and thought maybe I could help answer your questions. I know you're unhappy with the decision. It was Lindsey's, but I support her."

"Have a seat," Lindsey told him. "It's obvious this is a hit button for you."

He nodded, and dropped into a chair. "I haven't changed my mind about it. I still think that's a big mistake. With Craig gone, we can't afford to let our clients think we're cutting back on anything. Besides, people have expectations."

"Oh?" Lindsey lifted an eyebrow. "Like what?"

"Like expecting us to keep our schedule and honor our commitments. Craig worked hard to get it all set up. There are important people involved, not the least of which is the man who is so hospitable as to let us use his home and houses us while we are there."

"With Craig gone," she repeated for emphasis, "I need to get a better handle on things and see how it all fits. I'm still not convinced we have to go offshore for those layouts. As I said before, we have plenty of tropical locations right here in the Fort Lauderdale-Miami area. I'd like to research what's available before we start chartering planes again and eating the expense of a foreign location."

"Ruben Madea will be very disappointed," Jerry warned her. "He's been extremely gracious about welcoming us into his home."

"Fine. I will personally thank him for his generosity, but I wonder if we weren't beginning to take advantage of it."

Jerry shifted in his seat, his irritation obvious. "He also sends a lot of clients our way."

"Make me a list of them and we'll review them."

"But—"

Taylor held up a hand. "Jerry, is there a problem here I don't know about? Some arrangement I should be aware of?"

He paused so long before answering, Lindsey's neck began to itch, her personal warning sign that something was not quite right.

"Is there anything I should know about this that isn't in the reports?"

"No." He heaved a sigh. "But those location shoots are a big attraction for the models, too. It helps us get both some of the top ones and the young fresh faces that draw the attention of customers."

"How did you meet Señor Madea?" Lindsey asked. "It's somewhat unusual for someone to offer their home frequently the way he has."

"Craig knew him. I think they met through mutual friends. Why?"

"Just curious. Like I said, it's an unusual situation." She cleared her throat. "Listen, Jerry. I've been doing this a long time and I know there are many ways to please clients. How about this? Put together a report for me of those shoots, what clients they are for and how many models we'll be using. I also want to have John Martino do a cost analysis of the models' expenses."

Jerry looked ready to jump out of his chair.

"Lindsey, please don't tell me you're looking to change modeling agencies. We worked hard to get the relationship with this one and have them send us their best models for each layout."

"I'm not jumping into anything," she assured him, "but I need to have all that information in front of me to make informed decisions. The sooner you get it to me, the smoother this will go."

Then, as if he'd decided that arguing with her wasn't the way to go, the creases smoothed out of his forehead and the corners of his mouth turned up in a smile.

"You're right. Let me get this together, because when you see my report, you'll see how making changes isn't the right way to go."

"I look forward to it."

"Something's going on there," Taylor said as soon as he left.

"You're right, and I have to admit I'm disappointed. And how did I miss all this in four years?"

"Because you weren't looking for anything and there weren't any problems. And Craig was apparently very clever at making sure of that."

"I wish I knew if he's pissed off because his gravy train ride might be coming to an end, or just irritated in general because I might change things? If he was part of this or just stupid?"

"When you get his report, shoot a copy to me. By that time John should have some information and we'll be in a better position to pursue this."

"Sounds good to me. And I always welcome your opinion."

Taylor laughed. "Noah will tell you I am always looking for an opportunity to give my opinion."

Lindsey looked at her watch. "Okay. Staff meeting time. Then I'm all John's. And yours."

"Good." Taylor nodded. "Today I'd like you to really dig into Masquerade again. Anything you can find. Any tiny nugget, I don't care what it is. What else do you have on your plate today?"

"This shouldn't take that long. After that I need about a half-hour to catch up on some stuff with my own clients. Then I'm good to go."

"Where's the best place for Noah to park himself? He has some business to take care of. Plus, he's going to use some other off-the-books contacts in addition to what Charley's doing to see what he can find out about Ruben Madea."

"Tell him he can use my office. I'm working in here with John and I'll meet with the staff in the conference room."

"Excellent. Let me know if I can help with anything." She started to leave, then turned back. "Also, we should get to the funeral early enough to mingle with the crowd. Who knows what we'll pick up? Even at a funeral."

Lindsey nodded. "Of course. I'm letting everyone in the office know we should make a good showing. The more the better."

"Good. All right." She glanced at her watch. "I'm expecting a call shortly so I'd better go get ready for it."

For a long moment after she left the room, Lindsey just sat and stared at her laptop.

"Lindsey." She looked up to see John in the doorway. "I'll say the same thing Taylor did. None of this is on you."

"I just can't believe Craig was doing all this practically under my nose and I didn't catch it."

"If he'd been hiding it from the beginning, then it wouldn't be obvious in normal business operations. Let's go back to square one and see what we find. Come on. Let's put that sharp brain of yours to work."

"I don't think it's so sharp at the moment, but you're right. We have work to do. Let me get everyone together for the meeting, which will be brief. Then I'm all yours."

Heat flashed in his eyes and when he spoke, his voice was deeper. "I hope you mean that in more ways than one."

Answering desire coursed through her, making her nipples harden and the pulse in her core beat in a heavy rhythm. "Maybe I'll show you tonight after this day is over."

"That can't come soon enough for me." He paused and lowered his voice. "For more than one reason."

The staff meeting was brief. Everyone had work to do and she didn't want to keep them from it. After she'd been updated on where everyone was, she refilled her coffee mug and joined John in Craig's office.

"I'm ready to dig in again," she told him.

They worked without a break for the next three hours, John taking apart Craig's financials with meticulous care, Lindsey looking for anything and everything on Masquerade. She also decided to do some research on Parrot Cay where the location shoots took place. There had to be something somewhere. She was so engrossed that she was startled when John broke the silence.

"Okay! I think I've got something here."

Lindsey saved her screen and sat back. "I'm glad one of us is having success. What have you got?"

"I won't bore you with how I got to it unless you want a lesson in complex accounting, but—"

Lindsey held up a hand. "Thanks, but no thanks. My brain is already frying, attempting to dig up stuff about this spa. Just the basic details, please."

He turned his laptop so she could see the screen. "It appears Elite wasn't Craig's first venture into marketing. Check this out."

She scanned the article he'd found abut Craig Wainwright and his former businesses. "I knew that, and so did Arroyo."

"When he and Natalia married," John reminded her, "she dumped a ton of money into the company, jazzed it up and helped him get top-tier clientele. They became friends with two other couples who helped him attract more."

"And who exactly were these couples?"

"Frank Podesta, George Merriam and their wives. Are you familiar with them?"

Lindsey nodded. "The three men have been friends for a long time, both business and social. There's no doubt they have money and influence. Podesta owns Capricorn International Shipping and Merriam runs an influential hedge fund. They both have huge estates, one in Miami and the other across the causeway on Black Swan Island."

John lifted an eyebrow. "I'm surprised the Wainwrights don't live in either of those places."

"I once asked Craig why they didn't move to Miami if they had close friends there. He said that was a place Natalie liked to visit but wouldn't want to buy a house there. But it is odd, especially if both Podesta and Merriam are somehow involved in all of this."

"If Craig was the front man," John pointed out, "he may have wanted a place equally as luxurious but less ostentatious. Not calling attention to himself."

Lindsey sat back in her chair and stared at John. "Do you get the feeling something's going on here that we can't quite get a handle on yet? Especially about Enescu and Madea?"

He chuckled. "Lindsey, I always get the feeling. It's the naturally suspicious nature that goes with my line of work. I'm about to dive into everything I can find about the previous firm, plus Podesta's and Merriam's financial situations."

"Can you do that?"

"Only if I don't talk about it. The original business gives me an in. It's perfectly logical for Taylor to ask me to do a financial health check on Craig, especially considering the method of his death."

She studied him for a long time, hoping that the little shivers skating over her were just a false alarm.

"This is getting more and more complicated, isn't it?"

John dipped his head in answer. "I'm afraid so. And I'm just beginning to scratch the surface. I'm sure what I find when I get even deeper into this will be much worse." He turned his laptop back to face him. "So. Back to Masquerade. Have you found anything more about it?"

She shook her head. "Barely. It's as if they're deliberately low-keying the place, so there really isn't much to tell. Talk about keeping a low profile. I can hardly find a mention of them anywhere. Not even an ad. And that in itself is telling, because what legitimate customer-oriented business doesn't promote itself? And why have a marketing agency if you aren't marketing?"

John nodded. "No one has so much business they don't need to look for more."

"I did a full search online first and nothing came up. Then I did a search for day spas in the Fort Lauderdale area. There sure are plenty of them, but none named Masquerade. They aren't even in the listing." She clicked her mouse and brought up the screen with the list.

"Maybe it's listed as something else? Some other kind of business?"

"Anything is possible, but why? Why not put it in the right category? It doesn't make sense if it's a legitimate business."

"Legitimate being the operative word," John pointed out.

"So then I tried other similar classifications. I even tried different spellings of the name, and—" She flapped a hand. "Never mind. You don't need all the minutiae. The point is, except for a listing in the phone directories, you can't find it anywhere. Why wouldn't they advertise? Why not be included in category listings? Why try to hide it?"

"You wouldn't unless you had something to hide to begin with."

"And needed a way to hide it," she added. "But what? That's the million-dollar question. And again, like Noah said, there has to be someone with a lot more power pulling all these strings."

"I'm going to start a search for their bank accounts as an extension of Wainwright's finances. It all falls under the Elite banner, so theoretically it's all good. I want to know how much income the place has, what their expenses are, where their cash goes. I don't know if all this was Craig's doing or he had someone with accounting smarts setting it up for him. They've buried the shell corporations under a lot of layers, and the accounts have to follow that trail."

"I'm getting an increasingly bad feeling about all this," she told him.

"Me too. I've seen situations like this before and it's not good."

"Damn." She sat back in her chair and blew out a breath. "If they have no visibility, what was Elite doing for them? We're a marketing firm. Our job is to promote the name or the brand."

Just then the intercom on Craig's desk sounded, interrupting them. Lindsey got up and answered it.

"Yes?"

"How are you two coming?" Taylor asked.

"John's doing better than I am, although maybe no progress is progress itself."

"How did your staff meeting go?"

"About as expected. They weathered the detectives questioning everyone, although they had plenty of questions of their own. Hopefully I've got them calmed down for the moment. Everyone's still very concerned, but they know work has to be done and clients don't wait."

"Good. Glad to hear it."

"I set up a new reporting system," she went on, "that I'm pretty sure will make things a lot easier to manage." She checked her watch. "Did you want me to order up some sandwiches, so we can have a quick lunch before the funeral?"

"I already tasked Sharon with that. It will be here in a few. I thought we'd eat where you're working and catch up on where we are."

"Sounds good."

She relayed the message to John, then took a moment to stretch and work the kinks out of her body. She was glad to have a break from the computer. Her eyes were beginning to tire and she was getting a crick in her neck.

"I don't know how you do it," she told John. "Stay glued to that computer studying figures all day."

"Would I sound like a nerd if I said I am so fascinated by figures that none of that bothers me?"

"Well," she teased, "a nice nerd. Okay?"

He laughed. "Okay."

But his humor disappeared once the food arrived, the Cantrells had joined them and he began to outline what he'd learned so far.

"I was afraid of something like that." Taylor put down her sandwich and took a drink from her bottle of water. "Okay. Let's have it all."

By the time he'd finished, no one at the table was smiling.

"I just wish I knew how my people missed it."

"Because they were looking for something different. Clean business. Good reputation. No financial problems. The usual due diligence process. And Elite's financial records are impeccable." He looked at everyone for a moment, as if choosing his words. "And something else. We have an unexpected problem here so I'm looking under the bed and in the closet, so to speak. I don't think that firm uses some of the websites I do. These are places I go to when I am looking for money hidden from my clients. Places where I can find hidden corporate tracks, bank accounts, other related items. The first thing I did was track the corporate papers. I'm not going to bore you with all the details right now. I'll put them in my final report. And I found something else very interesting."

"Oh?" Taylor looked at him. "We already have more interesting things than I'm happy with. What did you find out?"

"I felt confident doing this," he told them, "because it's attached to the structure of Elite. Natalia's money comes from a trust that is funded through a holding company that is sheltered through another holding company."

Taylor nodded. "The way people do when they want to hide money."

"Well, damn." Noah balled up his napkin and threw it on the table. "How many more surprises are we in for, John?"

"The fact that Craig did this so long ago," John said, "makes me believe he's been in bed with Madea for a long time."

"And he saw Elite as another way to handle his off-the-books enterprises, whatever they turn out to be. I just wish to hell we knew what he was dealing in." Taylor blotted her lips and pushed her plate away. "I think I've lost my appetite. It's almost time to leave for the funeral, anyway. I'm debating about whether we should go to the cemetery, too."

Noah picked up his drink and drained the last of it. "Let's play it by ear. But whatever we do, we should plan on dinner together afterwards. We have a lot to discuss."

"And I haven't even told you about the inconsistencies with Masquerade yet," Lindsey told them. "Things that if I'd been paying attention would have made me ask questions a long time ago."

"Great." Taylor grimaced. "A lot of people are going to pay the price for sloppy work because of this. I promise you."

"I called Charley Graham earlier," Noah told them, "and told him to add Podesta and Merriam to his list. He can find a gnat hidden under a log, so he'll get whatever we need."

Lindsey blew out a sigh. "I can't believe how complex this whole thing has gotten. You'd think running an agency this size with such high-profile clients wouldn't have left Craig time for anything else."

Noah just shook his head. "Whatever this is started long before Elite. But rest assured, we'll get to the bottom of it."

Lindsey had just finished eating when the phone in the office buzzed. Leda.

"What's up? We're just getting ready to leave for the funeral."

"There's a Detective Moran on the phone for you. Shall I put him through?"

"Of course."

Kevin Moran was pleasant enough, and courteous, but he wanted to meet with her and the Cantrells first thing in the morning. He'd spoken to everyone else and needed to wrap things up with them. Lindsey put him on hold so she could check with the others.

"We have to do it," Taylor pointed out. "We're the principal players in this and he's just doing his job. Ask him to come by at nine. That okay with everyone?"

Lindsey confirmed it with the man and hung up.

"That ought to be a fun way to start the day."

They cleaned up the debris from lunch and Lindsey made sure to tell each person she was leaving for the funeral and she'd appreciate them making the effort to attend. It was important that the agency show their support for Natalia. She was pleased that most of the staff agreed and began preparing to leave right away. She also instructed Sarah and Leda to let the answering machine pick up the calls so they could attend. She was sure Natalia would appreciate their presence.

"Actually," she told John when she was finished, "I have no idea if that's the truth or not, but I want Natalia to see that the staff had enough regard for Craig, and by extension her, to pay their last respects."

"Be interesting to see who shows up," Taylor commented. "I know they traveled in the well-heeled circles. I wonder just how many of those people made their money without any taint attached to it."

Lindsey and John rode to the funeral with the Cantrells in virtual silence, none of them having much to say. They had left before the others because, as Taylor said, she wanted a chance to read the crowd, especially Craig's closest friends.

"We may not find a thing," she said, "and his friends may have no connection to whatever Craig was involved in. But the Podestas and Merriams will be there so maybe we can do a little snooping. At least try to get a read on them."

"I know Podesta," Noah told them. "I'll make it a point to say hello."

The chapel at the funeral home was nearly full when they arrived, people in expensive clothing milling about, conversing in hushed tones. Noah and Taylor exchanged greetings with some of the people they'd met through business dealings in the area.

"The money in this room could wipe out the national debt," John murmured to Lindsey, scanning the crowd. "Craig Wainwright definitely moved in the top circles."

A tall, thin man wearing a black suit and somber expression directed people to sign the register of attendees. Another man stood by an archway draped with a black curtain, pulling it aside to allow two couples to walk back into the chapel while two others entered the alcove.

At the front of the room, the coffin sat on a platform, bracketed on either side by tall urns filled with flowers.

Other floral arrangements filled the space behind and on either side of it. Several people had paused beside the coffin and stood in somber silence for a moment before moving on.

"I think that's the alcove reserved for the family." Lindsey pointed to the arch. "I'm sure Natalia's in there, out of the way so she doesn't have to stand out here with everyone else until the last moment. It's enough of a strain without that. Let's go pay our condolences so she knows we're here. Then we can sit down."

John hung back. "I'll wait for you here. She doesn't know me from Adam and this isn't the time to make introductions."

Natalia, dressed head to toe in black, sat on a couch facing them. Her hair was drawn back from her face in a severe style and there was minimal makeup on her face. The only jewelry she wore were a diamond wedding band and her engagement ring, a solitaire with a stone big enough to use as a searchlight. On either side of her were two women also dressed in elegant, subdued money. They looked ready to whisk Natalia away at the first sign of distress.

Lindsey stepped up first. "I am so sorry for your loss. I am truly grateful for the years Craig and I spent working together. His loss is felt by all of us at Elite."

"Thank you so much." Natalia forced a tiny smile. "I know he appreciated all your hard work and thought very highly of you."

"Craig was very important to us," Taylor said, taking Natalia's hand. "We're doing everything we can to find out how this dreadful thing happened."

If possible, Natalia's face turned even paler. "But—but the police said it was an accident, brought on by those stupid pills he took."

"And we're hoping that's all it is," Taylor agreed, "but we've asked the police to do a very thorough job."

"Thank you for caring so much."

But to Lindsey, her voice rang false.

Back in the chapel, Lindsey was doing her best to overhear any conversation she could, just in case someone let a nugget drop by accident. It wasn't easy, what with everyone speaking in hushed tones and several different conversations going on at the same time.

"It's hard to tell who might be involved and who is not," she whispered to Taylor. "There are the Podestas and Merriams over there, by the two large urns."

"I'm going to say hello to Frank," Noah told them in a low voice. "And I recognize George Merriam from pictures I've seen. I'll be back in a minute."

"It's always possible no one here is involved," Taylor reminded her, "but after what John dug up today, I'm voting yes. There's a connection here. Definitely. I just have a gut feeling whatever was going on is a lot bigger than we're imagining."

"If it includes the sex trade," she murmured, "you can bet on it."

Lindsey was still trying to eavesdrop as she moved through the crowd, when the funeral director called for their attention and asked that they be seated. The four of them sat near the back, doing their best, Lindsey thought, to be unobtrusive. She sat there, quiet, letting the somber environment wash over her, when a whisper from the row behind her distracted her.

"We have to get some answers, and soon." A male voice, very low.

Every muscle in Lindsey's body tightened. She eased her hand over John's and gripped it tightly, hoping he'd get the message because she couldn't say anything out loud. His answering squeeze was his signal for "Message received and understood."

"We will, but not here today at the funeral. Have some sensitivity." Another male voice, a little deeper.

"We can't wait too long, or we'll be in trouble. People have expectations and operations cannot simply be halted like this, just because Craig is…dead."

"I hope you didn't have anything to do with that," the other voice murmured, the words barely audible.

"Damn it, no. I told you. But you know who might have and that really screws things up."

"I promise you that will not happen. There's too much at stake. Our partners would never stand for it."

"They aren't—"

"Ssh. Hastings is about to say something. We can't discuss this anymore, especially here. Later, I'll make a phone call."

More than anything Lindsey wanted to look over her shoulder without being obvious, but there just wasn't any way to do it. And of course not during the service. Natalia and her retinue were ushered in from the alcove and seated in front. The pastor of their church opened the service and the eulogy was delivered by a cousin of Craig's. She wondered why neither Podesta nor Merriam had been invited to speak. That was a most interesting question.

At last, they were requested to stand while the coffin was taken from the chapel and out to the hearse. Now she was able to see who had been sitting behind her.

She looked at them, stunned to see George Merriam and Frank Podesta rising from their seats.

Well, that validates what we were thinking. Holy shit!

She was sure now Craig had said or done something that made him a liability. But who had made that decision? And who had done the deed?

"Cemetery, right?" Taylor checked as they got into the car.

"Yes," Lindsey agreed, "but I have to tell you something."

"Let's get out of here first," Noah said. He set the electronic directions for the cemetery and wheeled the car out of the parking lot. "Okay, what's going on?"

"Two men behind me were whispering before the service began."

"I heard them, also. Thanks for the nudge, Lindsey."

"I wanted someone besides me listening, so I didn't get it wrong." She repeated what she'd heard, adding, "When I looked, it was Frank Podesta and George Merriam. And what they said fits right in with what we were discussing earlier today."

John pursed his lips in a soft whistle. "Heavyweights in the business world, including on the international stage. That means our sense that this was much bigger than we first imagined was right on target."

"Indeed, it does," Taylor agreed. "You know, they've actually approached me in the past about doing some business deals with Arroyo. Podesta even asked to set up a meeting on one of our visits to the area."

Lindsey knew that Taylor and Noah visited the Miami–Fort Lauderdale area twice a year. They had other interests besides Elite and, as a power couple, were much sought-after.

Noah pulled onto a wider street. "If you weren't so obsessed about never giving anyone more than a certain slice of the pie," he told his wife, "you might already be involved."

"And a damn good thing I am. Otherwise I'd be in the soup more than we already are. It makes every nerve in my body tell me we still don't have the full picture of what we're dealing with." Taylor leaned her head back on the headrest. "If my board of directors knew I'd allowed some kind of deep, shady business to go on with one of our subsidiaries, they'd ask for my resignation on the spot."

"Let's remember," Noah told her, "some of them were there during the big mess when you inherited the company. They're not in any position to throw stones."

"Maybe not, but I feel like throwing stones at myself. Damn, Noah. This thing has big international implications. I wonder if Natalia is aware of it."

He shrugged. "Hard to say. My first guess would be no, but anything is possible. John, as soon as we get back to the office you need to hit those accounts again."

"No kidding."

"And I'm going to put in another call to Charley Graham," Noah added. "I want him to put his people on this at once. I should have used them to check Elite, but who knew I'd need a high-level security agency rather than one that vetted businesses?"

"Enough with that. Stop beating yourself up. The system has worked up until now. These are some very high-level, devious people used to camouflaging everything they do. They were ahead of you before you started. But now we're getting on top of things, or at least making a good start."

Lindsey cleared her throat. "Here's a question for you. Well, two, actually. Or three. If Craig was hooked up with these people in something high-level and illegal, why get involved with Arroyo and take the chance of being found out? Second, who do you think killed Craig? Someone had to substitute those pills at some point and not too long before it happened. It wouldn't have taken too many doses to affect him the way it did."

"And your third?" John prodded.

"Why?" she asked. "What happened to make them decide they had to get rid of him?"

"If we find the answers to the first two," Noah told her, "I think we can figure out the third. We have some heavy work to do, people."

"We should collect our gear as soon as we get to the office and work from the hotel tonight instead of the office. Just in case." Taylor shook her head. "I'm not even sure the hotel is that secure. Who knows who might be around? And if these people are as high-level and sophisticated as we think, they could even compromise the hotel electronic setup and ghost what we're doing."

Lindsey wet her lips, wondering if she should open her mouth, but then thought, *What the hell. It's all about security.*

"Why don't we work at my house?"

Taylor shifted in the front seat so she could look at her. "Your house?"

"Yes. I have a big dining room table we can use, and I'm paranoid about security. I update the firmware regularly and keep the remote administration turned off. And change the password every month."

"Jesus, Lindsey." John chuckled. "Maybe you should be working for Liam at Software By Design."

She shook her head. "This is as much as I want to get into it. But some of the work I bring home is proprietary and I always have a fear of being hacked. So you're more than welcome to do this."

"I say yes," Noah told them. "It's up to you, Taylor, but—"

"I agree. Thank you, Lindsey."

"We should stop at the office so I can get my car and we can pick up our laptops. I can copy everything from our system that I'm working on onto a thumb drive. John?" He hadn't said a word yet, and she wondered if she should have opened her big mouth. "You okay with this?"

Taylor laughed. "I'm sure he will be. But, John? Do you want to stop by the hotel first and get your things? It might be easier for you if you just move into Lindsey's house."

Lindsey froze, not sure if she should laugh or cry.

"Uh…"

"I know you two think you're being so cool and professional about all this, but I also know you haven't slept in your room. Since I think it's safe to assume you aren't bedding down in the street or a cheap motel, and I happened to see Lindsey drop you off yesterday morning to shower and change, I think I'm drawing the right conclusions."

Noah chuckled. "My wife is better than any detective. And by the way, I think it's a great idea. Neither of us could figure out why you stayed away for four years, John."

He heaved a sigh. "Damn. I guess I'd never make it in the stealth business."

"Me neither," Lindsey agreed. "Taylor, please don't think—"

"Someday remind me to tell you the story of Noah and me, when all this is over. When you find someone who's right, jump on it."

Beside her, John relaxed. "You might as well check me out of the hotel. Jesus. It's a good thing I'm an accountant and not a secret agent."

Lindsey managed a smile, but she hadn't changed her mind. She'd enjoy this while it lasted, but when John's assignment was over, she'd still be the one to walk away.

Chapter Fifteen

Mia Silva stared at her parents, anger surging through her. She was twenty years old, almost twenty-one, and they still treated her as if she was twelve.

"I would like to go somewhere. For a change, without being driven by a bodyguard and watched every single minute. I would like to have some *privacy* for a change."

Arturo Silva stared back at her, the muscle twitching in his cheek evidence of the frustration he was feeling. A self-made billionaire who had left the streets of Mexico behind long ago, he had made it clear he did not want his daughter doing things that could put her in danger. And to his way of thinking, almost everything she wanted to do fit that description.

"I know what goes on in the streets out there," he snapped. "How dangerous it is. I worked hard to pull myself out of that. Do you think I want something to happen to you?"

She glared at him, then resumed her pacing. "It's just as dangerous for every other female out there, but you don't see them kept under lock and key, do you?"

"I know that every parent who is able to makes the effort. If you had an older brother, I'd feel a lot better about this."

"Oh, great." She threw up her hands. "So I'd have someone riding herd on me every single minute? No, thank you, *mi padre*. I can handle it myself."

"You are not going out there by yourself." Her mother's voice was unyielding.

Esme Silva could be just as indomitable a force as her husband. Sometimes even more so. Mia stared at the woman whose snapping black eyes and rich black hair were so much like her own.

"I won't be by myself. You know I am going with Sassy, Luz and Rubi. You had them picked up already. We will all be together." She closed her eyes and recited as if by rote, "We won't go off alone. We won't leave each other. We won't go off with strangers. We will have our cell phones turned on and ready at all times."

Mia was startled when her mother surprised her by laughing.

"I know we drill all this into you," she said, "but please know, it is just to keep you secure on the streets of big cities. Safety first."

"Mama." Mia heaved a sigh. "It is no safer anywhere else."

Her father relaxed a fraction and smiled at her.

"Maybe in part. But trust me, I will be worried every minute you are gone."

"I know, and we won't be out too late. You don't have to send Jaime, okay? We'll take a cab back and the girls will spend the night here, just as you asked."

Her parents had sent Jaime Roland, her father's driver-slash-bodyguard, to pick up her friends and bring them here so when she joined them they could head to the restaurant right away. A place she knew her parents had vetted to within an inch of its life. What they didn't know was they'd just be spending a few minutes there. She could hardly wait. She was in love with the color and energy of Miami and South Beach, a place where she came alive. She had to get out on her own. She just had to.

"Okay. Fine." But he still didn't look any too pleased.

Mia gave each of her parents a kiss and a little hug, grabbed her purse and danced out of the door. She was in the battle of her life to move into a place of her own, but damn it, she was going to win it. She couldn't spend her life locked up in the consulate. She and her friends, whose parents were just as suffocating, had secret plans to rent adjoining apartments. Everyone had a job, even her, despite her father's griping about it, although it wasn't the one she wanted. Working as a translator at the consulate was a long way from being a model, but it was the kind of job her father didn't object to. She'd been saving her money, had everything planned and this weekend she intended to make a very big pitch.

Her friends, waiting for her in the reception area of the consulate, rushed to greet her.

"Group hug!" she squealed.

They did so, but with great care, because of their hair and makeup. Then they turned to Jaime, who stood at the door.

"You are only to drive us there," she reminded him. "No hanging around and spying."

He just grinned and ushered them out and into the car.

"You all have your cell phones?" he asked when they scrambled out at their destination.

They all held them up obediently.

"And you will be ready at one o'clock when I return?"

"Yes, Jaime," they chorused, then made faces at him.

Mia watched him as he laughed then drove off.

"Okay," she said to the others. "Are we all set?"

"If your father finds out," Sassy said, "he'll skin you alive."

"I am almost twenty-one," she pouted. "It is time I stand up for myself."

"Okay, but first let's have fun, before he locks you away for the next ten years."

They entered the restaurant, waved off the hostess, made their way to the back and out through the rear door, then across the alley and into the nightclub that backed up to it. Well, Mia thought, maybe *nightclub* was too fancy. More like a high-end cantina, but they loved the place. They'd managed to sneak into it a couple of times before just as they had now.

The restaurant portion was upstairs in the balcony while the first level was a dance floor, complete with flashing lights and a high-energy disk jockey. A place where they could eat dinner, have a few drinks, a few laughs. Nothing outrageous or dangerous. Just a good time. They might be young, but they were not stupid, and they had scoped the place out good before their first visit, asked their friends and decided it was an okay place to spend the evening.

They climbed the stairs and were lucky to claim a table right by the railing. They ordered appetizers to start, along with a pitcher of margaritas, and sat back to enjoy themselves.

"Ooh, look!" Sassy squealed and pointed.

The hostess was seating two couples on the third level, the VIP level.

"OMG!" Rubi slapped her hands against her cheeks. "It's Nona! Right here. In this very place."

Mia caught her breath. Nona was an internationally known model whose face could be seen everywhere — magazines, billboards, whatever. That was who Mia wanted to be. A model like that. Posing for magazine ads and modeling in fashion shows. Mia had done two shows in the past six months, shows her mother had organized for fundraisers she was in charge of.

"I know you think this is such a glamorous life," her mother had told her. "It's not. It's long hours and hard work and sometimes with unpleasant people. I want you to have fun, so I hope doing these shows answers your need for it."

On the contrary, it had just whetted her appetite for more. And it was a glamorous life, no matter what her mother said. It was everything she was missing. But she'd have to do this with a great deal of care, find out how to work around it or her very old-fashioned parents would find a way to lock her up until she was eighty. She wanted fun and success. To travel to places and meet new people. To be the face of something, like other models were.

She couldn't stop watching Nona and her escort as they relaxed at their table. The wait staff danced attention on them, and it was obvious they were thrilled to have such a celebrity in their place of business. Nona's hair was swept back from her face in her signature style, just brushing her shoulders. She wore an electric-blue dress with a deep vee neck, complemented by pendant earrings. Every move she made was performed with such fluid grace.

Mia wanted so much to run up to her and ask her how she'd done it all. How she'd gotten her first job. What agency had she used? But she satisfied herself with surreptitious use of her phone to take pictures.

Sassy noticed what she was doing. "You're not going to stalk her, are you? God, Mia. Are you still hung up on that modeling stuff?"

"It's not *stuff*," Mia snapped. "It's what I want to be. And I know I could be a good one. Don't you have a dream? Something you want to do or be?"

Like her, all her friends came from wealthy families. But unlike her, their ambition was to have a good time, marry a handsome man who also had a lot of money, have babies and take their places in society. Mia wanted the same, of course, but not until after she'd made a name for herself. She didn't want to spend the rest of her days just as so-and-so's wife.

"Yes." She grinned. "I want to have fun. And you should, too. Come on, the deejay is starting. Let's dance until they bring our dinner."

As the notes of the first song bounced into the air, they hit the dance floor. Within seconds they were twisting their hips to the beat, arms in the air, heads thrown back. They were breathless when the first song ended and the deejay slid without a hitch into the second. But after two more songs, when they looked up and saw the waiter putting plates on their table, they headed back to the stairs.

"Wow!" Rubi shook her hair back as she bounced up the stairs. "This is great. Let's eat and dance some more."

Dinner, as always, was great, although it wasn't the food that drew them to this place. They chattered throughout the meal, catching up on gossip although they'd been together just a week ago and they spoke daily. The waiter cleared their dishes and refilled the pitcher of margaritas. Mia was sure, between the food and the exercise of dancing, the alcohol would have only a mild effect on her. Just enough for her to let loose and have fun.

She was sipping her drink and watching her friends down below on the dance floor when a man slid into the chair opposite her. An unbelievably sexy and good-looking man, dressed impeccably in a sport jacket and slacks that screamed money.

"I've been watching you." He smiled. "You make a great impression."

"Me? Oh, well, thank you but —"

"Forgive me, I am doing this all wrong." Reaching into the inside breast pocket of his sport jacket, the man pulled out a slim leather folder and extracted a business card. "Please. Take this. You will see that I am legitimate."

Mia looked at the pasteboard card and rubbed her thumb over the embossed printing as she studied it.

"Dax Fornell," she read. "Bella Donna Models. Miami. New York. London."

Her pulse accelerated a tiny bit. New York. London. Glamorous places she was dying to visit, but at the moment had little chance of seeing. Why did she have to be born to such old-fashioned parents, anyway? She was sick of the old-fashioned restrictions everyone in their social circle or extended family adhered to. The timeworn rules and regulations imposed on females her age. By this time in her life she should be able to spread her wings if she wanted to.

"We are looking for some specific types," he told her, "and you fit the bill. You have a nice fresh yet exotic look that our clients will pay high dollar for."

"This is...very flattering." She kept staring at the business card.

"We represent some of the top marketing agencies in the country, and you can earn anywhere from two hundred and fifty per hour to ten thousand dollars per day." He smiled. "Interested?"

Interested? *Is he kidding? A chance to be independent. This is like a gift.*

"I have to think this over. You understand. How would I contact you if I am?"

"Just call the number on the card. We'll have you come in and do a test shoot to see if your incredible looks translate to the camera. Then we'll go from there."

From the corner of her eye, she saw her friends leave the dance floor and head up the stairs.

"I have to think about this. But I promise I'll call you."

The man rose from his chair. "I look forward to it." He nodded at her friends. "Ladies. Have a pleasant evening."

"Ohmigod," Luz squeaked, leaning forward. "Who was that sex god and what did he want with you?"

Mia looked around, as if someone might hear her, although with the pounding of the music words didn't carry very far.

"You are not going to believe what just happened. I'm going to need your help."

Chapter Sixteen

Lindsey was glad that John had volunteered to drive on the way home. She couldn't believe how exhausted she was, and she told him so.

"It's mental," he reminded her. "And that can be a lot more tiring than physical. You've had a very rough couple of days."

"No kidding." She leaned back against the seat and stretched her arms above her head.

"I'm sure I can figure out a way to relax you after we're finished tonight."

Images flashed through her mind and that damn pulse in her sex woke up and was soon so heavy she had to squeeze her thighs together. She hoped she could get through the work session without embarrassing herself.

"You two go ahead and set up and get started," Taylor said as soon as they were at Lindsey's. "Noah and I have some phone calls to return but we'll join you as soon as we can."

"No problem," Lindsey assured them.

She fixed coffee for herself and John and they spread out their stuff on her dining room table. By unspoken agreement, they each pulled up the things they'd been working on and went at it. After a few minutes, Lindsey sat back in the chair, lifted her mug and took a sip of the cooling liquid.

"At least with this topic, I'm getting somewhere," she told John.

He hit Save and slid his chair closer to her. "What did you find?"

"I know Charley Graham is working on this, and he'll find a hell of a lot more than I will, but I wanted to get a picture for you and me. Whatever I find might help us connect the dots to Craig. I wasn't sure which of the two men to start with so I typed both their names plus Craig's in the Search bar. Then I checked whatever came up to see who was mentioned more times with Craig. It actually didn't take that long. I found a bunch of items right away linking Craig with Frank Podesta. Take a look."

She clicked slowly from screen to screen, bringing up mention after mention of Craig Wainwright and Frank Podesta supporting community initiatives. Hosting fundraisers with their wives. Creating joint business enterprises. Appearing at top society functions.

One particular page she enlarged and highlighted.

"Look here. See this? This is a personal piece on the Wainwrights and the Podestas when they co-hosted the fundraiser for St. Julian's *for the tenth year*. It also mentions that Natalia Wainwright and Isobel Podesta are not only very close friends — they are both also from Colombia."

"Colombia is certainly the heart and center of a great deal of illegal activity, especially drugs. That doesn't mean either of these women are involved in it, although it tickles my brain."

"Mine too. And if they are such good friends, how come Natalia didn't call Isobel Podesta instead of me the night Craig was killed?"

John stared at the picture of the two couples on the computer screen.

"Good question. I'm also trying to trace the source of the money Natalia provided for Elite. I'm pretty close to that and some other things. A lot of money has passed through the shell corporations to offshore accounts. And I've just scratched the surface." He pointed at her computer. "Now, with this new wrinkle, I'll have to broaden my search."

Lindsey stared at him. "John, what the hell are we looking at here? This is a lot more than just a spa that tries to hide itself."

"No shit. I have a really bad feeling about this, Lindsey. And whatever it is, it's obvious it started way before Elite."

"I'll bet Podesta's shipping company is involved somehow. Don't you think that's a good possibility?"

"Shit." John ran his fingers through his hair. "That's not good."

"Because?" she prompted.

"Because whatever they are hiding, whatever merchandise they might be dealing in, they have access to worldwide markets. You know how easy it is to hide drugs and guns in those big shipping containers? Double shit."

"Listen." She sat up straighter. "Someone had to set all of this up."

"True," he agreed. "You can't, for example, just pick up the phone, call a terrorist leader in the Middle East and ask him how he'd like a bunch of guns shipped to him."

Lindsey couldn't help laughing. "No, I'd think not." Then she sobered. "There has to be a way to find out if any of the people involved traveled overseas, to any of the key locations."

"Let's get Noah involved in this. He can get hold of Charley Graham in Tampa. Just like I can dig up numbers, Charley can ferret out information. He's got unlimited contacts, and his contacts have contacts. He should be off the phone soon, I hope."

"Taylor, also," Lindsey added.

"And here's Noah now," John nodded at the man as he walked into the dining room.

Noah looked from one to the other. "What's up?"

"Actually, I'd like both of you, please," Lindsey told him. "This is important. Will Taylor be free soon?"

"I'm done for a while." Taylor took the chair across from Lindsey. "What's up?"

"Problem with someone or something?" Noah asked.

Before Lindsey could answer, her cell phone rang. She looked at the readout. "It's Leda. I checked on everyone before I left and made sure I answered any questions, so let's see what's come up." She hit Accept. "Yes, Leda? What's going on? Please don't tell me we've had another disaster."

"No, just a message from Mrs. Wainwright I thought you should hear right away. She just called and asked me to let you all know that she's leaving town tonight and will be gone for several weeks."

"She's what? She's leaving? Just like that?"

"Yes. I wrote it all down," Leda assured her. "She said she has to get away from everything. It's too painful staying in that house. Too many memories of her husband and the dreadful accident. She sounded really upset and apologized for leaving the way she is. Didn't know how long she'd be gone but she appreciated us understanding her need for this."

Lindsey scowled. "I guess I can understand. Sort of. A death is bad enough but one like this really can mess you up. Still, she must have estate things to wrap up."

"She did leave the name and phone number of her attorney in case there are any legal things to handle. His name is Bryce Miranda. I'll text you the phone number if you need it before you get back to the office."

"Okay, thanks for updating me." Lindsey disconnected the call then stared at the phone for a moment. "Well. That's really weird."

Taylor frowned. "What's up?"

Lindsey repeated what Leda had told her. "Don't you think it seems strange?" she asked the others.

"So she's taking off." Taylor shrugged. "Strange, but she's free to do whatever she pleases."

"What about the estate?" Lindsey asked. "When someone like Craig dies, even if it's from natural causes, there's a lot of red tape to settle things. And what about that big house? She's just going to close it up and take off? Leave everything?"

"There really aren't any legal things for her to handle with Elite," Taylor reminded them, "because of the way the agreement is worded. But yes, there always loose ends."

"I still say it's odd that she just picks up and leaves as if she's going on a vacation."

"Maybe it's her way of dealing with her grief," Taylor suggested.

"This is probably not very nice of me to say," Lindsey said in a slow voice, "but I can't help feeling, with everything else that's come up, that Natalia Wainwright might have just been putting on an award-winning act as the loving wife and supporter of Elite. That there's some underlying reason for this so-called trip."

"You may be right. Are you familiar with her attorney? Bryce Miranda?"

She shook her head. "I can ask around, if you want."

"I've heard of him," Noah acknowledged. "He only handles seven-figure clients. I'd guess he was Natalia's attorney first."

"There could be another reason," Taylor suggested. "Maybe someone's threatened her and that's why she's hightailing it out of town. If Craig was for sure into all this nasty stuff, and one of his so-called friends killed him, she might think she's next."

"But why?" Lindsey looked around the table. "What's going on here that we're all missing?"

Noah pulled out his cell phone. "I know the police here are doing an excellent job but not fast enough for me. And this is probably not the only thing on their plates. I'm going to have Charley send a couple of people down here to start looking into everything. I also want him to put some people on Masquerade. I want to know everyone who goes in and out of there and what goes on after hours."

"Good. I don't care what it costs." Taylor looked at her tablet, where she'd been making notes. "John. We need to ramp things up here and widen your search."

"I take it you want me to dig into Craig Wainwright deeper and wider along with everything else." He grinned. "My specialty."

"Why don't we order some food?" John suggested. "We didn't stop on the way here to pick anything up and I don't know about the rest of you, but I'm getting hungry."

* * * *

For the second night in a row, they sat around Lindsey's dining room table, and, while they ate, dissected the little bit of conversation Lindsey had overheard. Then they went piece by piece through everything she and John had found online.

"This is like one of those balls of twine," she mused. "You pull one end of a string and the whole ball unravels into a real mess. Okay. You know that Charley Graham is on this. Whatever there is to find, about Craig, Podesta and Merriam, if anyone can dig it out, he can. I also added the name of our so-called host on Parrot Cay. I want to know everything about him and that island, up to and including how many trees grow there and how many moles on his body."

"I know I keep repeating myself," Taylor said, "but it still bothers me that the firm I use didn't find out any of this stuff about Craig."

"Like I told you," Noah reminded her, "they were looking for different things. And exotic location shoots under normal circumstances don't ring any warning bells."

"He's right," John agreed. "They found records that showed Craig sold his earlier businesses. They didn't look any further because there weren't any red flags attached to the deals. They wouldn't have thought to check what happened to those businesses and learn that Craig still had his fingers in them."

"Or wonder why he thought it necessary to bury everything under so many layers. How far have you gotten with the money trail?"

John woke up his tablet, where he'd made notes as he'd gone along.

"Okay. I'm working backwards here, because I don't know where the original starting place is. I've gotten as far back as ten years before the inception of Elite. At that time Craig was a part owner of Top Shelf Advertising with George Merriam and Frank Podesta. Right about then he met and married Natalia, who gave him the money to buy out his two partners and Elite was born. They expanded their clientele, added more high-end clients and the revenue increased a lot."

Lindsey took a sip of water. "I'd like to know where Natalia came from. How did they meet? Why did she want to spend that money so Craig could have his own company? I'll never believe she was so altruistic she just wanted to, in effect, buy him a business. And where did he get the money to start Top Shelf with those two men?"

John put his now empty plate aside, opened his laptop and booted it up. In seconds he was typing, his fingers flying over the keys, nodding at whatever he was looking at.

"Okay, here it is. Top Shelf was funded with money from a company called Litton Industries." He looked around the table at everyone. "Incorporated in Delaware. Big surprise, right?"

"Was Natalia part of Litton?" Noah asked.

"Her name doesn't appear on the incorporation papers, only the names of the attorneys who drew it up. That's not unusual. But then I found more than one transfer from a company called Galaxy Investments to an offshore account and from there to another Delaware corporation, then to Litton and finally into a trust fund for her."

"Damn." Taylor shook her head. "A lot of work to hide the source of the money."

John nodded. "Indeed. All Natalia's visible money comes from the trust, which she tells people is set up by her family in Colombia. A way for them to get their money out of the country and the government's hands. So she says."

"So when we did our due diligence," Taylor said, "all we would have found was the so-called family trust, the direct line to Natalia's bank account and from there to Elite."

Lindsey closed her eyes for a moment. "I feel as if I really didn't know the man at all. As if the whole time he was playing some kind of part, and the real Craig Wainwright existed outside these offices. Why didn't I see it? I'm supposed to be such a good judge of character."

"I think that's on me even more than you," Taylor pointed out.

Lindsey just shook her head. "I'm not sure I'll be able to trust my judgment anymore. What if he hadn't been killed? What if we hadn't discovered the anomaly regarding Masquerade? What if—"

John reached over and pressed two fingers to her lips. "I repeat. Don't beat yourself up about this."

"John's right," Noah added. "And, Taylor? You did your due diligence. It came back clean. We didn't know how much dirt it was hiding, so let's move forward and see if we can fix this thing. What's next, John?"

"I'm looking for Litton's money trail. Where did the funds come from to set it up? Where else did they go besides Natalia's trust fund? And where else was Craig getting money?"

Taylor pushed her plate away, forehead creased in thought. "Can you get into Masquerade's bank account?"

John laughed. "Are you kidding? I can get into anyone's bank account. Haven't you ever gotten a notice from your bank that your account's been compromised? There are hackers all over the planet who have designed algorithms to crack passwords and get into accounts. It's much easier than you think."

Taylor just shook her head. "One of the first things I'm going to do tomorrow is call Liam Benedict and have him create hackproof passwords for our bank accounts and financial records. And write new proprietary security software for Arroyo. Good lord!"

John just shrugged. "You've seen me do this before, Taylor. It's nothing new."

"Yes, but always before you've started with more specific information than we gave you this time. And you knew all the people involved."

"Yes," he agreed, "this is a little more complex." He grinned. "But not unbeatable. I like a challenge. Just as long as you promise to bail me out of jail."

"No jail time," Taylor assured him. "All of this relates to the corporation. The suits have us covered." She sighed, something she almost never did. "John, you know how important it is to follow the money trail. And it seems, in this particular situation, there are a lot of trails."

"Yes. I'm also going to see what I can find about Podesta and Merriam and if their finances and Craig's cross in any way."

Lindsey cocked an eyebrow. "You think whatever this is, they're all in it together?"

"*I* do," Taylor interjected. "I have the sick feeling that whatever is going on goes far beyond Masquerade, although it might start there. That whatever the spa is part of is only part of the bigger picture. If we only had some clue what it is they're hiding."

"I can do something there," Noah told her. "We funded those scholarships for children of active police officers—I think the commissioner might do me a favor or two."

"You think he would? And not say anything to anyone?"

"I think if he has a chance to clean up a dirty mess in his own back yard he'll probably jump on it. I'll call him first thing in the morning."

"Thank you. I have to protect Arroyo, even if it means closing Elite completely and reopening in a different set of circumstances."

Lindsey stared at her. "You'd do that?"

"And more, to protect Arroyo. You know that."

Noah chuckled. "She took on the bad guys in the Mexican jungle, so yeah, she'll do whatever it takes."

"Oh, I definitely want to hear about that one of these days. Okay. Tomorrow I'm going to sit down with Jerry Ortiz again. I haven't been satisfied with either his attitude or the two meetings we've had. Time to get tough. If something was going on with those trips, you can bet he's in it somewhere."

"No doubt," Taylor agreed. "You think you'll get anything from him?"

"I have a feeling if he thinks he's really in the hot seat he'll open up. For a consideration, of course. He impresses me as someone who runs from trouble and avoids taking the blame like the plague."

"I agree. Let's see what applying a little pressure will do."

John pushed his plate aside and opened his laptop. "Meanwhile, I'm going to pull up the files I've been working on and walk you through them step by step. I gave you the broad strokes. Now let me fill in the spaces."

It was after eleven by the time they had the basic flow chart put together. Lindsey had been diagramming as John gave them information. When she was finished, she sent it to everyone at the table, so they could all look at it together.

"There's still a lot of spaces," Taylor commented, "but I see a pattern beginning to emerge."

"Podesta, Merriam and Craig have been friends since their days at the University of Miami," Lindsey pointed out, "so there's the beginning of the connection. That's probably why they went into business together. But why sell out to Natalia and go their individual ways?"

John shrugged. "I'm guessing because something came down that opened a bigger door for them and it worked better for the other two to start their own businesses. And look at those businesses. International shipping and finance. Transporting illegal goods around the world and moving money from place to place. What better setup can you have? Especially if you're getting even richer from illegal funds."

Taylor looked at her watch. "Well, children, I think we've put in a full day and should quit for the night. Tomorrow will no doubt be another bitch of a day."

The Cantrells had barely left before John pulled Lindsey into his arms.

"I prescribe a hot shower and a massage," he told her. "Especially the massage."

Desire bubbled up inside her as his words conjured up images of the two of them naked in a shower. Her nipples popped to attention and she had to squeeze her thighs together to contain the pulse beating in her sex.

John looked at her, the same dark desire flaring in his eyes, and a muscle twitched in his jaw. He cupped her cheeks, his palms warm against her skin, and tilted her face up to his.

"You've carried the bulk of the stress so far, Lindsey. Let me make you feel good."

"But—"

He touched the tips of his fingers to her lips. "Hush. Dr. Martino is on the job. Relax and enjoy it."

Erotic pictures kept flashing through her mind like a video. She visualized his hands roaming everywhere on her body, his mouth doing dangerous things to her—sucking her nipples, licking her clit, thrusting inside her needy channel—and desire, hot and greedy, consumed her.

John wrapped his fingers around her wrists and tugged on her hands. "Come. Sit. Just…sit. Leave this to me."

"But…"

He led her into the bedroom, where he sat her on the edge of the bed. "Just stay like this for a minute. Please? Close your eyes and empty your mind. Forget about Elite, Arroyo, Wainwright, everyone and everything else." He kissed the shell of her ear and murmured, "Think of soapy bubbles sliding over your body and my hands doing wicked things to you."

"Oh, god," she whispered, closing her eyes and letting more sexy images play through her brain.

"Not god, just me." He brushed a kiss over her lips. "Be right back."

She sat there as directed, eyes closed. She heard the sounds of the shower starting, then John was back, his hands urging her to stand.

"Don't open your eyes yet." He kissed the closed lids.

He undressed her in slow motion, caressing her skin as he bared it little by little. By the time she was naked, she was trembling with need.

"Okay, now you can look."

She swallowed a tiny gasp. In the intervening moments he'd shed his own clothes and stood before her in his glorious nakedness, dark hair curling on his hard chest, arrowing down his flat stomach to the nest of curls surrounding a thick, glorious cock. She reached out a hand to wrap her fingers around his shaft, but he circled her wrist and moved her hand away.

"Uh-uh. This is my show. Come on."

He led her into the bathroom where hot water steamed from the rain showerheads, creating a warm cocoon. He tugged her into the enclosure where the water could pour in soft streams onto her body.

"Close your eyes," he told her again. "No thinking. Just feeling."

In a moment his hands were gliding over her skin, coating it with fragrant body wash, the soothing scent of hyacinth drifting to her nostrils. She stood as still as a statue, hard as it was, while his hands glided over every single inch of her body, rubbing, caressing, stroking. She sucked in a breath when he palmed her breasts and rubbed the slick substance onto her nipples, pinching them a little while he did it. Then he skated a hand over her mound and slid one finger between the lips of her sex, teasing the tip of her clit before moving on.

When her entire front was coated, he turned her and began the same process with her back. When he stroked the cheeks of her ass and slipped his fingers through the crevice between them, it was almost more than she could bear. Her legs trembled and she had to press her hands against the cool tile of the shower wall to steady herself.

"Eyes still closed." John's voice was right near her ear and in the next minute he traced the shell with the tip of his tongue.

Then he proceeded to rub and knead and stroke every single inch of her body until she was so weak with desire she wasn't sure she'd be able to continue standing. The sluicing of the water over her skin as John rinsed her off did nothing to ease what she was feeling.

"Hold still now," he said, when all the soap was gone. "And remember. Keep those eyes shut."

She wanted to tell him she didn't think she could open them if she wanted to.

When she heard the crinkle of foil she was tempted to look but John touched his mouth to hers, placing a light kiss on it, and she just let herself enjoy the feeling. In the next moment he lifted one of her legs and draped it around one of his hips. Then he reached between her thighs to spread the lips of her pussy and very slowly eased his thick cock inside her.

Oh, god!

She was so aroused she came at once, her orgasm enhanced by his fingers rubbing her clit again and again. She gripped his shoulders, little mewling sounds escaping from her mouth as her body shuddered again and again. Her inner walls gripped John's very swollen shaft, spasming as she came and came and came.

She had barely taken a breath, little aftershocks still rippling through her, when he coaxed her up again, still teasing her clit — only now he added his mouth, sucking first one nipple then the other. She gripped his shoulders so hard her nails dug into the skin, but he never let up for a moment.

This time when she came he palmed her breasts, pinching the nipples hard, increasing the intensity of her orgasm. The tiny aftershocks hadn't yet stopped when he gripped her leg again with one hand, pulling it tight to his body. Holding her in place with the other, he began to drive into her, hard thrusts that hit that sweet spot inside every time. The second orgasm had barely finished before she felt, shocked, another one begin. This one reverberated through her entire body.

She could sense him holding himself back just a little, waiting for her to catch up again. Then it was hard and fast, over and over, until they exploded together. The walls of her pussy squeezed him over and over as his cock pulsed thick and heavy inside her.

At last, spent, they just stood there, her leg wrapped around him, his head on her shoulder, breathing ragged, while the gentle shower poured down on them. When the pulsing in his cock stopped, he eased himself from her body and lowered her leg, massaging the thigh muscle to relax it.

Then he kissed her, such a gentle touch it was like a brush of air over her lips. She still had her eyes closed while he killed the shower, lifted her out with him and dried them both off.

"Now you can open your eyes," he teased.

When she did she saw so much emotion on his face it nearly brought her to her knees. This was a side of John Martino she'd never seen. How the hell was she going to handle this, anyway?

"Still worried about Elite?" His mouth curved in a small grin.

She sighed. "What's that?"

"Good girl. I think we can both get a good night's sleep now."

When he slid them both into bed, he pulled her against him. His body was spooned around hers and one arm wrapped around her waist, his hand cupping her breast.

"Sleep, sweet girl," he murmured in her ear.

And she did.

Chapter Seventeen

Identifying the girl had been easy after all. Sadly, Dania found her in the National Missing Persons Database, along with far too many others. Daisy Winston's roommate had filed the report three weeks ago. She'd said the girl had been offered a job with a modeling agency and it was a big deal. She was getting a trip to the Caribbean and everything.

Dania had to make a conscious effort to tamp down the murderous rage surging through him. He and the detectives from Fort Lauderdale and New York had come to the conclusion that this was another version of grabbing girls for the sex trade. But, they all agreed, this was taking it to a new level, because all the girls were between the ages of eighteen and twenty and without question model material. So this was more than just 'grab a bunch of females and sell them off to a whorehouse somewhere'.

The first thing Dania did was call the roommate and give her the sad news. He hated doing this stuff. It always depressed him as much as the people receiving the news. This time was no exception. When the friend had calmed down at last, Dania made arrangements for her to come down and make a formal identification of the body. Another depressing act.

"I-I'll have to call her parents," she stammered, tears evident in her voice. "Oh, god. She should never have left home. Maybe none of us should."

Dania wanted to say, *Not until you learn how cruel life really is,* but he kept his mouth shut. This was no time for a life lesson. Daisy's death was education enough.

He was still sitting there, scrolling through the others in the database, looking for similar reports, when his phone rang.

Detective Rolf Andrews was with the New York Police Department and according to what he told Dania was focused on missing persons, with special attention to girls of this age. What he had to say made Marco tighten his grip on the phone and pray they were all making something out of nothing. *Jumping to conclusions.*

"The friend who filed the report insisted she went to Miami and she calls every single day. She just called again, asking me if we'd heard anything." His sigh echoed over the connection. "I hated to tell her that usually, unless the person is found within the first few weeks, the case just languishes in the database. There are too many ways for people to disappear to spend a lot of man-hours on it. But damn, she's a persistent pest. Asked for the number to call in Miami. I figured we'd have better luck if I called you myself."

"Totally understand."

"I don't hold out much hope, but let me tell you what I've got. Maybe it will ring a bell with someone else who disappeared in your area. Especially since this girl was headed in your direction." He paused for a moment. "The friend who filed the Missing Persons said Arianna had been offered a contract by a modeling agency, with a photo shoot in an exotic location in the Caribbean. Do you know if these other girls were in the same situation?"

"At least one of them was. I'm going to check through all the rest of them and see what I can come up with. Do you know the name of the agency?"

"Yeah. Bella Donna. They're a pretty big outfit. Their models appear in some very high-end ads. I can't see them involved in something like this. They're too visible. But the girl who filed the report swears her friend called her on her cell, said she just had a few minutes while they changed planes in Miami."

"I think the modeling agency has an office in Miami, too. These girls are too similar, as are their stories. Too coincidental. But I'm with you. How would a prominent agency like Bella Donna be connected to this? They pay their models a ton of money. Why would they dabble in the sex trade? Still, I'll have to look into it."

"Same here," Rolf agreed. "If you find out anything, please let me know. I think we need to coordinate on this."

"Listen, a friend with the Fort Lauderdale Police Department called me a couple of weeks ago about the same thing. I'm going to dial him in on this too, okay?"

"You bet. If it's this widespread, then we'll need a lot of help bringing down what looks like a massive organization."

"Yeah. Damn." Marco tightened his fist. "They look so young and innocent."

"Well, someone's after them, that's for sure. You know, it used to be these people who provided girls for the sex trade just scooped them up wherever, drugged them and sold them off. Maybe the buyers are more specific now. Paying more money for better goods."

"Jesus!" Marco felt sick.

"Listen, I'll put a list together from our database, those who fit the profile who've gone missing in the past three years and shoot it to you. If you'll do the same, we can see how many of them got a gig with Bella Donna. And have your friend in Fort Lauderdale do the same."

"Works for me."

He exchanged cell numbers with the other detective and they both hung up. Then he typed Bella Donna Agency in the Search bar of his computer and watched the website load. He was still sitting there surfing through it when Jon Alpert came into the bullpen and sat down at the empty desk next to him.

"Find out anything on your phone call?"

Marco sat up. "Maybe something." He told him what he'd learned from Rolf Andrews.

"This is more than just some missing girls," Jon observed. "And I'm willing to bet the number of missing girls is bigger than we imagine. While you do that, I'm going to check the national database for other girls who fit this profile and see what I can come up with. You checking out the modeling agency?"

"Yeah. Interesting." He scrolled back to the main page. "Before you do your thing, take a look while I click through the pages. Their models are in some pretty top-tier ads and also work in the gold standard fashion shows. Tell me if you notice the same thing I did?"

"The ages?" he asked at last.

Marco nodded. "Those missing girls fall right into the age range Bella Donna hires. And the looks are pretty much the same."

"Yeah, but I'll bet if you check other agencies, you'll find the same in a lot of them."

"But how many other agencies have a bunch of their models go missing?"

"You don't know for sure if any of the other missing girls are hooked up with Bella Donna."

Dean shrugged. "Well, there's a sure way to find out. Match the names of the ones we've identified with the list of models, and hope they still have pictures of them up on the site."

"Maybe they think the girls just asked for a few days off. That's possible."

"I dated a model once. Very briefly. That job consumes their lives, one hundred percent. They don't just ask for days off." Marco rubbed his jaw. "Besides, I can't imagine, after an agency has invested in a portfolio for a girl, taught her how to walk, wear makeup, pose, all that stuff, that they'd just say, 'Too bad, so sad, I wish you luck.' And just let her leave."

"Well. One way to find out. Let's pull the list, see how many of them told their friends they got a gig with Bella Donna, then go talk to the people at the agency. Rolf Andrews is going to do the same in New York. You and I both know sometimes the most information you get is what the person being questioned doesn't say."

"Got it. Let's get busy on this. You want coffee?"

"From here?" Marco snorted. "Not if I want to keep my stomach lining. When we leave here I plan to stop for some real stuff. I'll even pop for one for you."

As he sat there, compiling a master list of girls eighteen to twenty-one years of age who had gone missing in the last three years, he hoped and prayed he was wrong about this. That, far-fetched as it might be, all these girls had somehow decided to play hooky from their lives and would show up unharmed. But his gut was telling him something different.

Chapter Eighteen

How could I have been so stupid?

Mia Silva huddled in the bedroom, hugging her arms around herself and trying to calm herself down. She was such an idiot. She should have been smart enough to know that things didn't happen the way this did or as fast as this did. But she was just so damn tired of her parents stifling her and never allowing her to do what she wanted that when Dax Fornell, the agent from Bella Donna, had approached her, she'd jumped at the chance.

First she'd been thrilled when she'd called the number he'd given her and he'd said she was just what his clients was looking for. But when he'd invited her to a photo shoot at an estate in Miami Beach with some other models, she'd had a hard time containing her excitement.

"I know this is a bit unusual," he'd said, "but we have an opportunity coming up to put you and three other girls into a layout for a major designer. The major partner in the firm is here along with the potential client. This would be a great opportunity for you. If they like you, it could mean major assignments right out of the gate."

Ohmigod!

That was all she could think of. Lucky for her, both of her parents were planning to be out at an event that night. Dax had said he would send a car for her, but she didn't want it to come to the consulate. She was afraid if they knew who her family was, they'd kill the deal, not wanting to get involved in a possible political situation.

Instead, she called Sassy, the only one of her friends she'd told about this, and asked if he would mind getting her at Sassy's house. And Sassy, being a good friend, had picked her up and brought her to her home where a big black sedan arrived at three o'clock. She was glad to see it was Dax Fornell. At least she was with someone she knew. He drove her first to a spa called Masquerade, where he told her all the girls were getting full beauty treatments before the photo shoot.

Full was right. She was waxed, plucked, creamed, showered, had her hair styled and was given thong panties and a minidress to put on.

"Just until you get to the house," the woman in charge told her. "You can take your own clothes with you for later. But the wardrobe mistress will have outfits for you for the shoot."

Then cars returned to pick up all the girls and transport them. Again Dax was her driver, but this time another girl, Asia, just as excited and nervous as she was, rode with her. They squeezed each other's hands in excitement and anticipation.

The house Dax brought her to was enormous, a sprawling mansion bigger than her father's, on a large landscaped plot. It was situated right on the waterfront, with a lawn sloping down to the water and a dock with a slip that anchored a very large cabin cruiser. Lights around the pool sparkled in the fading dusk.

Mia was awestruck. Her parents' mansion was nothing to be sneezed at, and she'd been around money all her life, but this was the top of the ladder. A little shiver of excitement raced over her skin and deep inside her a pulse began to thrum with a slow, steady beat.

This is it! This is really going to happen!

She'd just have to figure out how to break the news to her parents, but she'd do it. It was a given.

"Miss Silva?"

She looked up at the man who had stepped out onto the patio and was holding a tall frosted glass out to her.

"Club soda." The man grinned. "Bella Donna does not like its models to drink with clients. It might give the wrong impression."

Wow! Okay, so nothing to worry about on that score.

"Okay." She reached for the glass. "Thank you."

"If you'd come inside now, the photographer is setting up around the pool. He may want to do some nighttime shots around the pool, too. Does that work for you?"

"Of course."

"Good. If you'll come with me, the wardrobe mistress is ready to help you."

Wardrobe mistress! A thread of excitement wiggled through her.

And it had indeed been exciting, changing into the glamorous outfits and posing for the photographer.

She'd been a little uncertain about the very teeny-weeny bikinis, but the wardrobe mistress had assured her bathing suit layouts were the most popular. Bella Donna had specified they wanted pool shots tonight, and Dax reminded her of the popular sports magazine that did them every year.

They'd taken what she thought was a gazillion pictures before the wardrobe mistress came to help her change into a cute shorts and top set. But then the woman couldn't find the right outfit and disappeared from the room. Mia needed to use the rest room and she figured it wouldn't hurt to just slip out for a minute. But there were so many corridors in the house it was easy to get lost, plus she had no idea where any of the bathrooms were.

The other girls who had been at the pool with her had been taken off for makeup or whatever, and she hadn't seen them since. Was something wrong? Was it her? Was she being cut from this? How would she get home? Her stomach was jumping with nerves and her mouth was dry as she tried to decipher the situation. She passed a door that was open a crack and she paused when she heard men's voices. Maybe they were talking about her, so she stopped to listen.

And almost fainted from shock.

"...the best one yet, Dax," someone was saying. "She'll be number one in the order of selection."

Order of selection? For what?

And Dax, the man who had smooth-talked her and given her his card, who had brought her here tonight — what was up with him? Was this whole thing a scam? For what?

Oh, god, how did I get myself into this?

"You know Enescu decreed an auction tonight rather than delivery as a group. He has individuals with millions waiting to buy these girls. Good work, Dax. This is the best crop you've brought us, and this one will bring the biggest price yet."

Biggest price? Buy these girls?

Mia's stomach cramped and chills of fear raced over her skin. What was going on here?

"There can be no trace of any of this," a woman said. "I can't afford it. This was a stupid thing for you to do and I am tempted just to get rid of her and avoid all problems."

Mia strained to hear, because the woman sounded so familiar.

"Calm down."

This was a deep male voice, belonging to the man who owned the house and who had welcomed her so properly. Frank. Big, with an air of power and far from friendly. Even when he smiled, he frightened her. He had scared Mia enough that she'd thought about asking Dax to just take her home. But then everything else had moved along and she hadn't had a chance

"We've made millions with this," another voice broke in. "Perhaps it's time to take a break. Craig's death has put us all under a spotlight. That was a foolish move to make."

"It was necessary." The woman spoke, and this time Mia was sure who it was. She nearly fainted with shock and fear. A very important woman in the whole Miami–Fort Lauderdale area. Uber wealthy, and some said from South American aristocracy. How was this possible? Was she maybe just hearing things? This woman would never be involved in something like this. Would she?

"Not for us." That was Dax. "We have a smooth operation going, and none of the missing girls have come back to haunt us. There's too much money to quit. You were the only one who had a problem, and I'm sure there were other ways to solve it."

Missing girls? Oh, oh, oh.

Mia stuffed her fist in her mouth to keep from screaming.

"It's done and I expect everyone to deal with it," the woman snapped. "You've never had a problem with anyone else we had to get rid of."

"No one else has had the same visibility, nor did they bring the wrath of the Arroyo Corporation down on us." Dax's voice was getting angrier and louder. "Jesus, Nat, these people have international clout. They can kill this whole thing worldwide and we could end up in prison."

"Enough." That was Frank.

"Yes, enough," the woman echoed.

"I'm talking about you, too," Frank said. "We worked for years to build this setup. Found the perfect vehicle to find the girls who would bring the best prices. Set up a process for selling, and with one stupid move you may have jeopardized us all."

"He wanted us to get out," she protested. "He wanted to destroy everything because he said he was sick of thinking about what happened to the girls."

"He didn't mind it when the money was rolling in. And when he had his pick of the girls to use first."

"Listen, Dax," the first man was saying, "are you sure we aren't going to get our dicks in a wringer because of her? That one's parents have money and clout. They can make a big stink."

"Once she's gone, she's gone. No trace. What can they do? Buy her back?"

The men laughed.

"But," the other man continued, "her friend knows about this."

"We'll take care of her friend if we have to. Meanwhile, calm down. It will all work out. Let's relax and enjoy another successful event. The buyers are all set. We just sent off the pictures for a preview, so calm down."

"Don't tell me to calm down," the familiar female voice said. "This is your mess, not mine. I had to clean up my own already. I'm not taking care of anyone else's."

"It will be fine." A different voice.

Who's this? Oh, yes. The man Dax had introduced her to as a silent partner in Bella Donna. The money man, he'd told her. What was his name? She wanted to remember it in case she managed to get out of here alive.

"Then let's do this. We're not taking them out to Alex's boat until tomorrow night. Lock—"

"Tomorrow night?" Nat interrupted. "Why was it changed? We need to move them tonight."

"You want to tell that to Alex Enescu," Frank sneered, "be my guest. He says change of plans, I say fine. Me, I'm locking them up and waiting for tomorrow."

Mia had to squeeze her hands together, twisting her fingers, to stop shaking. She wanted to throw up, but she knew she couldn't allow herself that luxury. Instead, she had to find a way out of here.

I am such a freaking fool. If I can just get out of this, I'll never leave the house again. I don't care if I'm almost twenty-one, I have a lot to learn before I try this again. And please, god, I promise to learn if you'll just help me get away from here.

Which of course she had no idea how to do. They'd had to drive through an electronic gate to get into the grounds of the house and she had no idea if there was any other way out.

"I'll give you thirty minutes to get her and the others out of here and on your boat. Then I'm taking care of it."

"Really? Look what happened when you tried to clean up the last mess. We have a bigger one to deal with."

"Not my fault," she snapped.

"Children, children," an unfamiliar voice broke in. "There's plenty of time to squabble later. Right now, we'd better take care of our immediate problem. Is that facility shut down nice and tight?"

"Yes," the woman answered. "And we transferred the merchandise still remaining. I still think that's a mistake. It will be a signal to them."

"They were already asking questions," the money man said. "And when news comes out about the disappearance of our latest little bargain here, they'll get the police to take that place apart with a fine-toothed comb. I've always said it was a mistake to handle it the way he did, but Craig refused to listen to me."

"Good thing he's not around to object." Dax's voice was edged with irritation.

"Fortunate, you mean," the woman snapped. "I would have had it handled. This just was not the right time to do this. Remember when it comes back to haunt us that I said not to do it. We could have weathered anything they asked. Right now, get the girl," the woman snapped. "Let's go from there."

"One thing," Frank told her. "We'll have to use a different place for processing the girls. Masquerade's under a spotlight now, ever since that woman Arroyo insisted on bringing into Elite stuck her nose into it."

"Which never would have happened without Craig's unusual death. Jesus, Nat, couldn't you at least have figured out a way to off him that didn't put us out there where people could ask questions? Those pills were a fucking stupid idea."

"If it was your neck on the line," she retorted, "you'd be singing a different song."

Mia took a deep breath and pulled herself together. She wouldn't get anywhere standing here frightened and shaking. She was still dressed in the stupid bikini, and she had no shoes on. But wandering through the McMansion just now, she'd discovered the kitchen had a back door. If she could slip out before anyone found out and set the extra alarms, maybe she could find a way off this property. She had to try. Otherwise she was dead.

Move. Now.

She tiptoed on bare feet down the hallway toward the kitchen, concealing herself around the corner until she was sure the room was empty. *Good!* The kitchen staff who'd served drinks and hors d'oeuvres were probably out by the pool. Mia had heard *The Man* say they'd be having dinner out there when the shoot was finished. She scooted into the room and over to the door that she'd discovered led to a back porch and the rear lawn. She eased the door open, letting out her breath when no alarms or bells sounded.

Then she was running as fast as she could to the rear of the lawn, to the trees bordering it, hoping there was some kind of road beyond them. She'd climb a wall if she had to, even in her bare feet. Anything was better than what these people had in store for her. She prayed as she put more distance between herself and the house, running faster than she ever had. Ignoring her bare feet.

Please let me get away from here. Please.

Chapter Nineteen

Lindsey had Elite business to attend to in the morning, and John was anxious to dig deeper into everyone's financial setup, so they were at the office early. Taylor was there working on Arroyo business, and Noah had gone off to meet with the two agents sitting on Masquerade. He'd received a call from them about nine-thirty and hustled off to join them.

They were all absorbed in their individual tasks when he returned and pulled everyone into Craig's office, where John was working, and closed the door.

"Here's a shocker," he told them. "Masquerade is shut down."

"Closed?" Lindsey repeated the word. "Just like that?"

"Apparently so. The agents sitting on it will be here shortly and I'd rather you get all the details directly from them, but—" He was interrupted by a knock on the door. He opened it to find Sarah standing there.

"The two gentlemen you were expecting are here."

"Good. Thanks. I'll come get them."

When he returned, two men were with him, dressed in jeans and dark polo shirts.

"We've got pictures," one of them said.

"Good. Everyone, meet Tim Blackburn and Harley Greer. Gentlemen, have a seat. How about some coffee?"

Tim shook his head. "We're carrying a night's worth of coffee," he joked. "But it was worth the caffeine to get this."

"Fine. Then let's get to it."

"We got there about six last night," Harley told them, "in time to relieve the team before us. According to them, all the other customers had left by then. There were only a couple of cars in the lot, but the previous team said a whole group of young girls were delivered there about three this afternoon. Then the cars left."

"They got pictures." Harley lifted the camera. "And video. Then, about an hour after we got there, a bunch of black cars rolled up again in the back. The rear door opened and seven girls in skimpy clothes were ushered out by four women and delivered into the cars, which then took off."

"We got pictures of that, too," Tim assured them. "You said the place opens at nine in the morning, but the staff usually get there about an hour before. We were curious, so, even though our replacements showed up, we hung out for a while."

"We were damn curious," Harley added. "So we stayed until we called you, about thirty minutes ago. No one ever showed up and the place is closed tighter than a drum. And get this. We called the number and there's a recording that says it's closed until further notice."

"Shocker," Taylor said.

"Okay." Noah sat back in his chair. "Here's the way I see it. Everything was going along smoothly for whoever is running this delightful enterprise. Then Craig somehow gummed up the works and the decision was made to get rid of him."

"But by who?" John prodded.

"Good question. We'll come back to that. So someone gets some contraband hard-on pills and switches them with Craig's regular meds. It screws him up enough that he crashes his car and kills himself. We on this so far?"

Everyone nodded.

"John, you've put together quite a trail from clients, real or otherwise, to Litton to numbered accounts back to another shell corporation then moved so many times you need a permanent road map. So now we have a possible money trail for illegal trade in drugs, guns and women."

"Girls," Taylor interjected. "The ones men like them are after are little more than girls."

"True," Noah agreed, and the others nodded. "And if Enescu and Madea are involved, you can bet it's big, widespread. I don't know how Craig got involved in this to begin with, but I have a feeling he wanted out and that's what triggered his death."

"This isn't the kind of death these guys are usually involved in," Tim Blackburn said. "Their favorite is an attack by 'person or persons unknown' who beat the mark to death."

"Then maybe this is someone outside their inner circle," John suggested. "I'll have all of that ready today, at least in basic form. If the cops want more, I'm happy to refine it."

Taylor rubbed her forehead. "Where do Podesta and Merriam fit in? Podesta I get, because they can ship the girls anywhere in the world his freight vessels travel. But Merriam?"

"He could be cleaning the money through his hedge fund operation?" John suggested. "Those could be some of the accounts I'm finding. All I have to do is dig a little deeper to be sure."

"God." Taylor rubbed her temples. "I'm sorry I ever thought bringing Elite into Arroyo was a good idea. I must have had blinders on. And you can be damn sure the person on my staff who brought them to me is not going to be pleased at all."

"Take it easy." Noah rubbed her shoulder. "They worked very hard to create a respectable image for the company and make it appealing so they had a cover for what they were doing."

"Well, I suggest we all be careful," John told them. "We've put a kink in their operation and they won't take too kindly to that."

Lindsey stared at him, wide-eyed. "You don't think they'll come after any of us, do you?"

"Too high profile, but you never know what desperate or angry people will do."

"I'd give anything to know where Natalia fits into all this." Taylor leaned forward, resting her chin on her hands. "Surely she had to have some knowledge."

John nodded. "And that's the sixty-four-thousand-dollar question. She sure ran off in a hurry. Where did she say she was going?"

"She didn't," Lindsey answered. "Just that she had to get away from all this mess. She's not even answering her cell. Maybe she's hiding from us."

"Or from somebody."

"Okay." Noah glanced over at Blackburn and Greer. "I think you guys can head on back to Tampa, along with your teammates. Thanks for flying down here and getting this done."

Tim Blackburn shrugged. "There wasn't a whole lot for us to do. Have you got equipment here, so we can give you copies of the pics and the video?"

Noah rose. "Sure do. Come on, we'll take care of it right now. And, Taylor? How about giving our friend Kevin Moran a call and inviting him over to see these? If he thinks we're way off base, he'll tell us, but I don't think we are."

Taylor nodded. "Okay. John, I think you know what you need to do today. And, Lindsey? Your major role is going to be keeping everything sane here at Elite. After Charley's men leave, you and Noah and I need to huddle on how to deal with the fallout that's sure to happen. I want to talk to Jerry Ortiz again. I'm not sure he's as lily-white as he'd like us to think."

"Sounds good to me." Lindsey pushed back from the table. "I'm going to get some coffee. John? Refill?"

"Please." He chuckled. "Maybe I should just mainline it today."

Detective Kevin Moran arrived soon after lunchtime, apologizing for not getting there sooner. Leda ushered him into Craig's office and let everyone know he was here. He dropped into one of the armchairs and accepted a cup of coffee with a grateful smile.

"I would have been here sooner, but I got a call from a friend of mine on the Miami–Dade police force. The body of a young girl washed up on the beach a couple of days ago. No marks on her so he's assuming she swam to shore from somewhere and didn't make it alive."

"Damn." Noah shook his head.

"No kidding. Anyway, he found her in the National Missing Persons Database, called the cop in New York who had taken the report and the two of them began discussing some other cases. Marco Dania, the Miami-Dade cop, and I have worked a number of cases together before, so he called me and asked, out of curiosity, if we had anything to add. Sadly, I did. I won't take up your time with the details, but there seems to be a significant number of girls around the age of twenty of a certain type who go missing after being offered a modeling gig."

"We had a feeling." Taylor looked at everyone who nodded. "It came up when I had our forensic accountant over there, John Martino, going through all Craig's financials plus his accounts. Lindsey, you want to take it from here?

"We focused on a spa, Masquerade, one of Craig's clients." She went on to tell him what she and John surmised and her impression on her one visit.

"You'll find this interesting," Noah told him. "I had a couple of private investigators watching the place since last night. Mostly because it is a client and if there's any stuff it reflects on us. Let me get you the pictures and video they took."

Moran looked at them, the muscles in his face tightening when he saw the shots of the girls.

"Like I said, it seems we're all dealing with the same problem. We seem to have a sudden abundance of young girls, around twenty, being offered hot modeling jobs. Supposedly the jobs are in the Caribbean, on some private island, and they never come back. My boss has contacted the FBI offices in Miami. This is a real hot button for them. In fact, they've got a message on their home page with a number to contact at once with information on human trafficking. They'll probably want to talk to all of you, too."

Lindsey caught her breath, knowing everyone else was thinking the same thing she was. *Does this have anything to do with the photo shoots in the Caribbean on Parrot Cay?*

"Any idea on who is contacting them?" Noah asked. "Is it an individual or an agency?"

"Don't know yet. It's not on the reports, but the three of us are going to start checking with whoever filed reports and see if they know. You know, this has to be some sophisticated operation, because they just used to scoop them off the streets, invite them to parties and ship them off."

"We all said the same thing," Lindsey told him.

"So." He looked at each of them. "When you called, you said you had information for me. One of you? All of you?"

"Actually, all of us," Noah answered, "in pieces, and some of it is supposition, but I'll be the spokesman for the group."

He ran through it all with him. The feeling there had to be more to Craig's death than just the wrong pills. The question of how he got them. John Martino's scouring of the financial accounts. The secret cell phone. The introduction of Ruben Madea and Alex Enescu. Then the revelation and assumptions about Masquerade.

When Noah finished, Moran just sat for a minute, a stunned look on his face. Then he swallowed the last of his coffee and held out the cup.

"Could I beg a refill?"

Lindsey smiled. "Sure thing. I'll get it."

"I think I need it to absorb all of this." Again he studied each of them. "Do you people always do this when there's a change in top personnel?"

Taylor laughed. "When you're responsible for an organization the size of Arroyo, you're always suspicious of everything. It's how you stay in business."

"I guess you're right." He pulled a little notebook and a pen from his jacket pocket. "Okay, let's go through this again, if you don't mind."

This time he asked questions, taking them over some things two or three times, until he had what he wanted. Finally, he sat back in his chair.

"Well. It seems I have a lot of work to do. If you don't mind, Mrs. Cantrell —"

"Taylor, please."

He dipped his head. "Taylor. I'm going to ask the district attorney to get a court order for the financial accounts Mr. Martino here has been working on, and ask him to explain his findings to my lieutenant and the district attorney."

John looked over at Taylor. "It's really up to you. I'm game for anything that will trap these bastards."

"Do it," she told him. "I feel the same way."

"Another thing." Moran looked at his notes again. "If we can dig up information on this so-called modeling agency, can we run it past you to see if you know anything about them?"

"Detective," Taylor said, "we want to do anything we can to find answers here and hopefully find these girls. So yes. Any time."

"One more thing." Moran pulled out his cell. "Can I have the cell phone number of one of you, and do you mind if I share it with the other two detectives I'm working with?"

Noah rattled off his. "Any calls should come to me."

"Okay, then. I guess that's it for the moment, but I'll be back later."

When he stood, everyone else did as well.

"You've given me some pretty significant information for which we'll all be grateful. I'll call and let you know when I'm on my way back."

"You didn't say anything about your research on Enescu and Madea," Taylor pointed out to her husband.

"I don't have anything concrete yet. Let's wait while Charley Graham digs around a little more. He's got connections out there he can utilize."

"Whatever you say."

"I notice you didn't mention anything about Jerry Ortiz, either," Lindsey commented.

"I want you and I to talk to him first, so I know what we might be getting into."

"Good idea," she agreed. "Listen, I know it's the middle of a workday, but I sure could use a glass of wine."

"I vote for that. Let's go across the street for linguine and wine. It'll help us get through the day."

And a long day it was. After lunch, somewhat fortified by the wine, Lindsey spent significant time going over the details and status of all of Craig's clients. She was also looking for anything that could be the least bit squirrely, something that she might have missed the first time around. She also made personal calls to those she still hadn't connected with. She and Taylor wanted a meeting with Jerry Ortiz, but he seemed to have disappeared, and no one knew where he was. Kevin Moran showed up late in the afternoon to get copies of the financial information.

By the time the day was over, they were all battling exhaustion. Everyone else had already left by the time Lindsey, John and the Cantrells shut the office down for the day.

"I think I'm too tired even to eat," Lindsey said as they walked out to the parking area. "And I'm burned out on takeout."

"We'll worry about it when we get home." He slid his hand beneath the fall of her hair to rub her neck. "I'm thinking a hot shower and something to relax us."

"Mmmm. Sounds good."

"Why don't you just crawl into the passenger seat and I'll drive?"

"Another good suggestion." She turned, stood on tiptoe and brushed a kiss over his mouth. She had to keep reminding herself this was just temporary. She was going to be very careful about putting herself out there again with this man, although she had a feeling it might already be too late. *Fine.* She'd enjoy the hell out of it while it lasted, send him back to Atlanta and nurse her bruised heart when she walked away from him before he could do it to her again.

Chapter Twenty

"Go take off your clothes."

Those were the first words John said when they walked into the house.

"What?" Lindsey stopped at the entrance to the living room and stared at him. "What did you say?"

"I said take off your clothes." He took her messenger bag and purse from her and set them on a small table. Then he put his hands on her shoulders and turned her to face him. "Go on. You are tired and worn out and so tense your muscles are tighter than a virgin's. I happen to be an expert in fixing that. Go on. Strip and lie down on your bed."

She hated following orders, but the thought of those big, strong, warm hands on her, soothing her body, sent waves of longing through her.

"Okay. I should tell you it's not necessary, but I'd be lying. Go on. Clothes off. I'll be right behind you."

She put her heels in the closet, her clothes in the laundry hamper and pulled back the covers on the bed.

Then she stretched out on the silky sheets, resting her head on firm but fluffy pillows, and waited. In seconds the mattress dipped as John climbed up behind her. Was he naked? Had he taken off his clothes?

When he bracketed her with his legs, she had her answer in the bare warmth of his skin.

"Close your eyes," he told her. "Just close your eyes and feel."

He tugged her arms so they were stretched out by her head, then trailed a line of kisses down her spine. Just the touch of his lips set the walls of her sex quivering so hard she had to squeeze her thighs together. He spent a lot of time tracing her spine with his lips, licking the skin and taking little bites of her shoulder before trailing down the length of her torso again.

Warmth washed through her, making her nipples ache and her sex thrum with need. His touch was magic as he kneaded the muscles in her arms and shoulders, kissing her shoulders and taking a tiny bite of flesh at the nape of her neck. Never would she have thought such a thing would be so erotic it made every part of her body scream, for his mouth, his tongue, his hands. When he placed tiny kisses the length of her spine then traced the line with the tip of his tongue, every nerve in her pussy sparked and heated.

"Relax." He pressed his mouth to the nape of her neck. "Don't tense up."

"Don't tense up?" She gave a hysterical little laugh. "When you're doing those things to me?"

There was that low, rough laugh again. "It's supposed to relax you. Just close your eyes and go with it."

"Okay." She drew in a deep breath, held it, then let it out and fell into his touch.

"Think of soft clouds," he murmured. "So soft you hardly feel them. Your bones are liquid. You couldn't move if you tried. That's it. Just like that."

She was surprised, as she listened to his voice and felt his warm hands on her, that she was able to relax, and her bones became almost liquid. He worked on her back and her arms for a long time until her muscles felt limp and molten. She was floating, with no desire to move, until he slipped his hands down to her butt and squeezed the round cheeks. That would have been okay except, as he squeezed, he slid both thumbs into the warm crevice there and pressed against the hot, tight opening there.

"Remember when I fucked you there, darlin'? When I slid my cock into that very sexy, dark place? Remember how good it felt? You screamed the house down, so loud I was afraid we might wake up your neighbors." There was that low laugh again.

God, she remembered that night. Their last night together, when he'd coaxed her into trying things beyond her boundaries. That had been one of them, and the orgasm that resulted had shaken every bone in her body. She'd dreamed about it for way too many nights afterwards. Nights when she'd wanted him beyond belief and tried to push him out of her mind.

"Uh-oh. You tensed up. I know you liked it, so you must be thinking of afterwards. Get that out of your mind. I'm not leaving, Lindsey. This is just the beginning for us. Believe it."

Oh, if only she could. With an effort she forced herself to relax, back into the state she'd been floating in before. He massaged the cheeks of her butt, giving them a gentle squeeze, massaging then stroking them, before sliding his thumbs back in between them again and rubbing in a gentle motion on that tight opening. Now the walls of her sex began to pulse, a slow but steady thrumming that reverberated throughout her body.

It went on for such a long time she could do nothing but close her eyes and fall into a conflicting pool of relaxation and need. She could almost fall asleep, if it were not for the intense need gripping her, the hunger for him, the desire that grew and grew with each stroke and caress.

She hung there, on the edge of reverie, when without warning he shifted his body, sliding backwards and urging her up to her knees.

"What—" She blinked. "Why? What's—"

"Just go with it," he repeated the mantra. "I promise this will cure whatever ails you."

She let herself go limp again as he pulled her to her knees and arranged her so her head rested on her forearms crossed in front of her. She felt his legs between hers and his knees pressing as he separated her legs even more. He pressed a kiss to the base of her spine even as he slid two fingers into her greedy, waiting sex and returned his thumb to that aching rear entrance.

Put it in, she wanted to shout.

Instead he continued tormenting her, fucking her wet sex with two fingers while his thumbs teased her rear again and again, until her entire body was shaking. And still he kept it up, pushing her to a place she'd never been before, where need and desire and pleasure and relaxation all bubbled together in an erotic cocktail. His body was hard against hers as he leaned forward more and placed another trail of kisses on her spine.

Please. Please. Please.

She thought she'd only said it in her mind until John chuckled.

"Please what? Please do more? Please stop? Please fuck you?"

"Yes!" She nearly screamed the word. "Please fuck me. Now!"

"But this is supposed to relax you," he teased.

"I'm relaxed, damn it. I'm relaxed."

He pressed his lips to her ear. "Okay. Then let's get you really relaxed."

She heard the rip of foil and the light snap of latex as he rolled on a condom. Then his fingers spreading the lips of her sex and at last, at last! The pressure of his thick cock as he eased it inside her.

Oh, god!

He filled every inch of her, his thighs pressing against hers, his hands gripping her hips to steady her. Then it began. In and out. Back and forth. Thrust and retreat. Again and again and again, but his movements so slow he drove her out of her mind.

Pleasepleasepleaseplease.

She didn't know if she was screaming in her head or out loud. The heed to come was so strong she was sure if she didn't she'd lose her mind.

Then, at last. At last! He increased the pace, his thick cock dragging against the walls of her sex, again and again and again and...

Yes!

She exploded, her inner walls squeezing him so hard she could feel every throb as he pumped into the condom. It went on and on and on, until she had no strength and no breath left and John had emptied himself. He collapsed and rolled to the side, still inside her, taking her with him, spooning around her.

"Feel how connected we are?" he breathed into her ear. "That's the way we'll always be, Lindsey. Just like this."

Oh, god. If only she could believe it.

But one thing she did know. She was one hundred percent relaxed.

Chapter Twenty-One

Mia huddled in the shrubbery, hugging herself and rubbing her arms in an attempt to get rid of the goosebumps. She was shivering and shaking, and her feet were killing her from running barefoot over gravel and whatever else was on the ground. The brick wall that fronted the estate had only extended a short way on either side of the property. The rest of it had been enclosed with chain link fencing disguised with shrubbery. She'd cut her feet climbing over it and she had another big cut on one thigh, but desperation overrode pain. And she was out of there. That was the most important thing.

They had to be combing the property for her, right? She huddled against the shrub-covered fence, hoping the greenery would conceal her. Had they discovered her missing yet? Probably the wardrobe woman had sounded the alarm when she couldn't find Mia. In the next second, she heard voices that confirmed it.

"Where the fuck did she disappear to?" Dax's voice, harsh with irritation and anger.

"You're asking me?" An unfamiliar voice. *Maybe one of the other men who was watching the shoot? Who are they, anyway?*

"Yes, damn it. I'm asking you. You and Doug were supposed to be watching her like hawks."

"We don't follow them into the bathroom," the nameless man snapped. "That was supposed to be Stella's job."

"Regardless of whose job it was, she's fucking gone and we're all in a pile of shit if we can't find her. I don't intend to let some little piece of garbage bring me down."

"Then you'd best get your ass in gear and find her, or we're all dead. Enescu texted he's got the buyers all lined up and he expects the auction to go off as planned. Frank's got his boat ready, so let's find this bitch."

Someone kicked the fence and Mia had to bite down on her lip to keep from screaming.

"Well, she's not here," the stranger said. "Let's move along. We need to comb this entire side of the property. She can't get anywhere in that nothing scrap of an outfit, no shoes, no phone and no money."

Mia crouched there, almost afraid to breathe, until they moved away. The sound of their voices faded until it became non-existent. But now what? There were no sidewalks here, and she didn't want to walk in the middle of the road, where she could easily be seen. Besides, she was sure, when they didn't find her on the property, Dax and one or two of the others would be out looking for her in cars.

She couldn't stay here forever. Sooner or later they'd decide to check the outside of the fence — then someone would find her for sure. The night was a typical Florida tropical night, warm with a slight breeze, but Mia felt chilled to the bone. She had to clench her jaw tight to keep her teeth from chattering.

She had no idea how long she stayed there, crouched so long her muscles cramped. But eventually she felt safe enough to ease along the outside of the fence. She was sure a car or two would be coming along any time now, but how would she know if it was someone who would help her or someone from the house who would drag her back and punish her?

It was still full dark out and, despite the decorative streetlights, there were enough shadows to hide her as she moved along the street. She remembered from her arrival that they'd driven over a causeway and there was water on either side of the street.

Mia also remembered having seen a police car cruising along the street, probably to keep the riff-raff from bothering the residents. She wondered what they'd say if they knew the riff-raff was living in some of these houses. Right then, she was thankful these people had all spent a gazillion dollars in landscaping, so she had places to conceal herself.

Her head ached and her feet were killing her, all the cuts stinging and maybe even infected from walking barefoot. She was about to do something stupid, like try to find some thick shrubbery where she could lie down, just for a few minutes, when she saw the lights of a vehicle moving at a slow pace down the street. *Is it them? Someone from that house?* When she saw that it was a police car, she could have wept with relief. Half walking, half crawling she moved out into the road, hoping he'd see her and stop before he ran over her. Caught in his headlights, she waved her arms at him, and he slammed on the brakes.

In seconds he was out of the car and lifting her off the road. Praying he wasn't hooked up to those people, she collapsed against him, sobbing.

"Help me. Please help me."

Chapter Twenty-Two

Detective Marco Dania hung up his phone and looked at his partner, Jon Alpert.

"That was Moran over in Lauderdale. Remember he called earlier to tell us his boss had brought in the FBI? Well, they've arrived. He wanted to give us a heads-up they'll be contacting the lieutenant about coordinating this mess."

"My guess?" Alpert said. "They'll want a joint task force with the three departments involved so everything is in one place." He rubbed his jaw. "This thing just gets worse and worse. Some of these girls have been missing for as long as two years."

"I know." Alpert raked his fingers through his hair. "Imagine the agony their families are suffering."

"Daisy Winston's parents are due in tomorrow" — he looked at his watch — "make that today, to formally claim her body."

"Her friend sure was a mess." Dania rubbed his jaw. "What a tough thing to have to do at her age. I can't imagine—" He was interrupted by the ringing of his phone. "Marco Dania."

"Detective, this is Bolling on the front desk. One of our patrol officers just brought someone in that you need to come and see right now. And I mean right now."

"What? Who? Are you—" But the clerk on the front desk had already hung up. He jumped up from his chair, motioning to his partner. "Come on. Bolling says he's got something for us downstairs."

Alpert scrambled after him. "What?"

"Didn't say. Let's go."

They hurried down the stairs two at a time and raced to the front desk, where Bolling pointed to a small room just off the lobby. It was a room where they put people waiting to speak to someone. What was waiting for him inside made every nerve in his body stand at attention. A young girl—yes, that was what she was, young and a girl—was huddled in a chair and wrapped in an old quilt. Her feet were soaking in what he assumed was warm water, her skin was whiter than printer paper and a police woman sitting with her was trying to urge her to drink from a cup of something hot.

Dania knew the woman, Patrol Officer Nora Hayden, and nodded to her.

"I just finished my shift," she told Dania, "and Bolling asked me to help with this young lady. She's pretty terrified."

He nodded, and when he spoke, he deliberately pitched his voice very low and soft.

"Hey, Nora. You have a guest for us?"

She nodded and held the cup up to the girl's lips so she could take another drink.

"Meet Mia Silva. She ran out and stopped one of our patrols in the middle of the road on Palm Avenue, scared out of her mind, scratched and bruised all to hell. She needs a doctor, Marco, but she keeps shaking her head when I suggest it. Says she won't do anything until she talks to the man in charge here. Neither the chief nor the lieutenant is here at this hour. But we all know the two of you have been working on this missing girls situation. That's why I had Bolling call up to you."

"Good thought." He took Mia's hands in his, holding them gently. "The first thing I want to tell you is you're safe here. Whoever you ran from can't get to you here."

When she looked at him, the fear was still etched in her eyes. "Are you sure? I — I don't know who to trust."

Nora set the cup down and squeezed the girl's hand. "Honey, I promise you can trust these two men. They're two of the best we've got."

She drew slightly away and hunched into the quilt. "They won't let those men get me? Come and pick me up?"

Nora shook her head. "Not even a possibility. These two men have been working on other cases just like yours. They want to catch these men and put them away."

And maybe you can help me, Dania was thinking, as the image of the body of Daisy Winston flashed in his brain.

"Okay. I believe you."

"Why were you there, Mia? Was there something going on?"

She looked down at her feet. "I did a very stupid thing. It's just… It sounded so exciting. They promised me a big modeling job and even set up a photo shoot for me."

Dania had to exert every bit of self-control not to pump his fist in the air and shout. *Finally. A possible lead in this fucking, stomach-turning case.* He crouched in front of Mia, trying to make himself as nonthreatening as possible. He had many questions, but protocol came first.

"Do you remember the name of the agency?"

"Yes. Bella Donna. They're one of the biggest. It would have been a dream come true." Tears welled in her eyes. "But it turned into a nightmare."

I'll just bet it did.

Mia took a deep breath, studied Dania's face as if memorizing it then gripped the comforter harder and nodded. "There's more. There are still girls at that house. Locked up."

Dania tried not to let his feelings show on his face. "The rest of them? There were more girls where you were?"

She nodded. "I heard someone say they were going to lock them up until tomorrow. Then they're supposed to take them out on someone's boat to deliver them. They talked about an auction."

Alpert whispered, "Shit. We have to move on this."

"No kidding. Listen, you should call Moran and dial him in, he can pass it along to the Feds." Alpert hurried off and Dania turned back to the girl. "Okay, Mia. Sweetheart. Do you remember the address where you were taken?"

"Yes. It was in a plaque on the gate. Four-seventeen Palm Tree Lane."

Dania swore. That address was very familiar. Frank Podesta, owner of Capricorn International Shipping.

Leader in local and state and even national society. Major donor to many things, including police scholarships.

Holy fuck! The shit is really going to hit the fan.

"And the man who owns it? His first name is Frank. I don't know his last name."

"That's okay," Dania assured her. "We know it. Unfortunately."

"Or anyone else's except the man who drove me. The one who approached me to begin with. His name was Dax. Oh!" She sat up a little straighter. "And there was a woman. Her name is Nat. That's all I know."

Dania squeezed her hands. "Sweetheart, that's plenty. Now, I need to put some things in motion, so we can save those other girls."

"I'll do it," Alpert said. "You finish up with Mia."

"Okay. But I'll be right there."

Alpert started to walk away, then turned back. "You should call one of those big shots at Elite and ask them if they know of Bella Donna. Didn't Moran give you a number?"

"Yes. I have the cell of one of the Arroyo big names."

Alpert made a face. "That ought to be fun."

"Tell me about it. Let me just get Mia squared away here."

"I'll be okay," she told him in a soft voice, "now that they can't get to me. I want you to save the others."

"My partner is working on it. How old are you, Mia? Do you live alone? Is someone looking for you right now?"

She shook her head. "I live with my parents." Her mouth tipped up in a sad grin. "That's part of the reason I got so excited about this. They are very, um, restrictive. My friends and I are planning to get an apartment." The smile disappeared. "Maybe not so much now."

Dania swore under his breath at what these bastards had done.

"Okay. Then why don't we get in touch with them? They must be very worried by now."

She frowned. "What time is it?"

Dania checked his watch. "Almost one o'clock. In the morning."

"They'll just be getting home from a party. And they think I'm out with friends."

Of course.

He wanted to shake all these dumb young women with stars in their eyes.

"No problem. Why don't we just give them a call? Just give me their phone number and I'll call them."

She sighed. "Esme and Arturo Silva. This won't be pretty. They'll tell me I'm old enough to have been smarter than this." She gave him their home phone number as well as their cells.

Sweet Jesus. Dania looked at Nora, who had been sitting there, arm around Mia, the whole time. From the expression on her face, it was obvious she, too, recognized the name of one of the wealthiest, most connected Mexican industrialists living in Miami. *These bastards picked the wrong girl this time.*

"I'll call them," Dania said. "Nora, you stay in here with Mia, but she needs to have those feet and scratches attended to before they get infected."

"There's a first aid kit behind the front desk. If you can get it real quick before you go off to make the call, I can take care of it. Then tomorrow her parents can have a doctor look at them. Oh, and there's a little stack of Miami PD T-shirts there—we keep them for these sorts of emergencies. Grab one of those so she can cover herself up."

Dania was already dialing Noah Cantrell's cell phone as he grabbed the things from behind the front desk.

"Yes?" The voice was abrupt, brusque. He was sure he must have woken the man out of a sound sleep.

Dania identified himself. "This may sound like a stupid question, but does the name Bella Donna mean anything to you? A modeling agency?"

There was full silence on the other end of the call.

"Fuck."

Dania wanted to say he agreed with him.

"Yes," Cantrell said, "that's the agency Elite uses. What's going on?"

He told him about Mia and what she'd related to him.

"God damn it," Cantrell swore. "All right. We're going to the Elite office and tearing that place apart. We'll pull every single thing we have on Bella Donna and get it to you."

Dania breathed a sigh of relief. He'd been afraid they'd give him a hard time. Deny the possibility. Refuse to help at all.

"Thank you. Very much."

"You're pulling Detective Moran in on this, right? I'll call him when we have everything together."

"I— Thank you again."

"No thanks necessary, I want to get these bastards worse than you do. Before I'm finished with them, they'll be ruined."

Dania realized the call had ended when he had nothing but dead air. He shoved his phone in his pocket, his mouth twisted into a grim smile. He'd hate to be on the receiving end of anything Arroyo

Corporation could dish out. There'd be nothing left of Bella Donna when they got through.

Next he dialed the cell phone for Arturo Silva. He figured the father would be less hysterical and he was right. Despite a slight tremor of concern in his voice, the man was all business.

"Is she unharmed?"

"A little scratched up from running barefoot and hitting some shrubbery but otherwise fine."

"Good. We'll be there in less than half an hour."

He found Alpert upstairs in their offices with both their sergeant and Lt. Cat Henrique, who had hightailed it to the station after Alpert's call.

"I already got a call from the FBI, Dania," she greeted him. "They are sending someone to be part of the rescue team here, and of course they'll be joining us when we haul the bastards back to the station. So, come on, get up to speed. The wheels are turning on this rescue operation. Give me the short version of everything you learned from the girl."

He filled her in on everything and told her he'd already contacted the people from Elite to confirm the modeling agency. She suggested hauling them in as material witnesses until someone explained to her about the Cantrells and Arroyo and their involvement.

"Fine," she agreed. "As long as they're cooperating."

The head of SWAT was also there and they were all huddled over a big desk, laying out their plans. A request had already been made for a search warrant.

"We'd like to do this with as little fuss as possible," Lt. Henrique told him, "but we have no idea what kind of fire power they have there. Also, if we have to be buzzed through the gate, we don't know what kind of reception we'll get or even if they'll open the gate. We'll try playing nice, but if they give us a hard time, we will definitely let them know that any harm coming to those girls is the end for them."

When Bolling rang him to tell him that Mia's parents had arrived, he excused himself.

"I'll be right back, Lt. The Silvas are here."

Enrique nodded. "Get their permission to interview the girl. We need a layout of the house. Anything she can remember will help."

"Got it."

Esme Silva had taken Nora's place and was sitting beside her daughter, arm around her. Arturo stood in front of her, a mixture of anger and relief on his face.

Dania managed to calm everyone down and persuade the Silvas to let them interview their daughter before they took her away.

"I want to tell them," she insisted, more settled now that her parents were here. "I'm almost twenty-one, I can speak for myself. They wouldn't do it until you got here. Don't stop me from this. Please."

With one parent on either side of her, her eyes focusing on the floor, she told them everything from the time Dax approached her until she escaped Frank Podesta's house.

"I'm shocked Podesta is involved in this," Arturo said. "Although I guess nothing surprises me anymore. Evil lives everywhere, when money is involved."

Alpert took notes throughout the whole recitation. By the time the Silvas left, the two detectives had enough information that they could create a rough diagram of the house and grounds, plus the best guess of how many people were inside.

A very chastened and still frightened Mia walked out huddled between her parents. She might be twenty years old, but Dania was aware from their conversation it had been a very sheltered twenty years. The details of the sex trade had frightened her, to which Dania thought, *Good. Maybe she'll think twice about shit like this from now on.*

By the time he got back upstairs, they were getting ready to rock and roll. He strapped on a vest, checked his ammo and listened to their final instructions. Rolling through the sultry tropical night with a convoy that consisted of the SWAT van and four other vehicles, Dania thought how incongruous their environment was with the deadly nature of their task.

At last they reached their destination. Lt. Henrique rolled up to the gate and pushed the intercom button.

Dania, sitting in the car behind the van, let out a long breath.

Here we go.

God. Please don't let any of the girls get hurt.

Chapter Twenty-Three

To Lindsey, it seemed her world had turned upside down and was spinning on its axis. Taylor and Noah showed up at seven in the morning, bearing pastries and decisions.

"We're invading you," Noah joked.

"Hiding out is more like it," Taylor joked.

"I hope it's okay." Taylor sighed as she unloaded her laptop and tablet. "The hotel is too public and Elite is...well...too visible right now. In fact" — she looked at Lindsey — "I'm keeping the Elite offices closed for a few days. Maybe permanently. We'll see. The staff will still get paid and the account managers we trust we'll put to work hard carrying their clients through the mess. Lindsey, you and I will handle the high-profile ones."

Lindsey nodded. "Sounds like a plan."

"We also need to find a new modeling agency." She made a note on her tablet.

"I want to take my time with that," Lindsey told her. "I'm not into scheduling extensive photo shoots right now. If we need one for a client, there are plenty of agencies in this area I can check out and people I can call for recommendations. And no more exotic location shoots."

Taylor chuffed a laugh. "Amen to that. By the way, did you see that Bella Donna is shutting its doors? They're under investigation by both the FBI and Homeland Security."

Lindsey shook her head. "Money. Some people have the disease so bad they'll do anything for it. A lot of people are going to suffer because of that."

"The one saving grace," Taylor pointed out, "is that the really good, well-known models will be grabbed up fast by other reputable agencies. But damn. What a mess."

While they worked, they monitored both the local and twenty-four-hour television news channels and online sites, still stunned at some of the things that had been revealed. Every news source was filled with the details of the late-night raid on Frank Podesta's multimillion dollar estate. Stock photos of Podesta were flashed on the screen at regular intervals. But the real shocker was the revelation that not only had Natalia Wainwright killed her husband, she was also the brains behind the whole thing. She was good at finding people's weaknesses and capitalizing on them, and Podesta and Merriam, with their constant hunger for more money and power, had been ripe for the plucking.

The Miami Beach police had also executed a search on George Merriam's house on Black Swan Island, where they'd found another group of girls hidden on Merriam's giant cabin cruiser, drugged and locked in the main cabin. Detectives Marco Dania and Jon Alpert, who had taken part in the raid on Podesta's mansion, had given out the information that Daisy Winston, the young girl whose body had been found on the beach, had swum from the island to escape what Merriam had in store for her.

Late in the morning, Kevin Moran, accompanied by FBI Agent Len Gerow, showed up at the house to see them and fill them in on what was happening. Noah had handed over the information they had on Alex Enescu and Ruben Madea earlier.

"Handling them will be a little more complicated," Gerow said. "Natalia knew them from her Colombia situation. Her family is uber wealthy, but the rumor is most of their money was made from illegitimate sources. She learned about what Madea and Enescu did before she ever came to the States, and wanted some of that pie. Saw how much money could be made and set about creating her own network."

"But you'll still get them, right?" Lindsey asked.

"Yes, but that's a little more complicated. We need to involve Homeland Security plus, for Parrot Cay, we'll bring in the Coast Guard. Even then it's iffy if we can succeed. People like Madea and Enescu are slippery as eels. They have the money and contacts to disappear and pop up again. Madea will buy another island and Enescu will hide out in Europe for a while, so we'll put the word out to Interpol. Hopefully we'll get them at some point, though."

"How did Craig get sucked into this?" Taylor asked.

"She relocated to Miami for a variety of reasons," Kevin answered, "met Craig at some swanky party and it was lust at first sight. But she also saw him as the perfect figurehead for what she wanted and Elite was born."

Gerow said, "Craig Wainwright was a good front for her. The kind of husband she needed. Knowledgeable about upscale marketing, well connected and hungry for money. Lots of money."

"So what happened? Why kill him? She had to know it was destroying everything."

"It appears he became disenchanted with the whole thing." Gerow shrugged. "The drugs and guns didn't bother him as much as the fate of the girls that began preying on him. He wanted to quit. He'd be a loose thread out there and Natalia and her partners couldn't have that."

"But his death meant she lost control of Elite. How did that help?"

"Oh, she found another firm whose owner was money hungry and not bothered with scruples. She had already made arrangements to buy into it."

"You got all the girls?" Noah asked.

Gerow nodded. "Thanks for the tip and thank you, Taylor, for making it happen. We met the plane from Parrot Cay when it landed. A surprised bunch of people got off, for sure. You know we got everyone at Podesta's house, but I wanted to let you all know we rescued the ones at Merriam's, too."

"Yes. We saw everything on television."

"More bad news, though." Moran looked around at everyone. "We went to Jerry Ortiz's house to question him. I'm sorry to tell you we found his body. Two bullets to the head."

"Execution," Gerow added. "I don't mean to be cold, but no more than he deserved." He sighed. "Well, I'd better get back to work. We've got a massive cleanup to do and it won't be pretty."

"What's going to happen with Elite?" Moran asked. "You know we'll be questioning everyone there as well as looking at some of the more questionable clients that John Martino pointed us toward."

"We discussed it this morning," Taylor told him. "We're closing it down and establishing a new company, wholly owned by Arroyo. We'll give everyone who's cleared severance pay and Lindsey Califaro and I will cherry-pick who we want to retain to form a new agency. Right now, we're reaching out to clients to see who we can save."

"Well, thanks for all your help. Sorry for the mess you had dumped in your lap."

Noah shrugged. "Goes with the territory. Arroyo will clean it up and move forward."

After Gerow and Moran left, Noah waved everyone back to their seats at the table where they were all set up. However, they all found it hard to concentrate.

"This is like the ripple effect when you throw a rock in the water." Taylor shook her head. "The more they find out, the more things keep coming to the surface. I'm glad I made the decision not to open Elite today and told all the staff to stay home. The press would be all over us. My people radar was really off with Natalia." Taylor sighed. "I'll be kicking myself for a long time about this one."

"Don't beat yourself up about it." Noah squeezed her hand. "I didn't see it either. She was a master at playing the role of the rich society wife."

"Lindsey?" Taylor looked across the table at the other woman. "You're okay with what I decided? Closing Elite, pruning the staff and creating an entirely new entity?"

Lindsey nodded. "I think that's the smart thing to do. Unfortunately, the name Elite will be tainted for a long time. No matter what we do, someone will always connect it. I agree creating something new is the best way to go."

"We'll give everyone who passes the smell test six months' severance," Taylor added, "and you and I will cull the best from the group."

"What about the clients who have campaigns in progress? I can handle them from here. I just need to make a trip to Elite to download stuff from my office computer and grab hard copies of anything."

"Sounds good," Noah agreed. "John, you still have stuff to do for the FBI, right? You'll work from here, also?"

Lindsey saw the question in his eyes when he turned to her. Of course he could work from here. And maybe she'd get in one more hot night with him. Satisfy her hormones before she told him to move along. Only somehow her brain wasn't getting the message and neither was her heart.

I won't change my mind. I won't.

Right.

"It's fine," she told everyone. "Let's get to work."

The day was long and exhausting, but Lindsey was grateful for the hard and consuming work that left no time for thinking about anything else. When she was focused on it, she wasn't conscious every single minute of John's nearness to her, or the electricity that always seemed to spark around them like a cloud of atomic dust. She had no idea how much longer he'd be staying. He had people at his office in Atlanta working on other projects, people he seemed able to rely on one hundred percent. But still, that was his home and soon he'd be returning there.

She'd stopped questioning if he would try to arrange some kind of long-distance situation between them. She would never be happy about something like that. Plus, she was still convinced in her heart of hearts that when this was wrapped he'd be on his way out of her life again.

Remember. You pull the plug first.

It had become her mantra, repeating in her brain over and over.

By evening, she felt confident they had as good a handle on things as could be expected. Taylor and Noah left a little after nine o'clock and while John finished one file he was working on, Lindsey took a hot shower and changed into a sleepshirt. Then, because she really needed a few minutes to herself, she lay down on her bed and closed her eyes, trying to sort out everything whirling around in her mind.

"Are you hiding from me?"

John's deep voice startled her and she opened her eyes to see him standing right next to the bed. His mouth curved in a very sexy grin, but the expression in his onyx eyes was a mixture of hunger, need and questions.

Lindsey blew out a short breath. "Just trying to air out my brain after today."

"It was a real pisser," he agreed. He kicked off his shoes and stretched out beside her.

"I think we'll have a lot more of those before everything settles into a new routine. How are you coming tracing the rest of the money?"

"Fine, but I don't want to talk about that. Not money, not Elite. Not any of that shit right now."

Butterflies began dancing in her stomach. What was on his mind? Was he leaving already?

Damn it, Lindsey, you're a corporate leader. A tough businessperson. Do not let him melt you into a puddle of mush then walk out again. You're stronger than that. And wiser.

She hoped. But everyone had their weak spot, and too bad for her that John was hers.

"W-what *do* you want to talk about?"

He rested his hand on her thigh just below the hem of her sleepshirt and slowly began moving it upward. If he kept doing that, her brain would freeze and all her good intentions would dry up.

"You've been withdrawing from me," he murmured, his mouth coasting over her ear. "You think I don't notice it, but I notice every single thing where you're concerned, Lindsey."

"Oh. You do?" *Crap.*

"Uh-huh."

Now his hand had reached her stomach and he slid the flat of his palm over her skin. Her nipples ached, the brush of the sleepshirt fabric almost painful against them, and her tiny bikini panties were no doubt already soaked. Damn it, but this man knew exactly how to flip every one of her switches.

Tell him now. Then you can have a night of outrageously erotic sex and move on.

Oh, but wait. He's still staying here, so what about that?

But she'd realized something during the past few days, something she'd been afraid to admit to herself. There was a lot of difference between saying, "I'll be in touch" and "I want to be with you. I was a fool last time." Nothing was the same this time. She could tell just by the way he treated her. If she didn't give them one more chance, she might miss out on the best thing to ever happen to her.

Go with your heart, Lindsey.

She took a deep breath and asked, "And what conclusions have you reached?"

"That I was a stupid fucking ass four years ago and what happened is still there between us like a big brick wall." When she didn't answer, he said, "I'm right, aren't I."

His hand had crept up to cradle a breast and he gave one nipple a gentle pinch, almost robbing her of the ability to think.

"Never mind." He nipped the lobe of her ear. "I'll talk. Then you can have your chance. Lindsey, I'm making arrangements to open an office in Fort Lauderdale."

"What?" She jerked upright, dislodging his hand with the movement. *Did I hear right?* "Say that again."

"Lie down and I will."

She eased herself back onto the pillow, but her brain was running a mile a minute. What was going on here? An office in Fort Lauderdale? So he did mean everything he was saying?

Oh, god, please, because despite everything I've told myself, I'm not sure I can walk away from him.

He was back to doing wicked things to her body with his hot hand.

"You think I don't know that what happened four years ago is still in your mind? That no matter what I've been saying, or trying to show you physically, you don't trust this situation?"

He finished teasing one nipple and went to work on the other.

"I— You—"

She had to squeeze her thighs together against the force of the throbbing in her now very wet pussy.

"Right." He pinched her nipple. Hard. "I'm not leaving this time, Lindsey. Not tomorrow or next week or even next month. Except when I have to travel to a client's location. And I didn't know any other way to prove to you that this time is for keeps."

"For keeps? Are you sure? Because if you're saying this just to get in my pants again, you can save your breath. My pants are yours and have been every night. Just not my—" She paused and took in a breath. "Just not the rest of me."

"Not your heart, right?" he guessed. "You think I don't know that? You think it hasn't been driving me nuts to know how badly I screwed up? But that's done, Linds. I want that heart and I promise you I'll take very good care of it. Otherwise, would I be opening an office here? The one that I'll work out of? And try this on for size."

By now his hand had slipped between her thighs and was cupping her sex, pressing the damp fabric of her panties into her wet flesh.

"Try what?" *God.* She was stunned to the point she couldn't even form a coherent sentence.

"Tomorrow I'm going to show Taylor the space I found and see if she thinks it would be good for both offices. That way you'll always know where I am and what I'm doing."

"What?" She tried to process it, but her heart was beating so fast. "You— That is— I mean—"

"Let's make it official all the way. Marry me, Lindsey. Marry me so we can spend the rest of our lives together and never waste another day. Take that leap with me, because I love you and I never want to let you go again."

And all her objections disappeared like so much smoke. What would she prove after this by shoving him away? Nothing, except her life would be empty without him. It was different this time. Even her bruised heart had to accept that. And she wanted this more than anything.

The words were out of her mouth before she could process them and make a decision.

"Yes." She let out a long sigh and the tension eased from her body. "Yes, John, I'll marry you, and spend the rest of my life with you."

"Thank god," he breathed. "Don't move. Just — don't move."

In seconds he had stripped off all his clothes, yanked her sleepshirt over her head and her panties down past her feet. His eyes never left her body as he rolled on a condom. Then, kneeling between her thighs, he spread her legs, slid his hands beneath her ass and lifted her to him. In one thrust he was inside her, filling every inch of her completely.

Lindsey closed her eyes.

This is it. This is where I belong. This is what I want.

He began to move in a steady thrust-and-retreat rhythm. As aroused as they both were, it didn't take long for them to reach the peak. A climax so strong it shook them both exploded, gripping them. The walls of her pussy spasmed over and over, milking his thick, hot, hard cock. It seemed to go on forever, and when it stopped, it left them both weak and spent.

"I love you, Lindsey. I've never said that to another woman. Ever. I tried to deny it but there it is. You live in my heart. Always."

She took a deep breath, let it out in a slow stream and said the words she'd been afraid to say before.

"I love you, too."

"This," he whispered, his lips jus touching hers. "This right here, us, together, is what we have for the rest of our lives."

"Yes," she agreed. "The rest of our lives."

Want to see more from this author? Here's a taster for you to enjoy!

Strike Force: Unconditional Surrender
Desiree Holt

Excerpt

Slade Donovan, code name Shadow, moved silently into the room where the men on his Delta Force team waited. Tall and muscular, he was the essence of a warrior, his dark brown hair slightly shaggy with a gray thread or two showing here and there, and the expression on his chiseled face said *Bring it on.*

Lowering his gear bag to the floor, he dropped himself into an oversized armchair and pulled out his laptop. *First things first,* he told himself. Mission completed. Men all accounted for. Time to reconnect with the outside world. He turned on the machine and waited for everything to load.

He was more than grateful for the satellite setup at their base camp that allowed them all to communicate with the rest of the world. It was a great way to maintain contact with his 'brothers' in the many Spec Ops groups, not just on newsy items but on ways to do things better. He also kept in touch with the foreman of his ranch back in Texas and with the few friends he'd been close with for years.

While he waited for the computer to boot up, he glanced around the room at his men, the members of Team Charlie, sprawled out on the battered furniture, weary and battle-hardened. They still looked rode hard and put away wet, as the saying went in Texas. This last mission had sucked a lot out of them.

Just yesterday they had come down out of the Hindu Kush, the mountain chain that stretched from Afghanistan to Pakistan, tired, dirty and spent, although eminently satisfied. Despite the intel fuckup, the mission had been a success. One more terrorist cell destroyed, one more maniac blown to hell. And the troops fighting for the people of Afghanistan had one less bad guy — and his followers — to worry about.

Delta Force, the Army's top covert combat unit, had counterterrorism as its main focus and they performed their missions with cold single-mindedness. Like the one they had just completed.

Once they'd landed, they'd gone through debriefing, badly needed showers, a hot meal and fourteen hours of sleep. Now they were just hanging out, guzzling water and making plans for their imminent leave. They were facing ten days to let it all hang out, battle their demons and refresh.

"Damn, Shadow." Trey McIntyre, code name Storm and the team's demolitions and firearms expert, flopped onto the beat-up couch and looked over at him. "That last mission was a stone bitch."

Slade nodded agreement at Trey's comment. It had definitely been a shitstorm of epic proportions. Angry at the poor intel, at the danger it had put them all in, at the possibility the mission would fail, Slade had kept it all together. They'd regrouped, adjusted their plans and completed the assignment. But hellfire. He wanted to throttle everyone who had put this together.

"Fucking A," he agreed. "I told the captain the intel on this one sucked. You all pulled off a miracle and I'm damn proud of you all."

"No shit." Beau Williams made a rude noise.

With his sun-streaked light brown hair and green eyes, he looked like a typical surfer, fitting his code name. Surfer. Nothing could be further from the truth, though. Beau was their sniper, a job that required incredible focus and discipline.

The *ding* of a bell let Slade know his computer was now up and running.

When he clicked on the email icon, a flood of messages rolled into his inbox. As he scrolled through them, the subject of one caught his eye. He'd been searching for something he and his team could do together on their current downtime, something to work off the residual tension. Maybe this was it. Last time he'd talked them into it, they'd blown away the competition. Maybe he could coax them out to the ranch and get them to do it again. They might have plans or not, but they were all so drained after the last few ops he wanted them to recharge as a team where he could watch over them.

"Okay, you guys." The others looked over at him. "I've got something here that might interest you."

"What's up?" Beau stretched and yawned.

"Remember that shooting competition we took part in two years ago?" Slade glanced at his screen again. "The one held just south of my ranch?"

"Yeah." Marc Blanchard—code name Eagle—grunted. "We cleaned their clocks."

Beau grinned. "No shit. What about it?"

"There's another one scheduled for next week, right at the end of our leave. Handguns and long guns. Just like the last one." He paused. "I don't know what plans y'all might have, but how about hanging out at my ranch again and we'll go win a few more prizes?"

His spread was south of San Antonio, where he ran a small herd of cattle and kept horses he could ride fast enough and far enough to clear his mind. It had become his refuge, a place to heal after each mission and reconnect with humanity. He'd taken his team there a couple of times when they'd really needed to switch off from everything to pull themselves together again.

Beau sat forward, interest sparking in his eyes. "I can always use a chance to dazzle people with my skills. But, uh, Shadow? Besides the competition, will there also be women while we're there? That's *my* top priority."

Of course. Beau didn't care where or what as long as there were women.

"Did you notice a lack of them the last couple of times?" Slade grinned. "Yes, there will be women."

"Then count me in."

"Me too," Trey echoed.

Marc was suspiciously silent. Still recovering from the disastrous end of an even more catastrophic marriage, bitterness had etched deep lines on his face and colored his entire personality.

Slade focused his gaze on him. "Marc? You in?"

The man was silent for so long Slade wasn't sure he planned to give him an answer. Then he gave a short, quick nod. "I'm in for the shooting. We'll see about the women."

Slade had discussed Marc's situation many times with Beau and Trey. They all worried that, when he had leave, the man just crawled into a hole for ten days and drank himself into oblivion. Still, he always showed up on time sober and sharp so Slade really had no cause to say anything to him. Yet. But he could still worry about him.

"And speaking of meeting women," Slade went on, "remember the JAG lawyer I introduced you to when you were at the ranch two years ago? Paul Hutton? Old friend of mine? We had dinner one night with him and his wife?"

"Is he providing the women?" Beau joked.

Slade chuckled. "Maybe. In a way, that is. He and his wife are having a party. If you all promise to clean up good and not pick your teeth in public, we're all invited."

"I'm guessing it will be a little different than the entertainment last time, right?" Trey winked.

Beau laughed. "I'd say that's a big Ten-Four."

Slade nodded. "No private sex club this time. We tried it at The Edge and you all passed on doing it again."

Beau nodded. "Not our cup of tea."

"I like my sex with no holds barred," Trey added, "but not with a lot of other people around. Call me simple, but I like my privacy."

"Is that so the rest of us can't see how inept a lover you are?" Beau teased. "Afraid your women will take a gander at us and leave you in the dust?"

"Ha ha ha. Very funny. As a matter of fact, I don't want *your* women to get jealous of my style."

"Whatever." Beau flapped a hand at him.

"But I think we're all agreed the club scene isn't for us, right?" Slade looked at each of them. "Speak up now and forever."

"Yes." Beau nodded. "Right."

Trey nodded his assent. Slade glanced at Marc Blanchard, who hadn't spoken a word. The man was in a very dark place and had been since the implosion of his marriage. Slade worried about him, a lot. He'd thought the visit to The Edge might have lit a spark in him, but Marc had disappeared into a private room with one of the subs and hadn't said a word about it afterward.

"Marc? You agree too?"

Marc just nodded.

"Okay, then. We'll head back to my ranch and make plans from there. Let me dig through my email and see if there's anything else on that might interest us."

Slade liked sex as much as the next man and had a healthy appetite for it. He lived by the motto—*We go abroad to vanquish and conquer for country. We come home and vanquish and conquer for us.* And why not? Tomorrow could be their last day on Earth.

Sometimes he wondered, though, if that would be the pattern forever. He was totally committed to Delta. It was his life. He had nothing left over to give to a relationship. Something he'd learned to live with. Sure, he'd seen others do it, but it required a mindset he didn't think he had. There were those who had retired from Delta Force, at least from active missions. They taught, trained others—any number of things. But could he do it? He was a warrior, after all. The leader of Delta Force Team Charlie. Up until now there hadn't been room for anything else. Could he ever adjust to a change?

But then, as he stared unseeing at the computer screen, *bam!* A memory popped into his mind. One that had been haunting him for five years. No matter how he tried, he couldn't get rid of it. He wasn't a man given to dreaming about women—except maybe for the occasional wet dream. But a trip to Chicago and a party with friends had ended in a night of the most spectacular sex with the most incredible woman he'd ever met. She had stunned him. Sucker-punched might be a better word. Blindsided him. Silky auburn hair, emerald green eyes and a body that had made his mouth water. Perfume that had tickled his senses, a low musical laugh and the satiny feel of her skin completed the package. She had been so put together on the outside, but wildness had sparkled in her eyes.

They'd come together as two strangers, looking for nothing more than the moment. A brief but explosively intense encounter. He'd wanted to wash away the devastation of his most recent mission and she had wanted — whatever she'd wanted. They hadn't spent a lot of time discussing it. In his hotel room they'd torn each other's clothes off in their haste to get naked. That first coming together had been hot and frantic and had blown his mind. He'd felt like a teenager on his first hot date.

Every moment of that night still haunted him, indelibly etched on his brain, on his senses. He couldn't forget her plump breasts tipped with rosy nipples, or the wet heat of her sex and the way it had clenched around him when she'd come. He swore he could still feel the satiny caress of her skin as she lay pressed against him, or the silken fall of her hair brushing his chest — and other parts of his body.

Underneath her proper exterior she'd been a hot, sensuous woman who'd liked her sex as rough as he did. It had been the best sex of his life, ever, hands down. He had definitely been up for more of it the next day. Worn out and replete, he'd vaguely remembered falling asleep with her in his arms, but when he'd awoken in the morning, she had been gone, leaving him with an unaccustomed emptiness. He'd asked his friends about her, but all they'd known was she'd come with some other people they'd invited. They hadn't recognized the name and apparently nobody else had known who Mandy Wheeler Baker was. Maybe she'd given him a fake name, just as he'd done to her. Women came and went in his life, and that was fine with him. The way he wanted it. He was married to Delta and had no plans to change that any time soon. But not even calling on all his personal discipline could get one time with that woman out of his mind. One night, for fuck's sake.

How was it possible that after five years he still remembered every erotic detail of those long hours? How many times had he replayed it over and over, like a video on constant rewind? She appeared in his dreams, as if taunting him, and his cock swelled and hardened every time. Other women hadn't been able to erase her from his mind. He was arrogant enough to wonder if she thought of him after all this time but pragmatic enough to know the chances they'd ever cross paths again were slim to none.

He wanted her with a hunger that ate at him. Worse than that, they'd made a connection. An emotional link. Whatever. He'd have thought with the passage of time that feeling would fade. Instead, it had just increased. Grown stronger. He couldn't get her out of his fucking mind. And if he did find her? What then? Where did they go from there?

"Hey, Slade." Trey's voice broke into his reverie. "You still with us? Where'd you wander off to?"

He shook himself back to the present, realizing with a start he'd zoned out right there in front of his men. Bad, bad, bad. "Yeah. I'm here."

"Good to know." Beau cocked an eyebrow. "You looked a million miles away."

"So we okay here? If nothing else, for ten days you'll get to eat terrific food, soak up some sun and not have to do a damn fucking thing."

Trey nodded. "I'm in."

The rest of them murmured their agreement, even Marc.

"Okay. Let's make some plane reservations. We'll fly into San Antonio. Then I'll have the ranch chopper pick us up."

"Sounds okay to me," Beau agreed. "Let's rock and roll."

In less than twelve hours they were on their way out of Helmand Province, making a stop in Madrid to pick up a commercial flight to the States. Long hours after that they finally landed at San Antonio International Airport where Slade hustled them out of the door and down a long walkway to the private plane terminal. A gleaming black helo awaited them, a familiar figure leaning against it, arms folded across his chest, white teeth gleaming in a smile contrasting with his sun-darkened skin.

"Glad you're home, bro," he said, slapping Slade on the shoulder.

"Me too. Look at the bunch of ugly mugs I brought with me again."

"Hey, Teo!" Trey shook hands with the man. "Think you can put up with us again?"

"As long as the boss pays me extra." He winked. Teobaldo Rivera was the ranch foreman, fiercely loyal to Slade and excellent at his job.

Whenever Slade brought his team to the ranch with him, Teo always went out of his way to make sure they enjoyed themselves.

"Okay," he told them. "Let's get loaded up. The beer's chilling in the fridge and the steaks are thawing."

It was a tight fit for five oversized males, but Slade figured they could handle it for the short hop to the ranch. As soon as the chopper landed, they were out of the cabin. Slade shoved his hands in his pockets and looked around. He loved coming home to the ranch. It replaced the family he didn't have and the home he'd lost a long time ago. The sprawling ranch house off to his right rose two stories from the lawn around it, shaded by ancient oaks and maples. To the left stood the enormous barn that held his horses, any cattle that might need to be separated in an individual pen, and Teo's offices. Behind that nestled the building that housed all the ranch equipment, including the portable pens for branding. And beyond that, as far as he could see, the endless rolling pastures meeting the horizon of the blue Texas sky. Pastures that contained the small herd of cattle he nourished and bred and sold.

He inhaled the familiar scent of horses and hay and Texas sunshine and almost at once the tension riding him began to ease. He loved coming home to this place. He could regenerate, rest, ride his horses.

And there were always women to hook up with whenever he wanted, women he'd met over the years. Too bad none of them replaced the one he really wanted. He could almost see her here on the ranch, in jeans and boots, walking to meet him, two small figures hopping along beside her, filled with excitement. But he didn't know her real name, didn't know where to find her and no one seemed able to tell him. So all he had was the memory of the most incredible night of his life, a memory that plagued him whenever he opened his mind to it.

Fucking damn. He needed to find that woman or get over her. He was driving himself nuts.

While Teo went through his shutdown routine, he and his men unloaded their duffels and headed toward the house.

"Let's get inside," Slade told them, "and I'll get you all situated." He grinned. "Then we can crack open some cold ones."

The large ranch house had four guest rooms plus the master suite, a situation that worked out well for them. The air was still sun-warmed, even though the sun itself had dipped below the horizon, but a soft breeze added a cooling element. The air carried the heady aromas of hay and horseflesh and cattle, a mixture Slade loved more than any perfume. The spread was his haven, the place where he could put all the blackness of his missions behind him and feel like a normal person. If he ever did settle down, the woman would have to love it as much as he did — *if* being the operative word. Did the woman he'd dreamed about so much — ?

Damn! He had to stop this. He was losing his grip here.

"I see Teo got the beer out?" he commented as he jogged down the stairs and out to the porch.

The men had dumped their gear in their respective rooms and were already out there waiting for him.

"Yeah," Trey joked. "We're trying to save you some, but you know how it goes."

Slade glanced around, realizing one of the team was absent. "Be right back," he told them.

Slade knocked on the door of the room Marc had dropped his things in. He'd wanted to give the man a moment to himself on the off chance he'd come on downstairs and join them, but it seemed he needed either prodding or dragging. Slade had hoped with such a peaceful setting, surrounded by the natural beauty of Texas ranchland, with a gorgeous sunset painting the sky, he'd feel relaxed. Maybe even looking forward to the ten days here. But nothing relaxed him anymore. While the rest of them kicked back and did whatever, Marc, the team's weapons and demolitions expert, often used his downtime in practice and refresher training. Considering the state of his personal life, Slade was glad the man was a disciplined soldier, committed to the job.

"Yeah?"

Slade pushed the door open. Marc stood at the window looking out at the scene below.

"Okay to come in?"

Marc shrugged. "It's your house."

"Hey, guy. That doesn't mean you can't have privacy."

If anyone asked Slade he'd say the man had too much privacy. Too much time to think about the dark place he couldn't seem to get out of. A place where the image of his naked wife, high on the drugs he hadn't known she was addicted to, was riding their equally naked neighbor and screaming with pleasure. He once told Slade, in a rare moment of confidence, he wished he could bleach his mind to erase that scene that played over and over like a video on a loop.

'That's what I got for letting my cock tell me what to do instead of listening to my brain.'

Slade knew some of the background. When Marc had met Ria, he'd been stunned by her beauty and swept away by her vivacious personality. Naturally quiet and introspective himself, he'd nevertheless been drawn to her at once. His total dedication to Delta Force had precluded any type of lasting relationship. Until then.

She'd told him she loved him and had made him believe it. The sex had been unbelievable, so hot it had scorched the air around them. When he'd had leave time between missions, he hadn't been able to get home fast enough to immerse himself in his incredible wife. The fact that she had chosen him when, he was sure, she could have any man she'd wanted, was in itself an aphrodisiac.

Slade and the other team members had met her, at a dinner where he'd proudly showed her off. None of the team members, including Slade, had been too enthusiastic about her, but that hadn't bothered Marc.

"You're just jealous," he'd ground out.

Then the roof had fallen in and his life had come apart. The scene he'd walked in on had been bad enough. He'd managed to control his rage to not kill the guy when he'd tossed them out into the street. But when he'd realized she'd been high on drugs rather than alcohol, he'd done a thorough search of the house, including her personal belongings, and found baggies filled with multicolored pills.

He'd called Slade, because he'd been out of his mind. Insane. Especially when he'd learned she'd been doing that for a long time, both the drugs and screwing anything with a dick. He'd been torn between wanting to kill her and kill himself. Slade had talked him down off the ledge and waited while he'd packed his things — not too many, he traveled light — and had walked him out of the apartment and out of her life. He'd found him an attorney who had told Marc to do whatever was needed to get a divorce fast.

He'd asked Slade not to ever bring it up again and had spent the rest of his leave holed up in a motel room, trying not to drink himself to death.

Slade wasn't an emotional person, but his heart ached for Marc, so damaged by a selfish, insane woman. He often wondered if Marc would ever get back to the point where he wanted to rejoin the living.

Now Slade cleared his throat. "Heavy thoughts there, Eagle. Admiring the great view?"

Marc turned, his mouth stretched in an imitation of a smile. "Just giving my brain a rest. Give me five and I'll be right along."

"I'll hold you to it. Beer's cold, so come on down."

Swallowing a sigh, he left the room and headed downstairs. He could already hear the others on the back porch where he'd left them. Maybe, just maybe ten days at the ranch would be the first step toward Marc regaining his sanity and equilibrium.

Home of Erotic Romance

What's hot this week from TOTALLY BOUND PUBLISHING

Sign up for our newsletter and find out about all our romance book releases, eBook sales and promotions, sneak peeks and FREE romance eBooks!

https://totallyentwinedgroup.us7.list-manage.com/subscribe/post

About the Author

A multi-published, award winning, Amazon and USA Today best-selling author, Desiree Holt has produced more than 200 titles and won many awards. She has received an EPIC E-Book Award, the Holt Medallion and many others including Author After Dark's Author of the Year. She has been featured on CBS Sunday Morning and in The Village Voice, The Daily Beast, USA Today, The Wall Street Journal, The London Daily Mail. She lives in Florida with her cats who insist they help her write her books, and is addicted to football.

Desiree loves to hear from readers. You can find her contact information, website details and author profile page at http://www.totallybound.com